A
FRAGMENT
TOO FAR

A
FRAGMENT
TOO FAR

A SHERIFF LUKE McWHORTER MYSTERY

DUDLEY LYNCH

Published by ECW Press
665 Gerrard Street East
Toronto, Ontario, Canada M4M 1Y2
416-694-3348 / info@ecwpress.com

Cover design: Michel Vrana
Author photo: © Larry Lourcey

PRINTED AND BOUND IN CANADA

This is a work of fiction. Names, characters,
places, and incidents either are the product of
the author's imagination or are used fictitiously,
and any resemblance to actual persons, living or
dead, business establishments, events, or locales is
entirely coincidental.

LIBRARY AND ARCHIVES CANADA CATALOGUING
IN PUBLICATION

Title: A fragment too far : a Sheriff Luke
McWhorter mystery / Dudley Lynch.

Names: Lynch, Dudley, author.

Identifiers: Canadiana (print) 20190110678
Canadiana (ebook) 20190110686

ISBN 9781770414990 (softcover)
ISBN 9781773053837 (PDF)
ISBN 9781773053820 (ePUB)

Classification: LCC PS3612.Y52 F73 2019
DDC 813/.6—dc23

PRINTING: FRIESENS   5   4   3   2   1

To my family.
One and all.

CHAPTER 1

My working eye — the other one was plastic — kept telling me I'd witnessed the world's first buzzard-cide. Or something akin to it. The bird's precipitous plunge had looked choreographed by the grim reaper.

The spectacle had unfolded not far below where I was parked — a turnout near the western end of the O'Mahony Ridge. This chain of boulder-and-brush-covered peaks ran for forty miles through the middle of Abbot County. The stricken buzzard had disappeared from my view beneath the stunted live oaks and mesquite trees at the point where the prairies ended and the ridge began. To the north, short-grass prairies stretched to the horizon, silent and empty. Usually, they spread out beneath cloudless skies.

At first, all I'd noticed was a kettle of the birds taking lazy swirls on one of our summer thermals.

Then this bird had veered away from the others. Flown two tight circles on its own. Stretched both wings. Drawn its feet and scrawny neck close to its body. Remained motionless for a second. Tipped backwards. And plunged straight to the ground.

You'd have thought the ill-starred bird had been attached to an anvil. Its fall was as true to vertical as a plumb line.

But a deliberate act?

I decided not.

More like an act of God. The animal shouldn't have been flying. Period.

Thinking about it, my inner choirboy dredged up a snippet from an old hymn: "Nevermore to roam. Open wide Thine arms of love, Lord, I'm coming home."

It wasn't unusual for me to think of old hymns. Or sermon titles. Or Bible verses. I was probably the only sheriff in the country — maybe the world — with a divinity degree from an Ivy League school.

Mine was from Yale.

Pretty expensive training for a sheriff. For certain, this isn't the kind of background you'd expect for a West Texas county's chief law officer. Or, in all likelihood, any other Texas county's. But then, I was used to explaining how my whole post-high-school educational experience had been shaped by the idea of being a preacher. When people asked me how I'd ended up being Luther Stephens McWhorter, *sheriff*, instead of Luther Stephens McWhorter, *minister of the gospel*, I'd tell them it was a long story. One probably best saved for another time.

Was it because of the pain?

That was part of the reason.

But it was more because of the risk.

You can't put much of a foundation for a new future in place if you keep obsessing over what you've lost.

I pushed those thoughts aside to concentrate on what I was seeing through my windshield.

The sight bordered on the majestic — if you were looking into the distance. *Red-dirt prairies meet green treed hills meet endless azure sky.* But the closer you looked, the more imperfections you saw. *Scraggly trees meet yawning gullies meet rock-strewn grasslands.* Only the azure sky carried over. One of my deputies had a puckish name for this whole area: "No Country for Old Radiators."

It was the vastness I loved about the country. And the isolation.

I could creep up the rutted gravel road, park my vehicle, and unpack my lunch. Ease my seat back when I finished eating. Watch the clouds drift by — if there were any clouds to be had. Luxuriate in the solitude and the stillness. And, most times, enjoy a nap.

On this blistering-hot day, it had almost worked that way.

I'd savored my ham-and-cheese sandwich, corn chips, and slice of store-bought orange spice cake. Peeled and nibbled down a banana. Poured myself more iced tea from my battered Stanley thermos. Directed the car's AC away from my face. Made a minor adjustment so my seat was less erect. And tried to decide whether to gawk or snooze.

But my thoughts wouldn't stay away from the buzzard.

I returned my seat to its upright position. Stepped outside to relieve myself. Brushed a few cake crumbs from my lap. Slipped back under the steering wheel. And aimed my souped-up Dodge police cruiser off the ridge.

I thought I knew where the buzzard had landed, and I wanted a closer look.

●●●

The turnoff was less than a minute away. By the first "welcome mat" on the left. Not that a cattle guard is that welcoming. The metal devices are like small bridges pockmarked with holes. If a bull were to misstep on the ugly grids, the animal could break a leg faster than a cat's slap. Hit one of the contraptions too fast in a vehicle, and you could destroy a transmission or oil pan. Or lose a few teeth.

I crossed this one at a prayer's pace. Started inching up the weed-choked road's twin tracks. Spotted a small whitetail deer through the live oak and mesquite trees. And prepared for my first glance of Professor Huntgardner's enigmatic old house since longer than I could remember.

No one lived there now.

The professor was — what? — almost ninety. They'd moved him to an old-folks home some years back.

His sizable house was odd. Always would be. Not because it *looked* odd. In many ways, though it was showing neglect, the boxy, cinnamon-brick, two-story house was still picture-perfect. In town, it would have fit well into any upscale neighborhood built in the 1920s or 1930s. In part, that was because of its deep, wraparound front porch, edged with low brick half-walls. The Huntgardner house looked odd because it was much too grand an abode to be so far out in the boonies. It was thirty miles from anywhere, and that was by gravel road. That nearest "anywhere" was Flagler, our county seat.

The professor's place of employment hadn't been any closer. The University of the Hills was one of three such institutions we had in Flagler. All were church-sponsored schools of modest enrollment. They were one of our two main claims to fame. The other one was the man now living in the White House. President Jim Bob Fletcher — James Robert, to anyone from outside Abbot County — had grown up here.

I'd once been a student in one of Professor Huntgardner's physics classes. Not a very good one — student, that is. I'd gotten my only *F* in two decades of schooling from Professor Thaddeus Huntgardner.

My dad had known Huntgardner too. After both of them had retired, I'd driven "Sheriff John" out to the Huntgardner place a time or two. And I'd been to it on a few other occasions.

But none of those visits had sent a morbid rewrite of verse 4 of Psalm 23 rocketing through my mind.

This one did.

Yea, I have walked into the darkest valley, and I have seen all evil . . .

CHAPTER 2

The nose often announces death before the eye can register it. For chemical reasons.

Putrescine and cadaverine, to name two. Powerful smells produced by decaying animal matter.

Think rotting meat bubbling in cheap dime-store perfume. Then imagine that smell a hundred times fiercer. Feel the stupefying stench as it coats your nose hairs, tongue, the back of your throat. Realize that holding your breath won't help. By the time you detect the unspeakable nastiness in the air, it's already seeped into your lungs.

I'd smelled decomposing flesh more than a few times as a law enforcement officer.

But I'd never lost my cookies.

Until now.

I braked hard and managed to get my door open part of the way.

Too slow.

I puked much of the packed lunch I'd eaten only minutes before onto my raised car window. Then staggered out of the car. Pivoted in a half-circle. Managed to put both hands on the front car fender. Leaned forward just in time to carpet-bomb the fender with more of my lunch.

The buzzards had been puking too. And peeing. And pooping. Mostly on themselves. As any rancher's kid knows, this helps to cool them off — and causes them to stink to high heaven. The white streaks on their legs and feet were from uric acid of their own making.

But this wasn't what was causing my distress. The horrendous smell had triggered that. Plus, realizing what the buzzards were feeding on.

Human remains.

The corpse closest to my car sprawled at the base of the short concrete stairs ascending to the porch of the house.

A half dozen buzzards milled around the prostrate body. When the buzzards weren't pecking at it, they were jostling each other. This allowed me only occasional glimpses of the victim's bloodied ribs. The denuded arm and leg bones. And the mangled areas where the face and scalp had been.

In two places in the porch shadows, beady-eyed black-and-red heads were popping up. Disappearing. Reappearing. Then vanishing again.

Over and over.

The knee-high brick shelf around the porch's edge kept me from seeing what had these birds so preoccupied. But from the way they were strutting and bobbing, my guess was the shelf was shielding two more victims from my view.

A fourth corpse lay draped across the open space framed by the front-door threshold. The body lay on its side, half-facing the yard. Or rather, its bones did.

What was left of one decimated arm angled upward, blood-stained as a butcher's stash. The face was gone, picked clean. The torso, nearly so. Jagged holes had been pecked in the back of the victim's eye sockets.

Other much smaller forms lay prone in the yard. More buzzards — deceased. A few were being eaten by their cousins. One of them could have been the one I saw fall out of the sky, the one I had followed.

I needed to sit down.

Breathe.

Think.

I wanted to consult someone, and I knew whose voice I wanted to hear.

But before that, I had to do something about my mouth. I reached for a bottle of water. Unscrewed the cap. Took a careful sip. Rinsed. Spat it out.

Another sip. Another rinse. More spitting.

Now I could risk a swallow.

I vomited again, this time on my car seat.

Fortunately, it was only a trickle. I wiped it off with a paper napkin left over from my lunch. Eased back into my seat. Rested my heavy arms against the steering wheel. My weary head followed, and I'm not sure how long it stayed there.

I needed to call my dispatcher at the Abbot County Sheriff's Department. But first, I wanted the comfort and reassurance of the special agent in charge of the Flagler field office of the FBI.

I managed to push the right buttons on my phone. Didn't know what I was going to say until I said it.

"Love you."

CHAPTER 3

"**H**old a sec, cowboy."

Special Agent Angie Steele didn't wait for a response. I'd violated a rule we'd both agreed on. *Work stuff public, personal stuff private, and never the twain shall mix.*

Addled as my mind was, I knew what Angie was about to do. Her office sat near one of the two front entrances to Flagler's two-story, art-deco-style federal building. She would steer for the nearest door. Bound down the short concrete stairs with her blond ponytail flying. Veer west on the sidewalk. And walk until she had some privacy.

This time, her tone was a bit sharper. "Sheriff Luther Stephens McWhorter, this an official daft day for you?"

This was my chance to give her information she could ponder. Advise me about. Follow through on.

Not able to manage a complete sentence, I supplied her with a word. The voice offering it sounded weak and remote. I had to think for a moment about whom it belonged to. She would have to decide whether to treat my word as a noun, verb, or adjective. And whether it was of any use to her.

"Puking."

Her reply skipped a beat but only one. "Tell me where you are."

Again, my battered mind didn't supply her with much to work with. "Smelling it."

She knew she needed to know more. "Smelling what, gentle one?"

There it was. The caring that lay under the tough outer shell of my Glock 22–carrying girlfriend. She was younger than me, so much so that some of my friends said I was robbing the cradle. I disagreed. I'd been born in 1977, so I was only eight years older. That isn't a chasm. We'd not even found it a distraction.

I wanted to tell her more, something useful, but I seemed to be flinging my words like errant paintballs. "Stink sticks."

At this point, a typical agent of the Federal Bureau of Investigation might have sighed from exasperation. But *my* FBI agent took charge.

When she learned I was sitting in my car, she asked if I could drive.

I told her not far. And not fast.

She instructed me to start driving away from the smell. When I could breathe good air, I was to stop and tell her where I was.

I thought I could make it to the cattle guard, and I did. Rolled up to the ribbed crossing grid. Pulled off to the right of the heavy iron fence posts and stopped a yard or two short. Put my patrol cruiser in park. Rolled down my window.

And heard the shots.

Someone back toward the house was firing a gun.

More shots.

Angie heard them over my phone. She again demanded to know where I was.

This time, I told her. She instructed me to keep my doors locked and the line open. She came back on twice to ask how I was doing. The third time she spoke, she said she was in line right behind my chief deputy. Both were speeding past the western Flagler city limits on County Road 16. Twenty-five minutes tops and they'd be here.

But the muscular four-wheeler raced up long before then. The big-tired vehicle was covered in orangey-red dust, courtesy of our West Central Texas clay prairies. The three teenage boys in the vehicle looked grim.

The driver was almost too big to fit behind the steering wheel. The other two were standing in openings in the roof. Each clutched a rifle with one hand and clung to the vehicle with the other.

The driver braked the vehicle to a stop a few feet short of the cattle guard and pointed back toward the house. "Ho-lee crap, mister! Buzzards are eating people back there!"

My thought wasn't the most sheriff-like.

Not my problem.

Then everything went black.

CHAPTER 4

The perspiring face hovering over my car seat was squarish. Huge, like its owner. And framed by a massive, high-crowned, brownish felt cowboy hat. The brim seemed to stretch straight across its wearer's forehead from one ear to the other.

It was a man-child's face, until I got to the burnt umber eyes peering at me through narrow slits. *Why did I feel those eyes gave you the answers you needed only if you knew the right questions to ask? And maybe not then?*

"Mister, you need to sit up and drink this."

It was one of those sports drinks that rehydrate. The bottle was cold and the taste sweet, although I knew this was masking a lot of salt. After all, that was the point.

I drank everything in the bottle, and he handed me another one. Cold and salty-sweet and reassuring like the first.

I felt like I should be asking questions. But the lineman-sized driver of the SUV got his in first. "You been to the house?"

I nodded. "Just long enough to be sick."

My caretaker-angel wasn't missing much. "Looks like you just ate." The snow-plow-shaped nose twitched. "Could be vasovagal syncope, you know."

"Vasso-what?"

"Sorry, sir. My dad's a doctor. Some people's blood pressure drops, and they throw up when they see a bad injury or something. That'd explain why you weren't out longer too."

Awake, I was. My eye was now seeing better. And my mind was beginning to have a sheriff-like thought or two.

The hole in the upper left rear fender of his vehicle. I could see it from where I was sitting. The bullet might have come from anywhere.

I asked.

My Good Samaritan glanced sideways only once before deciding one bald-faced lie at this point might be one too many. "Scottie's .22 went off when he jumped back in the truck."

"So nobody was shooting at you?"

"We were the ones shooting."

"At the buzzards?"

There was that sideways glance again. He nodded.

In Texas, you can be fined $15,000 and go to jail for killing turkey vultures — buzzards. But this wasn't a good time to have that conversation. The nervous trio standing around my cruiser might know more about my crime scene than I did. I needed to know everything they knew. Everything they'd seen and heard. A few quick questions wouldn't hurt.

Putting on a stern face wasn't difficult. It was the only kind of face I could muster.

He admitted they had been inside the old Huntgardner place twice already this summer, goofing off.

Each time they'd raised the same back-bedroom window to get in. And lowered it each time when they left. Never saw anyone else. Both times, the house felt like it had been deserted for a long time. Smelled that way too. The window shades were always down. And it looked lonely, although most of the furniture and the dishes were still there. On the whole, it looked freaky. That was one of the reasons they liked to visit.

And this time?

In the big fellow's words, they'd noticed early on that

"something was rotten in Denmark." They'd detected the horrendous odor as they drove into the backyard but hadn't started gagging until they had the bedroom window up halfway. That's when they slammed the window down and sprinted back to their expensive vehicle.

Scottie's rifle had gone off when he leaped over the vehicle's roll bar and into his back-seat riding hole. The bullet had gone into the fender. The buzzards and bodies had been visible in a blur as they sped past the house. The driver's plan was to call 911 when they reached the gravel road. He couldn't believe their luck when he saw a sheriff's car was already parked there.

I'd been hoping for more. "How'd you get to the house?"

The huge eyelids narrowed again. He was choosing his words with care. "Dirt road off the Sweetwater cutoff. Used to be the way you got to the ridge."

I knew what he was talking about. Two dirt ruts, actually. Riddled with washboards. Bad washouts in a couple of low places. A total no-go when it had been raining. "That's a good twelve miles of pretty rough traveling."

"Good rabbit hunting, though."

"You see anybody?"

The eyes giveth, and the eyes taketh away. This was when he told me a lie. "Saw some dust flying. But couldn't see if it was somebody."

I suppressed the urge to point out the obvious. Dust doesn't fly on its own. Of course it was somebody. It was going to be essential that we found out who.

And he'd tell me. By and by. Because the big guy and I had connected on some level. That was always a goal I had when I was interrogating people. But it was also a danger to be guarded against. You never wanted to lose your sense of perspective.

I had to keep my guard up most while I was dealing with exceptionally smart people, and I sensed that when it came to brains, this guy was in the upper echelon. But he might also be guilty of something. That's often why people tell lies.

I needed to go slower here. It wasn't only my mind that desired a time-out. At the moment, my stomach wasn't in the mood for hand-to-hand combat with resisting unknowns. But in the back of my mind, I found myself wondering why the giant I was questioning was being so evasive about the encounter his friends and he had obviously had on the road from the Sweetwater cutoff to the house.

I told him to pull their vehicle on through the cattle guard and park at the side of the road. We'd get back to them.

The approaching cloud of dust would be my chief deputy, Sawyers Tanner, and Special Agent Steele, plus whoever else was caravanning with them. More of my deputies, likely. And a couple of paramedics in their ambulance. It was time for me to get ready for an argument.

Angie was going to want me hooked up to an IV bag and carted off to the Flagler General Hospital ED. She was going to resist taking no for an answer. I could expect her to stand straight as a crossing guard to emphasize her authority. Switch to her special agent's face. Mask her emotions. Thrust her lower lip out and put her hands on her hips as she sized up her quarry-of-the-moment and evaluated her moves.

A trip to the ED wasn't in my immediate future.

I'd guzzle anything they asked me to drink. They could take my blood pressure as many times as they wanted. Listen to my heart if they couldn't already hear it. Peer at the whites of my eye, look at my tonsils, whatever. But the only place I was going anytime soon was back up that short, weed-covered road to Professor Huntgardner's unspeakably defiled old house.

CHAPTER 5

A ngie opened her car door. Stepped out. Stopped for a moment. Glanced behind her. Then turned back toward me and started walking in my direction.

Maybe she was anticipating defiance. Or perhaps she was only relieved at seeing me upright and communicating. Her first words suggested she still wasn't sure of her feelings.

"You stink."

I managed a weak smile. "Can't argue that."

"Your car too."

"Not been a premier day for smelling good."

She tried to lighten her tone. "Why don't we send both of you to a car detailer?"

I managed another weak smile but knew the time had already arrived to make McWhorter's Last Stand. "Tow my car, please. I'm needed here."

"You're needed a lot of places." She pointed to an approaching vehicle with its red lights flashing. "Right now, in the back of that ambulance."

Sometimes it was like that with Angie. It may have been why the bureau had assigned her to an outpost in the middle of fifteen of West Central Texas's most deserted counties. It was a savvy choice. The Wide Sky Country, as the chamber of commerce types liked to call it, was a good place for free-spirited folks. Maybe hard-spurring women most of all.

Our encounter might have been more heated had my good-natured chief deputy not repeated Angie's mistake.

Chief Deputy Tanner meant well. He'd taken one look at me and concluded, like Angie, that a seasoned hand in reasonable health needed to take charge. Three more of my deputies were walking up. I noticed that they were all dressed more for city duty than for traipsing through brambles and cactus patches. They were detectives. All my regular deputies must have been out on patrol.

My chief deputy watched them approach. "Listen up, Abbot County sheriff people —"

"Sawyers, stand *down!*" I shouted.

I shouldn't have been surprised that he had started giving orders the moment he arrived. That was one of the qualities I'd liked most about him when I'd hired him right out of college. His self-confidence. And the fact that he displayed a level of judgment in his decision-making that was unusual in someone so young. He was still only twenty-seven.

He was used to me skipping the niceties in our field conversations, but this time, the sharpness in my tone snapped his head around. The others, Angie included, also gave their hands and feet "freeze in place" orders and slowly turned to look in my direction. I was a bit surprised myself at the strength of my outburst.

Angie looked over at the youngsters sitting in their big-wheeled off-roader. "Got any names?"

I gave a slight shrug. "I don't. Too busy puking, passing out, and drinking stuff to ask them."

"The big one looks like he's ready for the NFL."

"The big one's my guardian angel."

"Think they're involved?"

"Don't think so. They seemed to be looking for rabbits, not Armageddon."

"You believe them?"

"They looked as pale as I felt when they drove up."

Her eyes studied my face, and she seemed to reach a conclusion.

She asked about the scene at the house.

I leaned against my car and thought for a moment about how best to sum it up. "Don't know how many dead we've got. I've seen two, and it looked like there were a few more outside. Every buzzard in this part of Texas is feeding on those poor folks. More victims in the house, I'm thinking. In the yard, the birds are keeling over too. Or falling out of the air."

Talking about all this was proving harder than I'd anticipated. I swallowed rough. An extra breath helped. "Don't know how to describe the smell. Catfish stink bait cranked sky-high, maybe. It's going to grab you, stick to you, penetrate anything you're wearing or carrying. So, I suggest anyone going to the house, get out of your regular stuff and into disposable clothing. Don't wear anything underneath or take anything unnecessary with you if you want to keep it."

I issued assignments.

My chief deputy would come with me. Or rather I'd go with him. I was going to need a car.

I had another assignment for Detective Matt Salazar. "Matt, you got a notepad?" I didn't wait for him to answer. He always had a notepad. With a hand-tooled alligator cover. He kept it in a rear pocket of his hand-pressed, custom-made jeans.

We needed to get personal info and written statements from the teenagers. I was pretty sure they'd find young Detective Salazar simpatico.

Detective Tobias Coltrane was a gravel-voiced retired military policeman. His graying burr haircut was as flat on top as the deck of an aircraft carrier, and his waistline was as trim as a ballet dancer's. He would be following Chief Deputy Tanner's car to the crime scene about a hundred and fifty yards up the road.

That left Detective Rashada Moody. She was the department's only woman deputy, only African-American deputy, only left-handed deputy, and the only one who had once competed for Miss Abbot County. Her sense of humor was smart and infectious. In fact, she had been the one to suggest calling her "Deputy Only." I could see her running for sheriff someday. And I couldn't imagine anyone more qualified to manage any crowd that might show up.

"Detective Moody, you stay at the cattle guard. You'll interface between us and the outside world." I patted my car fender. "And tell Dispatch to have this thing towed to the county garage. It stinks."

I issued one more order. "Nobody crosses the cattle guard without a respirator on. Activated charcoal is going to be the only thing between you and being useless at the house. Guaranteed."

The only decision still to be made wasn't mine. The FBI special agent had to decide what her role was going to be.

She told me as soon as she got off her mobile phone. "I've told D.C. where I'm at. They'd like me to tag along."

I nodded.

Moving to my car, I opened the trunk and found my protective overalls, a respirator, a pair of shoe covers, my blue latex gloves, and a small wipe dispenser.

The paramedics let us change in the back of the ambulance. I went first. They gave me two plastic garbage bags, one for my stinky clothes and another for my personal items.

The respirator went around my neck. I'd planned to let it dangle in place until I needed it. The feet masks and gloves went into my left rear pocket, and the narrow box of wipes went into the other rear pocket.

I was about to walk away from the muscular rig when one of paramedics asked me to wait. She stepped into the gurney bay. Opened a cabinet door. And extracted a couple of gifts for me.

One was a pill, accompanied by a cup of water. According to the labeling on the bottle, the medication was called ondansetron. She said it was an antiemetic that would take about thirty minutes to kick in.

The other item was a barf bag.

CHAPTER 6

I couldn't imagine a more Hitchcockian tableau. It was every bit as stomach-assaulting as when I'd seen it the first time. With one difference.

Entrails were now spilling from both sides of what remained of the bowel cavity of the victim on the sidewalk. From where we sat, it looked like the mess a toddler might make trying to eat spaghetti and tomato sauce for the first time.

Most of the movements we could see away from the victims were like a Kabuki performance.

A buzzard would spread its wings, flap, fuss, fly a few feet, land, preen, wait. Necks around this bird would crane, heads would pivot, and beady eyes would drink in the new development. After that, not much. Stillness returned and remained until the next bit of buzzard choreography erupted, repeating the movements of the first one.

Other times, a relocating bird crashed into a stationary one. This could start a whole throng of buzzards strutting herky-jerky around the yard, bumping buddies as they went. But stillness and silence soon returned.

There was occasional movement on the porch roof and up on the house's main roof. The beigey-black-tinted asphalt shingles on both surfaces were streaked with white. Buzzard toilets with a view.

Special Agent Steele and Detective Coltrane remained in their cars. They were waiting to see how we dealt with the birds.

My chief deputy was waiting to see too. "What now?"

"I know what the game wardens would do."

"Shoot the bastards."

I'd already considered that. "Well, they might use their twelve gauges to fire off a shell cracker. But they've got other stuff. Whistler cannons, rocket bombs. These creatures don't like loud noises. Especially if they don't know where they're coming from."

I reached up and tapped his siren switch. "This is what we're going to use. Give me a minute to tell everybody why it's about to sound like the Marines have landed."

I'd seen bats swarm out of caves. What happened next was kind of like that. Only our "bats" had wingspans up to six feet. And they had much less experience with mass exodus.

The birds in the yard and on the roofs had unimpeded egress. Once they got clear of each other, they were airborne and gone. All in a matter of seconds.

Not so, the others.

The birds under the porch overhang forgot which way was up. It was a survival-of-the-fittest donnybrook. Feathers flew. We could sense their rage and panic even if we couldn't hear their cries over our siren. It took about a minute for them to clear.

The buzzards inside the house had the hardest time of it. The door opening was only so wide and so high. And there was only one way out. Their instinct was to spread their wings. Six feet of bone, cartilage, and feathers fanning at the air. Like they were ice skating for the first time. Stagger, veer, and shove.

Their evacuation came in spurts. A torrent, then a trickle, then nothing. Until it started over again.

The parade of terrified birds kept coming. This meant only one thing.

There were more victims in the house than I'd feared.

CHAPTER 7

It was a surprise when the pump on Professor Huntgardner's water well fired up. We could not have been more shocked if a gunny sack of enraged rattlesnakes had been dropped on our heads. It sounded a little like that.

I hadn't wanted us to step over the corpse lying across the front-door threshold, so we'd come around to the back door, walking single file. Me first. Then Angie. Then Sawyers. Then Tobias.

We huddled at the back door, wearing our respirators. The breathing devices our department used didn't allow us to talk, so I'd brought a small wire-bound notebook and a ballpoint pen.

I extracted them from my overalls pocket, but Chief Deputy Tanner was the first to react. He grabbed the pad and pen out of my hands. Scribbled something. Turned the pad so we could all read it.

"What the hell?!"

We gave him a collective shrug.

I'd assumed the utilities at the house were off. No water, no electricity. But water was clearly running somewhere. And it seemed inconceivable that anyone could be alive in the house. Not after the bizarre exodus of buzzards we'd just witnessed.

Now, all those assumptions were vacated.

I took back my pen and pad. Wrote my own message. Waved everyone close to read it. "(1) Are we alone? (2) Where's water running?"

I issued assignments by pointing, first to a person, then to a part of the house. Each of us got a section. My responsibility would be the west end of the second story.

But what we saw a few steps into the kitchen brought us all to an abrupt halt. Angie and I exchanged a quick glance. The interior of the house had been trashed.

Destroyed.

Jagged holes had been ripped in the sheet rock of every wall we could see. Most of the ceilings were torn open or tugged down. The floors were awash in debris. The kitchen cabinets had been cleaned out, and not gently.

We proceeded with careful steps. Busy eyes. Super-cautious ears. We didn't have any choice. Every square inch of the house had become an obstacle course of rubble.

Our excessive caution wasn't necessary. One by one, our chief questions got answered with dispatch.

We soon realized that the reason the pump was running continuously on the house's water well was because the water was running in the upstairs bathroom toilet. I lifted the lid off the water tank and jiggled the float. The flow into the toilet bowl stopped. I was guessing the loss of water had been slow and steady. But it was enough to keep the pump out back cycling on and off, probably for days.

Like the bodies visible out front on the porch, the five additional human corpses we found in the house had been desecrated by the vultures. For the most part, down to the bone.

Nine victims total. Four downstairs. One upstairs. It wasn't possible to tell what they had been doing at the moment of their deaths. But from the shreds of clothing we could see, we were guessing they were all males.

I pointed toward the back door.

While it was still fresh on their minds, I wanted to get my colleagues' quick assessment of the crime scene we'd stumbled through. In my four terms as sheriff, I'd never seen anything like it, or, frankly, ever expected to see anything like it, in Abbot County.

I told everyone to meet up at the cattle guard.

CHAPTER 8

Angie suggested we confer in her SUV. It was roomier. I got in the front passenger seat and pulled the sun visor down. It had a mirror on the back side. When I flipped the mirror open, I could see the faces in the back seat. At the scene, I'd not bothered to take notes. But I had taken pictures with my phone. Angie had too. We both began flipping through our images.

Then Angie stopped. "I've never seen such extreme efforts to —" She hesitated. "Well, it's like Buchenwald or something. Like they were deliberately being robbed of their identities as well as their lives."

I agreed. "Didn't see any personal effects. Watches, jewelry, phones. No billfolds or anything in their pockets. Nothing lying around that might tell us who they are."

Chief Deputy Tanner was still in a profane mood. "Why all the goddamned house damage?"

I wanted the benefit of his experience. "What are you thinking?"

His answer surprised me. "Funny thing, but I got a feeling somebody was being punished. Like they were telling Professor Huntgardner how they really felt."

My eyes opened wider. *Lordy, is this whole thing about somebody's sour grapes?*

I wanted to hear from the others. "Real quick, no matter how far-fetched, what could explain this?"

Detective Coltrane went first. "Drug deal gone bad. Turf war, maybe. Might not even be about Abbot County. U.S. 283 is turning into a back-door route for the Mexican cartels. They're moving drugs from the border to Nebraska to Chicago via the Nebraska–Iowa interstates."

Angie spoke next. "Terrorists." She was likely piggy-backing on her boss's suggestion. "Not necessarily ISIS or anything like that. Homegrown terrorism. The modern equivalent of a range war, say. Maybe the idea is to frighten people away from living in these parts." She tacked on an afterthought. "Although I'm not sure any sane person would want to live in these parts."

My chief deputy stayed with his idea of personal payback. "Could be all these people are related. A family reunion, you know. Trying to divide up the professor's property. Turned into a deadly disagreement."

I nodded after each person spoke. But I was looking at another photo. I lifted my phone so everyone could see the screen.

"There was a portable white board lying face up on the living room floor. In its center, at the top, it had an insignia, a logo or brand — I don't know exactly what to call it. Or what it is. But it's obvious what the drawing depicts. And the date underneath it is significant."

I enlarged the image. "That's a mushroom cloud from a nuclear blast. And I still remember one of my history professors writing that date on the blackboard. That's when the world's first atomic bomb was detonated in the New Mexico desert. He called it an 'explosion heard around the universe.'"

July 16, 1945, was the date we were staring at on my phone. At that moment in Special Agent Steele's SUV, any noise at all would have sounded like a nuclear bomb going off.

I had no idea what the famous image and date had to do with nine suspicious deaths in a lonely old house in Abbot County's back country.

But I wasn't prepared to accept that it was a coincidence.

CHAPTER 9

On the way back to town, I told Angie more than once she drove like a Hittite charioteer.

Instead of keeping her eyes on the road, she kept glancing at me. "You don't quite look like the guy in the campaign photo."

I sent a scowl in her direction.

She would never quit razzing me about the photo I was thinking about using on my next election poster. She hadn't approved of my wearing the patch over my missing peeper. I'd lost the eye during my first year on the job while trying to subdue a drunk swinging a jack handle. She'd wanted me to wear my plastic eye in the photo and said she'd never understand why the touch-up artist hadn't removed the deep cleft that splits my snow-plow chin in two.

There'd been no touch-up artist.

I'd asked my photographer to do his best to make his subject look like a law enforcement legend. Rugged. Vigilant. Virile. I'd used those kinds of words. I wanted a campaign poster that didn't leave me looking like a mollycoddled, indoor dandy who had been groomed to be a preacher.

The truth was that if I was clean-shaven and wearing my usual white shirt and white Stetson with the narrow slotted black and white hat band, I stood a middling chance of being noticed at the grocery store. The fact that I stood a few millimeters under six-foot-two helped. But right now, I felt like I'd lost about six inches. "A shower would feel real good. And clean clothes. And a bowl of soup."

She squeezed my leg, but her hand didn't linger. She wanted us both to focus. This was one of those cases that can make or break a career. Especially if you are an elected law officer, and I was up for reelection next year.

Angie knew I liked to listen to myself talk aloud about a case. She knew this was one of the ways I problem-solved. Or at least, problem-surveyed.

I could depend on her to seed my thought processes. This time, she did it with a trick question. "Did you see the shoes the victims were wearing?"

The victims hadn't been wearing any shoes. No socks either. None of them. All were in bare feet. Nine unshod adults, nine dead ones. In a house surrounded by goathead sticker patches and prickly pear cactuses. What had been the point? Had there been a point?

"That's the key." I kept a poker face. "Find the shoes, find the killer." After what we'd been through in the past two hours, we were both entitled to a moment of levity.

Angie gave me her can-opener look. She wasn't in the mood for wit. I got serious again. "We may need Quantico's help with the identification."

She frowned. "The bureau's forensics people are the best. But they work fastest if they have fingerprints. Or even whole fingers. But I don't think your medical examiner can do that. The buzzards have eaten their fingers. The few that are left are so bloated they look like modeling balloons."

We both said the word "teeth" at the same time. Then realized that, again, to make comparisons, we'd need something we didn't have. Dental records.

We talked about DNA. The forensic people would be able to take samples. But, again, for identification purposes, we'd need something to match their patterns to before any identifications could be made.

I had something else on my mind. "What we do have are somebody's husband, father, brother, colleague, employee. Nine 'somebodies.' People have got to be missing these folks. Or are going to start missing them soon. Obviously, they've been lying in the house for days." I glanced at Angie again. "Can the bureau's missing persons program help?"

I could see Angie biting her cheek. "Maybe. But if no one has reported missing our victims, they aren't going to be in the program's files or on its website." She reflected for a moment. "Or on NamUs."

The National Institute of Justice's National Missing and Unidentified Persons System could be searched online by anybody. But again, you couldn't find anyone on it who wasn't there.

For the next mile or two, neither of us spoke. But it wasn't quiet. The road still roared. The car engine hummed, along with the AC. Rocks dislodged by the vehicle's churning tires kept thudding into its undercarriage. The reality of what we were leaving behind settled in. *So much we didn't know. Where do we start looking?*

At the edge of town, I realized that we could be at the Abbot County Courthouse in another ten minutes. My department offices were there. But I wasn't going straight to the office. Before I faced my office manager or anyone else in the department, I wanted a shower and a shave. And a chance to change into something that didn't reek of death or vomit. I asked Special Agent Steele to take me home. That would add another fifteen minutes to our drive. Then I had things to do that weren't going to brook any further delay.

I'd thought the motherly side of this comely creature I was

riding with would insist on a better plan. Maybe suggest letting her warm me up some chicken broth. Rub my shoulders. And tuck me in bed so I could get the rest my body craved. Point out that my associates would be more than capable of carrying the ball for a few hours in my absence.

But Angie had a knack for sensing my mood changes and managing them adroitly. I caught her looking over at me, but she wasn't going to ask what was going on in my mind unless I let too much time pass without offering to share my thoughts.

I did so as we were driving past the entrance to Flagler Memorial Gardens, the city's main cemetery. We'd buried my mother there. Then my father.

Seeing the well-watered Bermuda grass lawns and acres of tombstones had triggered memory of a conversation. A conversation with my dad. We'd been discussing his friends, and one of the people we'd talked about was Professor Thaddeus Huntgardner. He'd said that he'd always found Professor Huntgardner a strange one. Those were his exact words. I'd asked him why, and it was his answer that loomed large in my mind as we approached the city limits.

My dad had said the professor had secrets. If anything came of them, Flagler stood a good chance of being transfigured.

I'd repeated the word back to him. "He actually said 'transfigured'?"

Sheriff John had assured me this was the word Huntgardner had used. The next day, back at my office, I looked the word up. I wanted to remind myself of its exact meaning. As I recalled, *Merriam-Webster* said it meant "transformed into something more beautiful or elevated."

The only way to render Flagler's rocky, sparsely treed red-dirt prairie hills beautiful at all would be to move them to the fabled Texas Hill Country and redecorate them. The Hill Country started a hundred miles south of Flagler. And our little city was already perched atop some of the only high points in our part of West Central Texas. It would be hard to elevate it more.

I hadn't thought of my father's comment in nearly a decade, and wouldn't have now if he hadn't called out to me from his grave.

Professor Huntgardner was still alive. And nine people had just died frightful deaths in his house. Nine mystery personages who might have slipped into Abbot County like wraiths with bare feet. If this wasn't a transfiguring development of some kind, we needed to start looking for a real one.

I wanted to see how good the professor's memory was. See if he could still carry on a conversation, about transfiguration or anything else.

CHAPTER 10

At my house, Angie opened a can of chicken noodle and sent me to the shower. Two of my deputies were bringing me another car. I ate soup and saltines while speaking on the phone to the receptionist at Pecan Mountain Nursing Home. She said visiting hours ended at seven. If I hurried, I might be able to spend a few minutes with the resident in room twenty-eight.

But she warned me not to get my expectations up. "His Alzheimer's is fairly advanced. He'll probably forget who you are or mistake you for someone else. Or just sit there and ignore you. Unfortunately, he's off in la-la land a lot."

I already knew a little bit about what went on at the nursing home because of my chief deputy. Sawyers occasionally used his knowledge of the county's streets and roads to earn a few extra bucks doing deliveries for the nursing home's catering service in his off-hours. But I'd not been to Pecan Mountain before, nor had I ever met its developer. You'd need to be a hermit not to be aware of Garrick Drasher in Flagler. His primary claim to fame? A novel idea for making nursing homes more financially viable. His idea, as I understood it, was to turn them into 24/7 cash registers.

They had to have a kitchen, right? A big one.

Well, his idea was to make it even bigger. That explained Pecan Mountain Catering. It provided eatables for parties and banquets where food was ordered by the tableful, not the takeout-boxful.

And every nursing home needs vans to haul its people around. Why not use the vehicles when the old folks didn't need them for something else? That was the origin of Pecan Mountain Super Shuttle.

But the innovation that seemed to bring the spotlight to Drasher most often was his Oasis on the Prairie Café. Instead of a drab dining room for his residents, he'd built them a restaurant. By Flagler's standards, a classy one.

I'd been told the seating area was under a giant skylight. Every few tables had their own mini palm tree. There was a fountain with a pool for dropping pennies. And Drasher had imported a head chef from Dallas. His "Out West Gastronomics" menu had already drawn several national restaurant critics to town. For local trendsetters, eating at the nursing home's dining room was becoming de rigueur.

Copies of the menu were lying on the receptionist's counter. I helped myself to one and glanced it over. One of Angie's perennial complaints about Flagler was its lack of good places to eat out. But I had neither the time nor appetite for trying BBQ pork belly pot stickers or chicken paillard with spaghetti frites on this trip. I asked to be escorted to room twenty-eight.

Dr. Huntgardner gave no sign of remembering me, but I'd have recognized him anywhere.

He was in his trademark packable sun hat. I couldn't tell how much hair he had left, but his plunging white sideburns suggested it might be substantial.

The lines in his face were remarkable. Deep, commanding, mesmerizing. Like an artist had designed them, and a gravestone engraver had etched them. His cowcatcher mustache had been shaved into two parts in perfect symmetry with his nose. His eyes were silver agates. I'd always thought it was the kind of face an Andrew Wyeth or Andrew Salgado would have killed to be able to paint. Whatever the state of his mind, he was a photogenic old gent.

He was slouched in a tan overstuffed antique wing chair with wild paisley designs, watching people walk past his room door. For a moment, I felt a surge of hope.

It lasted about as long as it takes to order a burger at McDonald's.

"I'm Sheriff McWhorter, Professor. You might remember me and my dad."

His smile was so wide, it scrunched the skin above his bushy eyebrows together like an accordion's bellows. "Oh, you want my son. He's the professor. Comes every . . . every . . . every while."

I changed the subject. "Well, how about we talk about your house?"

He was staring again at people passing in the hall, and I wondered if he was going to answer. When he did, he seemed surprised that I was there. "Gone. Burned. Everything but the chimney." He shoved his glasses higher on his nose with his thumb. "What did you say your name was?" The impish grin reemerged like he'd said something brilliant.

My audience with the demented oldster lasted about five minutes. It was clear that there would be no transfiguring in this life for Professor Thaddeus Huntgardner.

As I was leaving, the receptionist waved me over. "Sometimes, Dr. Huntgardner remembers better. You might come back when Mr. Drasher is here. He and the professor talk a lot."

"Any idea what they talk about?"

"Mr. Drasher says hidden things."

Once again, I was staring at a grin from someone who thought they had said something clever. This one might be right.

CHAPTER 11

Angie sometimes stayed over, but she hadn't this time because she needed to get an early start. I was ten leagues beyond exhaustion when I crawled into bed, as tired as I could ever remember. Sleep had descended in an instant. So, I was lying there dead to the world when a flashing blue light started up somewhere in the front part of my house.

The flashes alternating with the darkness brought me awake. And the short, piercing screech of metal against something solid — floor tile or hardwood, maybe — caused me to stir on my pillow. I had a burglar.

My mind wasn't at its sharpest, but it was still happy to serve up a word for this: *Phantasmagoric.*

Well, think about it.

My patrol car was parked in front of the house, as it was on most nights. A billboard saying, "A cop lives here!" wouldn't have been any more obvious. So, this person was either brain-damaged, drunk, or foolhardy. Or else someone who had wanted entry into the home of the local sheriff in the worst way.

I don't sleep with a gun under my pillow. Two words explain why: trigger discipline. Anytime my finger touches the trigger of a gun, I want my mind awake. Sentient. Focused. Under my full conscious awareness and command.

To come awake, my brain needs at least about as much time as my Dodge Charger to go from zero to sixty: five seconds. Absent that, the odds that I'd shoot myself in the head as I move about in restless slumber are every bit as good as the next person's.

That's why I keep my Glock 22 in a gun safe that doubles as my nightstand. My reading lamp and my digital clock sit on top.

As my feet hit the floor, I noticed the LED display on my clock. It read 2:16 a.m.

I noticed other things too.

I noticed that I was pumped so full of adrenaline that it felt like I had never been to bed at all.

I noticed how easy it was to extract the Glock from my gun safe in the dark.

I noticed how the gun melded into my hand with all the familiarity of my morning coffee cup.

I noticed that my house shoes seemed to know where I would be lowering my feet. I slipped into them, then noticed something else.

Each time I took a step, I was anticipating the move that came next so intently that when I made it, it felt like I'd already been there. That's when I realized that when the stakes are high, what you can end up noticing may be otherworldly.

My bedroom door was the last door at the back end of the hallway. The opening to the kitchen was on the opposite side of the hallway about a third of the way toward the front of the house.

I had night-lights in the hallway and in the kitchen. Thus far, my unwanted visitor had not stepped into their beams because I had seen no shadows. And I'd spotted no one in the illumination of the flashing blue light sweeping around my living room with the regularity of a lighthouse beacon.

If I saw someone moving around, chances were high that I was going to fire my gun with deadly intent. That was something I'd always tried to avoid. So I called on my lungs to convey my resolve at being obeyed. "Sheriff's department! Hands in the air! *On your belly, now!*"

A couple of loud thuds issued from my kitchen. These were followed by a tinkling sound, then a sharp, high-pitched clink. Then another, softer clink.

I thought I knew what the causes of those sounds were. First, one of my kitchen windows had been broken. After that, the window screen had slammed against something hard, then bounced once.

From the start, I'd assumed the racket startling me awake had happened after my intruder had broken into my kitchen. Now, I understood that there had been no break-in in the kitchen. The invasion of my home had to have come earlier elsewhere in my house. The racket I'd heard in the kitchen was my intruder breaking out.

You needed a key both coming and going on all my outside doors because of the double-keyed deadbolt locks. The only copy was on my pocket key ring. When I shouted, my intruder had rushed to the back door but couldn't open it. He'd unlocked the low-slung kitchen window leading to the patio. Raised it. Broke one of the panes, likely injuring himself.

Dived through, body-slammed the screen, and rolled onto the patio. I heard the sounds of rubber shoe soles slapping against a concrete surface. The only glimpse I caught through the kitchen window was of a shadowy figure racing around the corner of my garage. He was about as tall as the bottom of the breezeway light fixture mounted on the side of the garage — a little less than six feet.

It was one of those split-second decisions, but I chose not to chase him. I was in my house shoes and pajamas. And it was dark outside.

I turned on a light, glanced around my kitchen and confirmed everything I'd suspected.

Instead of hurrying to get dressed, I called my nighttime dispatcher, Saul Peetson, on my mobile radio.

I asked Saul to flood my neighborhood with whatever deputies could be spared. All I could tell him to look for was someone who was about six feet tall and might have lacerations on his hands. "How soon can they get here?"

Saul was his usual efficient self. "They're on the way."

"I've got something truly weird to show them."

"Can I tell them what?"

"You can as soon as I figure out what it's all about."

I'd found the source of the flashing blue light. It was one of those cheap party lights that revolves like a temporary emergency beacon placed atop a cop's car. It sat on a black plastic base and was no more than four inches tall. I'd seen them advertised on the internet for less than five bucks plus shipping.

The light had been placed on my living room coffee table atop a handwritten note. I was holding it as I talked to my dispatcher. When he asked what was going on, I'd almost read it to him. But I decided I didn't want to give him, or anyone else listening to our late-night radio communications, a head start making jokes about the bone-tired sheriff's science fiction encounter.

They'd be making the jokes up soon enough, and I might be adding a few of my own.

Only four words were written on the note under the flashing light, all of them in labored block letters: "DON'T MAKE ROSWELL'S MISTAKE!"

When three of my night deputies arrived, I told them what I knew, asked them to make themselves at home, and went to my bedroom, closing the door behind me.

For the first time in my career, I chose to ignore trigger discipline. I slid my Glock under my pillow.

This time, despite all the excitement, I believe I went from sixty to zero in less than five seconds. The last thing I remember before falling asleep was a flashing blue light on the inside of my eyelid.

CHAPTER 12

I overslept.

My chief deputy had apparently left word that I was not to be disturbed for anything short of the Second Coming. So I didn't learn about the excitement at Pecan Mountain Nursing Home until I was about to leave for work.

Jeff Brailsford, my daytime dispatcher, said the bomb threat had been received about an hour before dawn. Anonymous caller. And from all indications, a malicious one, like most kooks who call in bomb threats.

Our hazardous devices squad had gone through the nursing home wall to wall, floor to ceiling, and found nothing amiss. Jeff said all the occupants of the home had been housed in a nearby school until the all-clear had been sounded. We were releasing audio of the call containing the bomb threat, hoping someone might recognize the voice. Detectives were listening to it too. By the time I got in, the sleepy-eyed occupants of the home had already been wheeled back to their rooms and tucked in their beds.

Since things had returned to normal, I decided to proceed to my meeting.

● ● ●

If no more than two people plus myself are involved, I can hold meetings in my office. The rickety old round table I'd picked up at a garage sale allowed for three chairs to be placed around it, while still leaving room between the table and my desk for people to squeeze by.

Meetings with more than three participants got assigned to a cleared-out corner of our situation room. It had a large white board and a cork board within reach. But no doors or windows and very little foot traffic. It was the closest thing I had to a conference room. So that's what we called it. Conference Room Corner.

I'd asked Helen Grainger, my veteran office manager, to request the presence of three people soon after eight o'clock. My chief investigator and CSI team leader, Doug Lewis. The medical examiner's field supervisor, Evelyn Thompson. And our game warden, Johnny Filo. When I walked into our ready room, I could see that all three had found themselves a chair in the conference area.

I started with my head forensic investigator. "Find anything in all that chaos, Doug?"

He yawned. Wide. It embarrassed him. "Sorry, haven't been to bed yet. We spent half the night lugging sheet rock debris out of the house." He looked at the ME guy. "That way, our medical examiner friends could at least get to the bodies." He scratched under an armpit without seeming to notice how awkward it looked. "Correction. What's left of the bodies." He handed each of us a single sheet of bullet points. And yawned again. "Stop me if there are questions."

He was balancing a beat-up faux leather portfolio on his knees. That's where his own copy of the list rested. "No blood spatter on the furniture or walls, bullet holes in the ceiling, discarded cartridge casings, footprints outside the windows, nothing that looked like a weapon. None of it."

He was tracking the points on his list with his index finger. I noticed the rest of us were picking up the habit. "Second, and I know the sheriff and others who were first-in have already been commenting on this, but there weren't any personal effects in the house. Nada. Nothing to tag, bag, or photograph. That we could find."

He glanced over the top of his reading glasses, but his eyes didn't fall on anyone. "Third, no usable fingerprints on water faucets, door handles, cabinet surfaces, tabletops, wood facades. No fingerprints, period, actually. They've been wiped, methodically. Most surfaces were coated with sheet rock dust, for that matter. Nasty stuff."

His finger had already moved to the next line. "Fourth, nothing of consequence was found outside the house so far. No wastebaskets or trash cans, footprints, tire marks, or signs of digging. We're just beginning to move out from the house into the surrounding fields, but so far, zilch."

Doug flicked his eyes in my direction but only for a second. "Fifth, the bodies — what's left of them. Not a lot we could do. We check for defensive wounds. See if there was anything under their nails. Photograph clothing. Search for drag marks. Note the location of wounds. Just not possible with these bodies. The putrefaction. And then the buzzards. Talk about destroying the evidence."

I'd never heard him so disinterested, so dismissive. Of us, of a crime scene, of himself. I attributed his laissez-faire attitude to fatigue and let it go. But I had questions.

"The bare feet?"

His mea culpa gesture involved tapping his forehead once with two fingers. "Oh, sorry. The feet. All the victims' feet were bare. Shoeless. And sockless. We'd have noticed this sooner, but their footwear was covered by a large piece of the kitchen ceiling. Actually, they weren't shoes. They were all heavy-duty construction boots. The kind that lace up through eyelets."

I thought his breathing changed and wondered what was coming next. "Funny thing is, we found too many shoes. Ten pairs. And we only have, you know —" like a kindergartener, he held up his hands, palms outward. With one thumb folded down. And wiggled his remaining thumb and all his fingers. "— nine bodies."

My mouth gaped open, but he wasn't finished. "Oh, yeah, hot plate and fans. The hot plate was under the sheet rock in the kitchen. Don't know if someone had knocked it to the floor or what. Had a coffee pot close to it. One of those Pyrex types. Lying on its side. Just enough coffee left for us to take a sample."

"And the fans."

"Oscillating type, like you'd sit on a tabletop or a counter. Good-sized fans. Six of them. Scattered around the house. Close to electrical outlets but none of them plugged in. Kind of a 'now you feel them, now you don't' scenario. Maybe they wanted the bodies to deteriorate quicker in the heat."

Baby steps. The house was beginning to talk to us. But the sheer chaos at this scene was overloading my staff. And me too. It took a moment to think what my next question should be. "Any drinking cups anywhere in the house?"

"Didn't find any. They must have used paper cups."

I sighed, summoning patience. "Find any paper cups?"

"I think a garbage dump is one of the things Chief Deputy Tanner and his guys are looking for out beyond the yard."

I wanted to hear next from the ME's representative.

Thompson said maggots had been feasting for days. "We think forensic entomologists at Texas A&M will be able to narrow the timeframe. We're going to send them samples."

Her best guess was the same as mine. Five days.

"They were way past the point of exploding from internal gases. Purge fluids had quit draining from noses and mouths, where there were noses and mouths. Skin and hair had sloughed off. And fingernails. But then, not counting bones, the buzzards didn't leave a lot behind."

Fortunately, she thought her boss, the medical examiner, would be able to take bone marrow samples from all the bodies. That would help them ID the victims.

She took a deep breath like she was finished, but I wasn't. "Can you use those samples to test for poison?"

Weary as Evelyn Thompson was, she could still wag her head. "We can't. But a forensic toxicologist can. Plenty of big bones available. They work best. And sometimes, some of the hair was left too."

I asked my Game Warden Filo how long he thought the buzzards had been feeding. "Not long. Doesn't take long."

He explained how forensic anthropologists at South-Central Texas State University had filmed a wake of American black vultures eating a donated cadaver. Took just five hours.

"Literally stripped every shred of flesh from the body. Reduced it to bone. But I think these had been feeding at the house longer than five hours. So many bodies. The fuller they got, the slower they went. These birds thought they'd died and gone to —" His faux pas embarrassed him. "Well, you know."

I rolled my chair to the writing wall and removed a felt-tip pen from a suction-cup holder. Turned my back on my colleagues. Wrote one word on the board in big block letters:

PROFESSIONAL

I turned to face them. "I'm pretty sure these deaths weren't accidental. And that the killer is a professional. Or killers, as it may be."

This thought had taken root yesterday when my three colleagues and I had put on our breathing masks and returned to the crime scene. It now seemed certain. Amateur murderers don't leave behind scenes like this one. Only trained killers do. After planning their criminal actions down to the most minuscule detail.

But this was in sleepy Abbot County. The sanctimonious, over-churched Sunday School capital of Texas. To paraphrase Bogart's character in *Casablanca*, of all the piety-drenched counties in all the world, why show up in this one?

Professionals?

I was sure I'd only heard the word used around the Abbot County Sheriff's Department a few times at best. Usually in reference to Flagler's occasional prostitutes.

CHAPTER 13

They say when the mind gets overloaded, blessed are those who can compartmentalize.

Sitting in my office after my conference room meeting, I wasn't feeling very blessed. And I thought I'd been pretty good at compartmentalizing. The delegating part in particular.

I'd delegated control of the crime scene to my chief deputy. Tanner had done some delegating himself, turning his command duties over to Detective Moody at about four o'clock this morning. He'd driven his car back to the cattle guard. Folded himself into his back seat. Rolled his windows down. And, cut a break by the nighttime drop in the heat, managed to sleep for five hours.

He was back at the scene now, leading a mixed crowd of investigators in ever-expanding circles, searching the brush surrounding the house.

Detective Moody had returned to the office. I'd given her another job. Keeping up with the information flooding in. But I told her to first go home and get some sleep. Knowing her, she'd be back at the office by early afternoon.

Delegating was not the right word to describe how Special Agent Steele fit in all this. A country sheriff doesn't give orders to an FBI special agent. Even if he knows how to reduce her to instant putty by nuzzling a certain spot on her neck behind one ear. But I knew there'd be no need to ask for her help. Knowing Angie, she was going to be an invaluable conduit between the sheriff's department and all things federal, if the Feds turned out to be involved. That's the advantage of having an FBI agent's office just down the hall from yours. And having an exceptionally close relationship with its occupant.

I fiddled with the hole in the fabric on one of the armrests in my rickety black leather office chair. Fiddled and fidgeted. And realized there was more than compartmentalizing going on.

What had happened in Flagler in the past twenty hours was giving me a new sense of purpose. I felt like my special mix of skills could be useful to my trouble-beset county in a way I'd not experienced before. And that was good, because my piety-drenched, middle-of-nowhere community appeared to be needing investigative skills almost never found in a country sheriff.

What had happened in Flagler in the past twenty hours felt far beyond the boundaries of everyday circumstances.

The blue light parked on my living room table — who knew what that was about?

Not to mention nine mysterious, shoeless cadavers reduced to bones by buzzards in a remote house that itself had been ravaged beyond belief.

And there was the bizarre memory involving my father. A memory that reached out to me from beyond the grave. A memory about a chat he'd once had with a perplexing college professor whose mind was now rotting from the inside out.

I'd had no training in law enforcement for dealing with this kind of weirdness. I'd had no training in law enforcement at all. Everything I'd learned about law enforcement had come from my sixteen years on the job. That wasn't rare among rural Texas sheriffs. Most of my colleagues, I'd guess, had pinned on their stars without so much as a single college credit.

That wasn't an accurate description in my case. I had a Mercedes of a university degree on my resume. A Master of Divinity degree from Yale, no less. And that came on top of two preparatory degrees at the University of the Hills, where I'd been awarded magna cum laude. For those reasons alone, I'd always be considered an oddity among Texas sheriffs. The fact that I was the third generation of my family to do so provided more fodder for the gossip mills.

But, day in and day out on the job, I'd always felt the advantages in my background outweighed the disadvantages.

I still thought so.

A divinity degree is a compartmentalizing degree. More than anything else, it prepares you to divide things between the known and the unknown and travel between the two.

To borrow an idea from the New Testament's St. Paul, Hebrews 11:1, it prepared you to navigate the substance of things hoped for, the evidence of things unseen.

But I was certain that the events that had unfolded in Abbot County thus far were only a foretaste, a trailer. I had the feeling we were being herded like lemmings toward some kind of abyss. And if we weren't careful, our smug, inexperienced little community was going to find itself shoved right off a cliff.

ooo

Helen was on the phone again. I could hear her telling a caller she'd have the sheriff get back to them. "No, he isn't dodging you."

Helen had been my personal assistant from the get-go. I'd inherited her, in fact, from my father.

On most days, she wore a pair of oversized earrings, usually silver, either dangles or pendant-style, and a splashy matching necklace, often inlaid with turquoise. She was wearing her beloved accessories again today. The jewelry was competing with a freckled neckline that showed almost too much, but never quite went too far. She was one of the most winsome sixtyish widows in Flagler. And she didn't tolerate upset in her office, not from me, not from anyone. Certainly not from Clyde Hazelton, managing editor of the local paper.

She gave me a report. "Clyde says he's feeling neglected."

I suppressed a grimace. "Is he the only one?"

"Hmm, think not." She started flipping through her call-back pad. "Let's see, calls here from the Associated Press, *New York Times*, CNN, *Dallas Morning News*, *Houston Chronicle*, *National Enquirer*, and somebody at a blog called *Oddliers*. They want to run a story called 'The Mystery of the Ninety Naked Toesies.'"

This time, I didn't bother to suppress my disgust. "Cripes, never assume the media's taste has hit rock bottom."

So the news of nine shoeless bodies in Abbot County was out. My guess was that someone had been listening to our radio traffic. Maybe reporters. All you needed to eavesdrop was a police scanner. We didn't encrypt our calls like a lot of law enforcement people, and our technology was still a bit dated, so it was easy to do.

Helen was waiting for me to decide. She knew we had to feed the news beast soon or it would devour us. "News conference? Courthouse steps? Five-ish?"

"Sounds good. Draw up a press release. Get the reporters to come to us."

Next I found the number for Pecan Mountain Nursing Home on my phone. The receptionist said she thought Professor Huntgardner was in his room but would check to make sure. Would I wait?

I would.

I waited. And waited.

I was about to hang up and try the call again when I heard her voice. "We're in a bit of a panic here."

No need to tell me why. I'd been tardy in realizing that we'd needed to keep close watch on the professor.

Huntgardner was not only not to be found at this moment. From what she had understood, he'd not been seen since the bomb threat evacuation. They'd taken the home's ambulatory residents to a nearby school gymnasium to wait out the bomb squad's search, and she wasn't sure he'd been seen there. Again, the truth hit me like the mother of all gas pains.

Of course not.

That was the other reason I was kicking myself.

Until now, I'd not tuned in to the fact that he was the reason *for* the bomb scare.

CHAPTER 14

The remains of the tenth person were discovered by Chief
Deputy Tanner and his helpers as they searched in the
mesquite and live oak thickets behind the Huntgardner house.

"Defleshed," I'd heard Sawyers say amid the static arriving
on my two-way radio.

For a moment, I wasn't sure if he was going archaeolog-
ical on me. The ancients sometimes removed a body's organs
and flesh before burying them. "Defleshed them" was the way
scholars sometimes put it.

But if my chief deputy had been trying to be pedantic with
me, he'd more likely have said it like most archaeologists do.
"Excarnated them."

Sawyers added, "Except for the bones and clothing scraps,
very little of the victim is left."

Sawyers said the remains were found about a hundred
yards north of the house. Judging from the shreds of clothing
scattered about, he was guessing this had been a *he* — we'd
have to see what the ME said.

We could assume this victim had died about the same time
as the others. Five days ago. Although this corpse had been
lying in the sun and could have deteriorated faster. I suspected
the buzzards had still been at work when we'd fired up our

"symphony of the sirens." Like the others, those birds would have lit out for Cheyenne.

Sawyers believed this victim had been run over. That was based on the damage to the bones. The tibia and fibula on both legs were broken, the pelvis was shattered, the spine looked anything but right, and the skull had multiple fractures.

My chief deputy wasn't saying it, but I was sure he was thinking the same thing I was: this person had been killed while trying to flee.

I asked about shoes. Sawyers said there weren't any. So we could suspect that this was the owner of the tenth pair of work boots in the house.

"Tanner, what about —"

A burst of static cut us off. I waited until the airways soothed themselves. Tried again. "Any other signs of activity?"

I thought I heard him say something about "entrail ration out here" but knew that couldn't be right. "Ten-nine, Tanner."

He repeated himself. "Grand Central Station out here."

"How so?"

"Lots of pattern evidence. Shoe prints. Tire tracks. Big suckers — dual rear wheel types. Could have been big pickups or rental trucks or maybe transportation vans. It might explain how these poor folks got to the house. The CSI crew's making casts now."

"Can you tell where they originated?"

"Not where they started, no. But I think I know where they were headed. To the old washout road that leads to the Sweetwater cutoff."

"So they were easy to follow?"

"Like I said, Grand Central Station."

I asked if they'd found anything else of interest.

It sounded like he hawked on hearing my question, but I knew it was the static. I repeated my question. "Anything else of interest, Tanner?"

"A garbage bag."

"Garbage bag?"

"Yeah, one of those big thirty-gallon plastic bags. Somebody tossed it to the side of the main tire tracks about halfway to the washout road."

"Anything in it?"

"Picnic stuff. Plates, drinking cups, plastic forks — that kind of thing, you know. Closed it back up so CSI could take a fresh look."

My mind was seizing any comforting thought that wandered past, no matter how remote. This time, it served up a variation of Neil Armstrong's bungled pronouncement on the moon. My variation? *One small step for a sheriff, one less mystery for mankind.*

"Good work, Chief. If you can get here, we're having a press conference at five."

I'd been facing the end wall of my office as I spoke into my desktop microphone, so I hadn't realized Detective Moody was back from her sleep break. She was leaning against the door frame, listening.

I exaggerated surprise. "You ought to be a detective — you're good at sneaking up on people."

She smiled her wide smile and got straight to the point. "So, we'll be telling the media we've got ten victims, not nine."

"Bet they already know."

I turned to my computer and typed in "tenth body in Abbot County." Google informed us that two of Flagler's TV stations, Clyde Hazelton's paper, the *Tribune-Standard*, and a British tabloid were already running bulletins.

She shrugged and turned to leave, so I ended up talking to her back. "I'd like you to join me at the press conference."

I thought that she'd return to my office, take a chair, and we'd talk about this. But she didn't.

She didn't turn around. Replied without taking another step. "And say what?"

"Probably nothing, but it'll look good."

The moment the words left my lips, I realized my comment could be taken more ways than the Manhattan subway. Had I sounded racist? No question, if that's the way Rashada chose to hear it. Egotistical? That too. Sexist? Glaringly so. Self-promoting? That, most of all.

When my detective did turn to face me, she offered her equivocal look. It wasn't hard for her to use that on me. The two times we'd had dinner before I met Angie, I'd found her skilled at leaving me flummoxed. Or amused. I'd always wondered what kind of item we might have become had Angie's transfer to Flagler not intervened.

"Nothing's going to leave us looking good on this one." That was when I knew she'd understood.

She hammered it home with another comment she flung over her departing shoulder. "The phone's beginning to ring, so I better help in the ready room instead. You can handle it on your own. Just tell reporters that Flagler's trying to grow up."

CHAPTER 15

I ran a quick eye over the motley crowd of reporters, recognizing all but four of them.

I suspected — correctly, as it turned out — that the four I didn't know were university journalism students. They looked young. And they sat together apart from the usual culprits: three on-the-scene TV reporters, two local newspaper reporters, four radio station reporters, and a few stringers for the *Dallas Morning News* and the *Fort Worth Star-Telegram*.

I started by noting that we were asking the media to urge people to call our "800" number if they knew anything. We were especially interested in knowing about anyone in the Flagler area who might be missing.

Forty minutes after our press conference ended, I checked in with Detective Moody.

She wasn't taking the calls herself. Four of our other deputies were doing that. Jotting down information and handing her the call slips. She already had four piles underway on her desk pad. She looked up to make sure I was watching. Then pointed to the first pile. "Missing relatives, neighbors, acquaintances — Texas only."

To the next pile. "Missing from outside of Texas."

The next one. "Suspicious people spotted in Abbot County."

And to a call slip sitting by itself. "This is going to be my 'Make the Pope's Horse a Cardinal' pile."

My surprise was real. "Your what?"

She sounded a little guilty. "Shouldn't be saying things like that on a day like this."

"Make the Pope's horse a cardinal?"

She looked around to see if I was the only one in earshot. "Old children's poem. Pope Leo the tenth was fat, but his horse wasn't. When he asked for advice on how to fatten up his horse, somebody suggested he make the beast a cardinal."

She pointed to the single call slip again. "Let me try again. Offbeat suggestions go in this pile. This caller suggested a psychic we should try."

Now that I understood it, I admired her attempt to inject a little humor. I was feeling the weariness. "I'd love for someone offbeat to tell us how to start solving this one."

She nodded and took another fistful of call slips from the deputy who had approached.

Plenty of reasons to be pessimistic.

But one in particular.

No matter how many call slips Detective Moody sorted through, or how well she did it, it wasn't likely to help us anytime soon. At the moment, we had no way of telling who any of our victims might be, even if we got a direct hit.

I'd have been more morose had I not known Special Agent Steele was due to arrive at my house in an hour or so. Before dawn, she'd been sent to Brownwood, a little over an hour's drive southeast of Flagler, to help with a drug crackdown. Business completed, she was motoring home. She had requested that I pick up green-chili chicken enchiladas from Casa Mariachi.

□ □ □

I bided my time at the restaurant's takeout counter. When my turn came, I picked up enchiladas, tortilla chips, salsa, napkins, and plastic tableware in a take-home sack and headed to my car. I didn't notice anything unusual at the time.

That may have been because I had been paying more attention to my nose than my eye. What's Spanish for "ambrosial"?

¡Olé!?

Fragante!?

Olores maravillosos!?

As I made my way back to my place, the odor wafting through my car confirmed Angie's good judgment, not to mention good taste, in requesting Casa Mariachi's green-chili enchiladas for dinner.

I wasn't in my Charger. The supervisor at the county garage said they were still cleaning it and airing it out. I was driving an almost new gray Ford Taurus we'd outfitted as an undercover unit.

Flagler straddled the eastern hills of the O'Mahony Ridge range. I'd bought a house in a subdivision that spread out over the top of one of those hills.

From downtown, I always got to my place by taking a winding four-lane street called Bison's Cut Drive and turning into my neighborhood after a couple of miles. I noticed the vehicle behind me not long after I started up the hill. A white pickup. Looked like a late model. Had heavy window tints. That's all I could tell.

I changed lanes. A couple of blocks behind me, this vehicle did likewise. I activated my turn signal and changed lanes again. So did the pickup. Looked like I was being tailed.

The hills of the O'Mahony Ridge aren't easy places to build houses. My subdivision, Wild Deer Estates, had a street layout like a spider chrysanthemum bloom. Only one way in, and once you were in, you had a choice of going all the way to the roundabout six blocks away and coming back out or taking one of the "petals," the petals being streets.

Only taking a petal didn't get you very far. The streets weren't very long. And they all had the same thing at the end. A cul-de-sac.

The limited navigation possibilities were one of the reasons I'd bought a house there. I thought it would be a good place for a sheriff to enjoy privacy in his off-hours.

I'd never had to chase anyone or flee from anyone in Wild Deer Estates, but of course, I'd thought about how I'd do it. Wouldn't chase or flee at all. Would bait a trap. Then spring it and let everything come to me.

I could do that because every two "petals" shared an alley. They had culs-de-sac at the end too. Some of them were curved. The one closest to the entrance to the subdivision was almost a dogleg. If I jammed on my brakes, backed into this alley like a stunt driver, and killed the lights in time, I had a good chance of going unobserved by anyone following me or chasing me. At least, going unseen until I wanted to be seen. Then I could dart behind my quarry as he attempted to exit.

Everything went as planned until the exit part.

The white pickup sped past, headed into the subdivision. A late-model Ford F-350. Big sucker. Dual rear wheels. The window tint was probably legal, but I couldn't see inside. Or, in the fading light, read the license plate. They could have been Texas tags. I'd know as soon as the truck reappeared.

I waited.

Two minutes. Three minutes. Four minutes.

Nothing.

I continued to watch the digital clock numbers tick by on my car's audio system. Five minutes, six minutes.

Nothing.

The smell of Mexican food was soaking up the oxygen in my car.

I wanted to go home.

Be off-duty. Have a tasty meal. Share news, strategies, doubts, fears and hugs with a wonderful woman I was hoping to be with for a long time. Feel safe and sheltered and protected from purveyors of mayhem and death, if only for the night. In my own house, my own bed. Was it too much to ask?

After nine minutes passed, I wasn't sure.

Had I been too clever by half? Too cocksure about my abilities to take advantage of my neighborhood's weird Google Maps signature?

I wasn't sure.

Could this have been one of my neighbors driving a new F-350? Someone visiting who had one? Or had I allowed some of the evil that had invaded Abbot County in the past two days to pass unchallenged a few feet in front of me and disappear into my own subdivision without confronting it?

Where had it gone?

I wasn't sure.

I could ask for deputies to respond and help me search. As a resident of Flagler, I was entitled to that.

My department also provided police services to Flagler. It was one of those city-county "metro" arrangements our voters had approved in the late 1990s. There weren't many of them. Las Vegas and Clark County, Nevada, had them. But at the moment, my deputies were like me — overextended. Exhausted. And I really didn't have anything concrete to tell them. Only suspicions about some weird behavior on the part of a driver. Or not. He — or she — could have been nothing more than a kid with a rich dad, a new driver's license and the bangle of all bangles.

Or I could start searching the subdivision myself.

I'd already put my car in gear when my phone went off. I knew the ringtone. It was Angie's.

She said she had gotten in earlier than expected. She was already at my house. If I didn't get there soon with the enchiladas, she was going to call in another order, go get them herself, and start eating alone.

"Where're ya at?" she asked.

"Just down the street."

"Then you'll be home in a jiffy."

"In a jiffy."

"I've parked in your driveway. You won't recognize the car. Mine's in the shop. This is a rental."

"What color?"

"Gray."

"What kind is it?"

"A Taurus."

"How new is it?"

"This year's, I think."

I told her to stay out of her car. Draw the drapes. Make sure the doors were locked. And keep her gun handy.

Her reply was vintage Angie sass. "Well, here's loving you too, Mister Luke."

But given how we both made our living, we had agreed on another rule. *Prudence until you know it's safe.*

She'd do what I asked.

CHAPTER 16

I'd had a relationship this serious once before.

Mary Austin had been a willowy blond. So was Angie. Mary Austin liked to pull her long hair back in a ponytail. So did Angie. Mary Austin favored pinning it toward the back, higher than you might expect. Angie did that too. I don't think these likenesses and some of the others had anything to do with my attraction to her. But who knew?

I'd never mentioned it to her, and I didn't plan to. It wouldn't at all be in keeping with my resolve to let the past be the past.

I was halfway up the front walk when she flung the front door open, took a few quick steps down the sidewalk, and stopped to eyeball the street in both directions.

She blocked my advance. Scowled up at me. And reached for the Mexican food bag. But she was wearing her gun. "Explanation, please, Marshal Dillon."

I grasped her left bicep — it felt only a tad less firm than a baseball — and decided to forgo any levity. "I think I was followed home."

"By what?"

"A new Ford F-350 pickup."

"So where'd they go?"

"Disappeared. Somewhere here in the subdivision."

I could see her attitude building. "Six thousand pounds of steel and rubber? In this itty, bitty place. Like Poof the Magic Dragon?"

"I believe it was Puff the Magic Dragon, not Poof."

"With the best law enforcement tracker since Cochise hot on its tail?"

"Cochise was an Indigenous chief, not law enforcement."

She gave me an exaggerated pout. "Well, thank goodness, the great Wells Fargo delivery man didn't lose the enchiladas."

"I need to give you the full story."

"Please do! Unless you think we need to turn the sofa over and get behind it with our rifles first."

After two years, I was getting much better at reading Angie's moods and real intentions. She only fired both barrels of her sarcasm when she was uncertain, tired, or hungry. I sensed at the moment it was all three.

"You had anything to eat since breakfast?"

"Energy bar."

"When was that?"

"Early afternoon, I think. The gangbangers in Brownwood were down for their naps."

I suspected that the energy-bar story was a fabrication or a half-truth.

She might have never had an energy bar. Or she might have opened one, then had to toss it in the gutter because a raid was starting. Or she might have eaten part of it, grimaced at the blah taste and offered the rest of it to a stray dog.

She was famished.

She had set the table. Or rather, spread dinner utensils on my bar counter. I could see a pitcher of fresh tea on the cabinet. I reached for two mason jars and began filling them one at a time from my refrigerator ice maker.

Angie moved the enchiladas to a baking dish and put it in the microwave. I was already wishing that I'd picked up sopapillas and flan too. I sensed a long evening of heart-searching introspection ahead, and yummy Mexican desserts would have gotten us off to a nice start.

I had my hand on the oven door when the microwave timer went off. Cochise couldn't have nocked an arrow any faster. I served up enchiladas. And counted two *hmm-mm*s, several *ah*s, and any number of smacking sounds before either of us said another word.

Then it was Angie who wanted the conn. Three green-chili chicken enchiladas had done wonders for her constitution, mental and physical. "I heard on NPR about your tenth body."

"Can you believe it?"

"At least you know who to return the shoes to."

"Just wish I knew who to return the body to."

"Oh, that's going to happen. What we have to hope is that we don't keep finding them."

"You heard that the professor has gone missing?"

Angie's eyes got wide, and her mouth flew open. She hadn't heard.

I told her what I knew.

She listened like I was supplying details on how we were going to kill Caesar. "Your town . . . isn't . . ." She didn't finish her thought, but then, she didn't need to. I was sure she was about to point out that my town was starting to look like it was something other than what it had always pretended to be: an open, welcoming kind of place, especially to newcomers.

But analyzing my community's psyche could wait. I had ten suspicious deaths to solve and a demented missing nursing home occupant with a shady past to find. And a young FBI special agent's crackerjack mind available, maybe for the entire evening.

I tried to dab enchilada sauce off her chin. "I'm not a conspiracy theorist —"

"You think, Sheriff Luke?"

She dodged my hand so she could look me in the eye.

"His house. Mystery number one. His dead house guests. Mystery number two. A bomb threat that empties his current place of residence. Mystery number three. The man himself goes missing. Mystery number four. Weird stories about the gentleman from your own father, a former sheriff. Mystery number five." She shook her head so hard her ponytail flew over her shoulder. "No, sir-ee, Mister Sheriff. A very good time for you to be a conspiracy theorist is my guess. I think your sanctimonious little town is losing control of its secrets."

I had a thought about all that. "I keep wondering —"

"Do you think your father knew what this is all about? Or even your grandfather?"

It was a habit she had.

At first, I'd been as annoyed as most people at her interruptions. Then I'd realized how much her mind thrived on possibilities. Watched for them, hunted them down, prioritized them, interpreted them, pieced them together. Her gifts had enabled her to write a prize-winning master's thesis at the University of Iowa analyzing Mark Twain's racist instincts.

It was possible that my father and grandfather had known what it was about. Only McWhorters had worn the sheriff's star in Abbot County in the past fifty-two years. But I sensed what she was asking was if my family could have been part of the ugliness that was surfacing. Maybe even one of the causes of it.

I didn't know and told her that. "Both my father and grandfather were true meat-and-potatoes Texans. Steady as rocks. If you needed it, they would give you the shirt off their backs. But they were also cowboys at heart. They didn't talk about a lot of things. At least to me."

"And now they're gone."

"A lot of people in Flagler are gone. Or will be going soon. I'm getting a hunch that this might be close to the heart of the matter. The truth is trying to get out —"

She finished the sentence for me. "— while there's still someone around who knows where the truth is buried."

□□□

Angie decided to stay the night. That was happening more and more.

Since Christmas, we'd both kept clothes and toiletries at the other's place. Our nocturnal discussions were becoming more intimate and confessional. Sometimes, we'd talk deep into the night. And cuddle. Love-making was rarer than I think either of us would have liked. But we were often too exhausted for such exertions.

I'd already begun to look at rings.

Angie fell asleep before she could cover herself with the sheet. I did it for her. Then lay awake for long minutes thinking about the pickup that had followed me into my subdivision. About the ten slayings that had happened in my county this week. About the mysterious and now-missing Professor Huntgardner. About the past and the cruel hand of fate.

It had robbed me of my future once. I'd go fighting into that dark night before I'd let it do so again.

I got out of bed. Went to the kitchen. Turned on the light. And had a sudden thought. An urge, really.

I walked outside to where our cars were parked. Got down on my hands and knees beside each of them. And did my best to see if I could spot anything amiss. I couldn't.

Back in the kitchen, I found Angie's car keys where she'd laid them on the counter.

I hid them on the top shelf of my cabinet. Then I located the pad I usually compiled grocery lists on. And wrote Angie a note. It was unlikely she would wake up before me, but I didn't want to take chances.

"I have your car keys. Don't leave the house without me. We may have a problem. Love, Luke."

I'd been thinking about the pickup. About its dual rear wheels. About my chief deputy's comment about dually tracks at the crime scene. About why a killer would go to the trouble of shadowing me as I left the office and following me for miles, only to disappear a few blocks from my home.

I intended to awaken early. The first thing I was going to do was call the sergeant in charge of our bomb squad and ask him to send someone to search both vehicles. I could have done it right then, but I wasn't sure if my fears about a bomber were an overreaction. We didn't need any more unwarranted excitement around the department. Especially in the middle of the night. We had enough as it was.

But at the first crack of dawn, I made the call. I couldn't think of anything that would plunge Abbot County even deeper into despair and confusion than a bomb planted on its sheriff's car.

Especially if it went off.

CHAPTER 17

My sergeant, Haskell Haines, responded himself, along with another member of the bomb squad. They pulled up to the curb in their menacing white-over-black truck. The vehicle looked big enough to be a local-haul moving van.

My deputies' lack of urgency reminded me of the mail carrier's. They'd stayed in the cab long enough to have ordered a pizza and gotten it delivered. I didn't think that's what they were doing. They mostly just sat there talking and pointing at the two cars in my driveway again and again. And consulting their laptop like they'd forgotten instructions on how to breathe.

Angie was up and dressed now, and we were both standing across the street from my house on a neighbor's lawn. Watching. Waiting. Wondering. It was all we could do since neither of us had our mobile phones or radios. At least my deputies had waved at us. Once.

By and by, Sergeant Haines stepped out the cab and walked over. He said good morning and informed us that a patrol car was coming to transport us to our offices. He didn't want us to return to my house until there was an all-clear. My neighbors for two blocks around were going to be ordered to leave too.

He saw the impatience on my face. "You never hurry a

bomb, Sheriff. And unfortunately, our Labradors only sniff out drugs. Deputy Ainsworth and I are going to put on our bomb suits and see if Andy can spot anything."

Our bomb squad hadn't been accredited very long, and it hadn't been called out that often. I'd never been with them on an assignment and wasn't all that familiar with their activities. Or their argot.

"Andy?"

"The most expensive gadget in your department, Sheriff. Andy is our robot."

"Why 'Andy'?"

"The manufacturer calls it the ANDROS F6A. It's the gold standard creepy-crawly for finding bombs. Even has a periscope."

□□□

I didn't get to see Andy find the bomb because Angie, the neighbors, and I were long gone. But Sergeant Haines said it was in plain view, taped to my gas tank. From the office, I radioed him for details.

"Nothing fancy. Four sticks of TNT and a tilt fuse. Didn't even have a timer. They were counting on it going off the first time you hit a bump. Probably when you went over the street gutter backing out."

"And if it had?"

"Well, we'd be needing a new sheriff, most likely. And other people could have been killed. Lots more injured too. If it had detonated, say, downtown."

"Can you find who made it?"

"Maybe. It helps that it didn't go off. We're going to ask Alcohol, Tobacco, Firearms, and Explosives to get involved. And the FBI."

That reminded me that I needed to talk to the FBI myself.

Angie answered on the first ring. "Special Agent Angie Steele of the HTBA bureau speaking."

I decided to play along. Serious talk at this point might be treacherous anyway, given the arrogant way I'd handled this situation from the first. "Excuse me, I think I have the wrong number."

She didn't miss a beat. "Boyfriends who forecast car bombs can use this number at any time."

So she'd moved past her pique at awakening to learn that her car keys had been hidden behind my mother's crystal dinnerware.

"And HTBA?"

"It stands for 'Happy To Be Alive.' And you are forgiven for spending all night thinking about car bombs instead of the beautiful creature sharing your bed."

We seemed to have abandoned the rule that the personal go unreferenced when someone else in the office might be listening.

I asked her where she thought I should focus my attention. I thought she'd use the question to joke around a bit more. But the time for joking was over. "I've been reading about Professor Huntgardner on the web. Very interesting. You knew he was a physicist, right?"

"Yes, I've never forgiven him. He gave me the only *F* I ever got in a class, college or otherwise."

"Then you know he started the physics department at Hills-U?"

"Seems like I did. Or maybe I just assumed it. I remember he lived and breathed the stuff."

"Then you probably heard him talk about how his passion for exploring and mastering — what did he call it? — 'the second Scripture.' That was his name, you know, for the physical universe."

"I do remember that, now that you mention it."

"And how his inspiration was triggered by the first atomic bomb blast in New Mexico?"

I paused for a minute, thinking. "The only time I can recall hearing the Trinity thing mentioned at Hills-U was by my history professor."

"Professor Huntgardner was just a teenager that morning. Said he saw the light from the blast just over the mountains. Said it profoundly changed his life."

I waited a few more seconds before I spoke again. My thoughts had gone elsewhere.

But Angie didn't seem to mind. In fact, she didn't wait for me to speak. "I find it odd that July 16, 1945, keeps popping up. I think that's where you should start." She segued again from the serious to the breezy. "Maybe you'll get a better grade in physics this time."

I could hear her smile over the phone line.

CHAPTER 18

It wasn't the Wikipedia article about Thaddeus Huntgardner itself that I found compelling. It was one of the footnotes to the article. And not anything that the footnote said, but what I found on a website referenced by the footnote. Two more clicks and I was reading from a media release dated June 1972. The University of the Hills had issued the release to dramatize the announcement of its new physics department:

31 miles north/northwest
of Roswell, New Mexico,
shortly before 5:30 a.m.
July 16, 1945

Thaddeus "Thad" Huntgardner took small steps in the darkness of his parents' kitchen. Not quite tiptoes, but almost.

Sometimes, he didn't move at all. Not until he felt something familiar. A chair, a drawer handle.

He could have flipped on a light switch, but that would have dispelled the mood.

He unhooked the screen door and eased into the

pitch-blackness of the backyard. He peered off to his left, to the east, but there was nothing on the horizon. Not yet.

He loved the waning moments of the nighttime like no other. It was why most mornings he arose at his house before anyone else and pondered life and things as he waited for the first appearance of dawn.

But at the very moment when history laid down one of its most eradicable markers, sixteen-year-old Thad Huntgardner was gazing to the west, not the east.

That's how he witnessed the light from the first sunrise that morning — the one that came from a godforsaken valley in a remote corner of a desolate Army Air Forces bombing range called White Sands. From a desert patch along a route the conquistadors had called the Jornada del Muerto: "Journey of the Dead Man."

At 5:30:45 a.m., the predawn sky flashed a brilliant yellow. Witnesses in every state and nation bordering New Mexico saw it. It was hotter than ten thousand suns and brighter than a dozen of the Earth's own warming star.

Thad was more than a hundred miles away, so he was not endangered by the blast or the heat. But at that instant, he realized he had been jolted across a threshold.

That's how it felt: like a lightning bolt.

In two years, he would leave for college, and until that moment he hadn't given much thought to what might give focus to his studies.

Now, he knew. He could feel it. He wanted to study what the universe was capable of. The kind of forces that had turned the predawn skies into a light

brighter than day — he could surrender his curiosity
and future to that.
    And he has.

I had no idea what this had to do with ten suspicious deaths,
a missing dementia patient, the Roswell note left in my living
room, and the duct-taping of a bomb to the gas tank of my car.

But I sensed that I needed to know a lot more about the
professor.

CHAPTER 19

They told me at the county garage why they'd kept my car so long. They had to take some of it apart.

Dismantle the inside of the door on the driver's side. Pressure-wash everything that could survive a wetting. Scrub it all down with liquid industrial cleaner. Do another rinse. Blow it dry. Then reassemble it. Some components couldn't survive being drenched. These had to be replaced. The motor for the power window, for example.

As I drove away, I noticed that some thoughtful soul had placed an air freshener on the dashboard.

Savoring the smell, I thought of Robert Herrick's poem. "Gather ye rosebuds while ye may . . ." *I got straight A's in English, Professor Huntgardner!* The interior of my car smelled like rosebuds.

Quite nice.

I was headed for the four-lane arterial that leads up the hill to the turnoff into my neighborhood, the one where all the drama had started yesterday evening. Only this time, I'd be turning left at the top of the hill, not right. I was not going home but to the University of the Hills. I didn't think glancing in the rear-view mirror several times as I went up the hill was being paranoid. This time, I saw nothing that caused me any concern.

The university's big granite sign marked its entrance. The Whosoever Rock, as students had called it for generations. I sped past the sign and steered for the new Bible Building. With its dazzling bluish plate glass exterior, it was impossible to miss.

I needed to talk to someone with an encyclopedic knowledge of all things past and present at Hills-U and I knew that would be Dr. Malachi Jepp Rawls. Three decades of Old Testament students had called him "the Prophet." His specialty was the book of Ezekiel. I'd considered him a friend as long as I'd known him. Maybe even a mentor. He'd told Helen I could have the first appointment after lunch.

Watching Dr. Rawls walk toward me had always been a unique sight. It was like watching a diminutive "weave artist" advance with a walking stick. Or a mercurial peewee football player parry and feint in the backfield. He was only about five-foot-four, which made his damaged leg all the more obvious. He'd had polio as a child.

He walked to the door to welcome me. Stuck out one hand and waved me to a chair with the other. "Saw you on TV last night."

In his office, the Prophet had a hat rack that I'd always admired. An elegant wood sculpture affair. The carver had chiseled the shape of a lush, leafy vine into the surface of a six-foot-tall butternut pole about three-and-a-half inches through and through. Like Jack's beanstalk, the sensuous design started at the bottom and wound its way to the top. On every visit to my friend's office in the past sixteen years, the first thing I'd done was park my Stetson on the rack's uppermost peg, the one angled toward his office window.

But not today.

The hat pole had been moved from beside the door to the end of his desk. Now, it was protruding into one of the few open spaces in his floor plan. This disrupted the traffic in the room, particularly for the Prophet himself. To get to his chair, Malachi had to walk out and around the hat pole.

This wasn't the only anomaly.

The venerable, taupe-colored trench coat he favored on nippy days for the entire time I'd known him was hanging from one of the hat pegs. Not its usual place. Usually, you could expect to find it hanging from a hook at the end of one of his floor-to-ceiling book shelves.

The new arrangement seemed a bit awkward. It looked like he wanted his coat within easy reach.

I gestured toward the hat rack. "Practicing a little feng shui?"

I thought he might chuckle, but he didn't offer so much as a smile. "There's a loaded pistol in my coat pocket. I decided that was better than sticking it in my belt. That's too visible when you don't have a license to carry."

For an instant, we stared at each other like two birds that had spotted a worm at the same time. Then our gazes went elsewhere.

I felt like I was watching a movie in fast-forward. It started with my friend being placed in a jail cell on gun violation charges. Malachi's eyes seemed to focus on the badge pinned to my shirt. After an interval, he decided to see if the conversation could be rewound. At least to the point before he'd tossed it off the bridge.

"You know, I've never been to the old Huntgardner house. Not once. Always found it strange that he would isolate himself so. But then, maybe not. He had an obsession with darkness, as you probably know. It seemed all consuming. I told him one time that he should write a physics textbook for blind people."

"What'd he say to that?"

"Laughed. Said that was his life calling — helping his students understand what the dark can tell you if you don't get blinded by the light."

"So you knew about his Trinity story?"

"Puzzled by it is more accurate. I came to Hills-U in the late '70s. Back then, he babbled about his little parable, as he called it, at every opportunity. In his lectures, speeches, interviews, conversations. Then one day, he just stopped. If someone else brought it up, he'd change the subject. He even quit letting the university use it to promote the physics department."

This gave me the opening I was looking for. "So can you think of any reason why his Trinity story would get ten people killed at a house he built to chase the darkness?"

Dr. Rawls's eyes were casting shadows again. That left me nonplussed.

I hadn't entered the Prophet's office expecting that he would have anything to hide. To my knowledge, he'd never lied to me, so it wasn't my intention to build a house of cards that could trip him up.

Was it the way I'd phrased my question? Had it suggested more than I'd realized? Did he think I was trying to make him take ownership of a theory for this crime and reveal more than he wanted to say?

Or all of this?

I repeated the question in my mind: *Can you think of any reason why his Trinity story would get ten people killed at a house he built to chase the darkness?*

Watching Malachi, I decided to change my own ground rules. My own expectations. I was going to adopt a different strategy. See where things went.

With no hat rack in easy reach when I'd walked into his office, I'd hung on to my Stetson. The hat had been resting in my lap. I stood and used it to gesture toward his hat rack. "Mind if I get rid of this?" I didn't wait for an answer. I went over and hung it on the top peg.

My move could be read in one of two ways: I had switched to being more aggressive, or I was planning to stay awhile. I didn't wait to sit back down before asking my next question. "When was the last time you saw Professor Huntgardner?"

My friend's eyes blinked in rapid succession. Several times. Five, six. I counted them like the FBI agent said he did when he was interviewing the Oklahoma City bomber. I knew the Prophet was about to lie to me.

"Just a guess." More rapid blinking. "Do you know when he retired? I probably saw him at the faculty reception that year."

"Did you ever share any students?"

"I'm sure we did. We both taught classes required for freshmen."

"Did any of your students ever tell you there was something weird about his interests?"

Malachi leaped at the chance to be sarcastic. "Oh, sure. Here I was, a guy who's obsessed about a book in the Bible full of incoherent visions, kaleidoscopic churning wheels, and desiccated bones. Just the person you'd pick to complain about a guy who was nuts about finding out why most of the universe is in the dark."

By now I was taking notes. "Universe in the dark?"

"You've not heard of the dark energy and dark matter thing?"

"Well, I've heard the terms."

"How about Stephen Hawking?"

"I tried to read *A Brief History of Time*. About all I remember is his catty quip. The one about needing a research accelerator as big as the solar system and thinking he probably wouldn't be able to get it financed in today's political climate."

"Then you probably don't remember what he said about dark energy and dark matter."

I saw a chance for a little cuteness myself. "No, I'm still in the dark."

If Dr. Rawls saw any humor in that, he kept it to himself. Or perhaps he was just excited about his opportunity to enlighten me. "We have decent explanations for only about five percent of the energy density of the known universe. Sixty-eight percent is dark energy, whatever that is. The rest is dark matter, whatever that is. Dr. Hawking said this darkness was the missing link in cosmology."

"Professor Huntgardner was interested in this?"

At this point, I could see my learned friend's sense of self-preservation catch up with his desire to come across as super-informed. "Well, that's what some people said."

This time, I was stunned into silence. I tried not to imagine how I looked as my mind trotted out three new suspicions about Dr. Malachi Jepp Rawls.

One, I now doubted he was the open book I'd always believed him to be. He had to be harboring secrets. They might be important secrets. Secrets that could push to the heart of the crimes I was trying to solve.

Two, I had reason to suspect the emotions he was feeling had him close to panic. He was trying to hide them. But his mouth had turned down. His forehead had developed deep furrows. And his eyes couldn't seem to find anything to focus on — they were flitting back and forth around the room.

If he didn't outright know the reason for the ten murders in that madman's enigmatic old brick house, it seemed like he had strong suspicions. And letting on that he suspected anything was making him as nervous as a germaphobe in a garbage dump.

Three involved my other hunch. My suspicion that the words in my question that had spooked him were these: "in a house he built to chase the darkness."

I was preparing to revisit all this with the Prophet when my phone rang. It was Helen. The urgency in my assistant's voice made it clear I needed to steer straight for the office.

CHAPTER 20

Helen wasn't sitting in her chair. The throne, as she referred to it, was occupied by a kid. His stuffed backpack sat abandoned at one corner of her desk, so I was guessing he'd come to the courthouse straight from summer school.

He was in his mid-teens and had sandy hair that looked a little like an abused Brillo pad. I couldn't tell about his smile because I wasn't seeing one. He and Helen, who was standing to his left, were transfixed by whatever they were watching on her computer screen.

She gave me one of her urgent "You gotta see this!" looks. "It's gone viral."

I sought more information. "What's gone viral?"

"On Twitter. My nephew can show you." She laid her hand on his shoulder. "Tommy, meet Sheriff Luke."

Still no smile. Serious kid. But polite. At least he glanced up, nodded, and said, "Howdy." Since he didn't remove his hand from the computer mouse, I didn't offer to shake it.

Of course, I knew about Twitter. The omnipresent Pony Express of cyberspace. The me-and-thee online social networking service that limited you to writing 280 characters in any given message. But if you knew how to execute the launch, it allowed you to send that message flying off to a jillion different people, or at least a few hundred, at the speed of light.

I'd been hoping for months to get at least a half-time social media person for the office. But it hadn't happened yet. Until it did, I'd been depending on my usual salvation: Helen. But I had the feeling that whatever was going on now had arrived on her radar screen with the aid of the young man sitting in her chair.

Tommy looked up at his aunt. "This tweet here doesn't make any sense —" He stopped speaking, swiveled his chair in my direction, and pointed back at the computer screen. "That's what they call those messages, Sheriff. Tweets. Like bird chirps. Because they are short."

I nodded. "Thanks for that."

The tweet was from someone calling themselves @donthinkzebras. It said, "Why isn't Sheriff McWhorter telling anyone about the anthrax?" It was being retweeted frequently.

I didn't bother to look at Helen. My whole body was telegraphing my consternation. Anthrax! We'd never had a case of the dread bacterial disease in Abbot County, much less had anyone die from it. At least, not to my knowledge.

"When was that tweet made?"

Tommy pointed at the screen. "Six minutes ago."

"Have there been others?"

"Loads." He used the power-scroll wheel on Helen's computer mouse until he spotted what he was looking for. "The first tweet using the #DOAFlagler hashtag appeared thirty-three minutes ago."

Again, I needed more information. "What else have they been asking?"

Helen signaled that she wanted to be the one to reply.

She said the first tweet had sounded casual, although, she added, it may not have been. It could have been a red herring.

Or a sick joke. This was the one with the #DOAFlagler hashtag. That tweet had asked if anyone else in Flagler had been approached by FBI agents asking if they'd received any unexpected packages with white powder on them.

"What happened next was like Chinese firecrackers. One tweet after another. Someone said they hoped Flagler wouldn't turn out to be another Bhopal. Another tweeter asked about evacuation plans for the county. People started speculating about where the anthrax could be coming from."

Looking over Tommy's shoulder, I saw that someone named @vengeanceisours had just posted a message. "Remember polio, Flagler! It took your kids once & anthrax will do it again!"

Helen froze, then leaned forward to catch my eye. She suggested that this conversation be adjourned to my office.

Tommy said he would do some checking around to see if he could find any other internet interest in Flagler and anthrax.

□ □ □

Helen rediscovered her voice first. "I don't believe Abbot County has had a case of polio in . . ." Her eyes angled toward the ceiling. "I don't know — fifty years. Probably more."

I knew that the dread polio virus had always been a master of ambush. Capricious to a fault about when and where and who and how it struck. When it did, it segued into an even more cruel, fickle creature.

Most of those infected felt like they had a mild case of the flu and quickly recovered. Only a handful of the victims — and they were nearly always kids — became paralyzed, usually in their legs, sometimes for life. An unfortunate few lost the ability to breathe because their chest muscles were paralyzed. Most of those victims died appalling deaths.

More than anything else, it was polio's diabolical whimsy that had made it one of the most feared diseases of the twentieth century. Texas had been an epicenter in America for the contagion. And Flagler, for reasons no one had ever adequately understood, had been an epicenter for the disease in Texas.

Helen's knowledge of how all this had affected Abbot County was much more vivid and extensive than mine. After all, she'd been born in one of the worst years of the Texas polio epidemic: 1952.

"My parents were too frightened to let us go outside. When people who had polio in the family came to see us, they had to stay on the porch. We couldn't go to church, either. Our church canceled its worship services when the news really got bad and people started dying. The swimming pool was closed too. And the picture show — unless we went to the drive-in."

I kept nodding, and she kept remembering.

"Airplanes were spraying everywhere and fogging machines in the alleys. Spreading DDT. I remember that because it stank so bad. Sometimes people wouldn't roll down their car windows — didn't matter how hot it was outside. Some wouldn't even use the telephone. They thought polio germs might crawl through the phone lines."

A peculiar look seized her face. She raised one corner of her mouth in a half-smile and started to sing softly with her West Texas twang.

She sang about getting rid of the housefly and the mosquito. Because they carried a bug that could make you terribly ill. About keeping the garbage can covered and not drinking from the creek. About eating sanitary food and keeping your utensils clean. And taking care to wash your hands and brush your teeth after every meal. All because this was how polio would be beaten.

She looked embarrassed, especially when she saw her nephew staring at her through my office's glass outer wall.

"I'd forgotten I knew 'The Polio Song.' When I was a girl, we sang it around the house — my sisters and me — more times than I care to remember. A guy named Red River Dave wrote it. Sang it over WOAI, San Antonio. It stayed on the radio for years. My mother taught it to us. She thought it would improve our hygiene. Make us safer."

"Dr. Rawls caught it, you know."

He and I had discussed this several times. How excruciating the muscle spasms and the treatments had been.

His doctors, like most doctors, had little idea how to treat infantile paralysis, as it was often called. So, several times a day, they'd wrapped his legs in old woolen army blankets soaked in hot water. They thought the heat and the dampness from their hot packs would help relax his rigid muscles. He said he'd go to his grave remembering the itching and the pain from the heat — and how bad the stench was. The torture went on for months and months, even on hot days. All this in an era with little air-conditioning.

The good news, he'd conceded, was that he hadn't needed to be placed in the dread iron lung.

Malachi said these clunky devices looked like miniature versions of a Jules Verne submarine. They were big enough that a person could be laid on their back in one, with portholes for attendants to reach through. They saved lives by alternating the pressure of the air around a stricken person's chest. Lowering the chest, then allowing it to rise, then lowering it again, unceasingly, around the clock.

I hadn't thought of that conversation with Malachi in a long time.

Any other time, I'd have been swift to get the Prophet on the phone. Remind him of our chat about polio. And ask how serious this threat about anthrax sounded to him. But after the conversation I'd just had with him in his office, a concern of a different kind was worming its way into my mind.

I'd not doubted some of the tweets Helen, Tommy, and I had read came from citizens with genuine concerns. But the whole discussion had an undercurrent to it that felt like manipulation. Like disinformation. Squirrelly.

I had no trouble putting exact words to what I was feeling. "Like somebody was trying to throw the dice so they'd turn up snake eyes."

The Old Testament was filled with such acts of deception. I was certain Malachi could tell you about a dozen of them in Hebrew, Greek, and probably Assyrian as well as English.

This whole episode felt like another instance of someone in Flagler stirring the dust because they were afraid of losing control of events. Or explanations. Or maybe just losing control period.

I could see Professor Rawls having such concerns. And being capable of pulling such strings. I'd not be discussing tweets about anthrax or polio with him.

But I would ask our Greek-born county medical examiner. Soon. It was only a two-block walk to her offices. First, though, I needed to dictate an official tweet from the Abbot County sheriff's office and get Helen and Tommy to send it out with the hashtag #DOAFlagler.

It would deny any and all claims of anthrax bacteria or polio viruses running loose in our county.

CHAPTER 21

How we'd gotten the irrepressible Dr. Konstantina Smyth for our medical examiner was a Cinderella story. Not that she'd come to Abbot County looking for her glass slipper. It was more her husband that she was trying to keep in her sights.

Mr. Smyth was British and a teacher of medieval history with what I'd concluded were modest skills. They'd met in Athens as undergraduates. In the two decades she'd spent getting MD and PhD degrees and credentialed in forensic anthropology, he'd traipsed after his ambitious wife without complaint.

When he was offered a job at Flagler's smallest college, she'd said it was his time. She didn't mind talking about it in her quaint second-hand English. "He has been the one deserving." It didn't seem to have bothered her that a world-class forensic anthropologist was heading off to podunk.

"Doc Konnie" was hard not to notice. She was a large woman with chipmunk cheeks, mischievous dark eyes, over-painted lips, and a chin that resembled half a donut. She'd consumed hefty servings of moussaka, pastitsio, and souvlakia in her forty-plus years.

"Yassou!"

I returned the big smile. "Yassou, yourself!"

"Always, I like this job."

"I knew you'd find this case intriguing."

"The bodies, there are so many."

My outfit was similar to hers because she'd provided it when I'd arrived at her office — a lab coat. And, given my recent medical history, she'd also provided a barf bag. It was jammed in my coat pocket.

"The job you are ready for, I see."

"And I see you've already been on the job."

"I will take a look. You will take a look?"

"I'd be disappointed if I couldn't."

Other times I'd been there, Doc Konnie called her autopsy room her industrial kitchen. She'd told me that was because it was larger than most such facilities. But I'd never been in it when more than two cadavers were out on display. If there were any others, they'd been wheeled into cold storage.

Not this time. The remains of all ten of our victims were resting on gurneys.

Most of what there was to see were the bones. For the most part, they were lined up on Doc Konnie's tables in the order Mother Nature had intended. *Back bone connected to the shoulder bone, shoulder bone connected to the neck bone, neck bone connected to the head bone.* As I looked on, the song played itself over and over in my head.

Sometimes the bones were connected, sometimes they weren't.

Doc Konnie had left a path through the shiny metal tables so she could walk to the center of the room, view all the gurneys, and decide which one she wanted to examine next.

"The elements, I have checked them. Preliminary, of course. A few are — how you say it — kaput. Missing. Smaller ones, in the most part. The buzzards, they must have eaten them."

"The bones, you mean."

"No, the elements." That's what it sounded like she'd said, but I knew she was mixing apples and oranges again. English and Greek. I'd learned in divinity school at Yale that the Greek word for yes looked like "neh" in our alphabet. And sounded like "no" to English-speaking ears.

She'd told me, yes, some of the smaller bones were missing.

"Everything, I have put in anatomical position. We will now take a look. You will take a look?"

"I'll take a look."

She summoned me to peer at the nearest skeleton's pelvis. "The sexual dimorphism — so pronounced. Every one." She gestured dramatically toward the nearest gurneys. "No pelvises here for having babies."

"So, they're all men?"

"Neh, all men, those."

This time, I provided the dramatics, sweeping an arm over the assembled tables. "Younger men, middle-aged, older?"

"We will take a look. You will take a look?"

Again, we approached a tidy arrangement of what was left of a human being. She pointed to the pelvis again — to a precise point halfway between the two hip bones. It looked like Mother Nature had filled a space between the halves of the pelvis with a hefty strip of grout that had turned to bone. "Pubis symphysis" — she spelled the words for me — "this is. It is changed, with age. This one, it is not so young, it is not so old. Others older, others not so much."

I knew when she wrote up her report, she might be more precise, but I got the point. Age-wise, we had a wider range of victims than I was expecting.

"Big question. How'd these people die?"

"All morning, I have been looking." She held both arms out. "Every gurney. Every specimen. From tip of phalanges to last zag in coronal suture on each one."

"From top to bottom, I get it."

"Neh, neh! Sharp force trauma, projective trauma, I do not see on these." For the first time, I'd become aware that she'd pushed one of the gurneys apart from the others. She'd been talking about the nine cadavers that were grouped together. "Blunt force trauma, I do not see on these." She gestured toward the nine tables again. "Strangulation, maybe, but there are no signs. Electrocution, heat related, explosion — that is difficult. Maybe I could see, but I do not. OH-kee, OH-kee!"

Or so it sounded. But I knew she'd lapsed into Greek again. She'd said "όχι, όχι!" No, no!

I'd learned not to rush Flagler's Greek-born ME when she was leading you through the thicket of possibilities. We were getting there.

She summoned me to follow her to the gurney parked away from the others. No introduction was necessary. This was the victim that my chief deputy thought had been run over.

The skeleton looked the part. And a lot more than the leg bones, pelvis, and spine had been damaged.

"The human body, it has two hundred and six bones. At least by time it is grown out. This one I think is grown out — more than thirty years. Another male. Hit so hard. See, everywhere, there are fractures. For itself, the skull has eight fractures. We will take a look. You will take a look?"

She had something to show me, so I followed her lead. She bent over the midsection of the skeletonized remains, so I bent over the midsection. And looked where she was pointing.

"This one, I have an idea how the death arrived. You can see that, neh?"

"I can see it."

"The photographs, we have already taken."

"I appreciate your leaving it in so I could see where it was."

"I will pull it out so you can closer look."

"That would be good."

She left to get one of her stainless-steel kidney dishes and a pair of tweezers. On her return, she leaned in and grasped a translucent piece of plastic the color of tangerines. It came from one of the hip bones and wasn't sizable — smaller than a pencil eraser. It slid around in the tray when she thrust it toward me but made very little noise.

"To the lab, we will send this. But this one, I will predict a guess on cause of death." Both her eyebrows and her eyes were dancing. "Blunt force trauma."

I agreed.

I was almost certain we were looking at a tiny piece of injection-molded plastic from a broken vehicle light. Tangerine-hued lights were most often from the front headlight assembly. If so, it would indicate that our tenth victim had been run down by a forward-moving vehicle. One probably accelerating.

I handed the tray back to her. "For the lab."

She swept an arm in the direction of the other gurneys. "I will hope the lab tells us information on these gentlemens too. From the few blood samples we have got. And the garbage bag, maybe. Everything to the lab. We only find the cause of death that way, I think."

"Unless your sharp eyes see something else here."

"We will be looking. I find something, you will come take a look?" She arched one brow and studied me.

"Anytime you call me."

CHAPTER 22

Walking back to the office from the ME's, I realized I didn't mention anthrax to Doc Konnie. She'd kept me too entertained to remember it. But then, I was convinced my suspicions about it being disinformation were correct. What had Helen called it? A red herring.

Even if the claims in the tweets were real, an abandoned house thirty miles from town would have been the best place for an anthrax outbreak. Especially since everyone who had entered the house after we'd found the bodies had been wearing protective clothing and a respirator.

My mind kept seeing plastic. A jagged tangerine-colored flake of it.

If we only had a witness.

Then I remembered we might have one. The big kid at the cattle guard, the one who'd kept plying me with rehydrating fluids. He'd said he'd seen something. I'd felt he wanted to tell me more, but for some reason, he'd held back. Knowing it would keep, I hadn't pressed him. Now I would.

I slipped my walkie-talkie off my duty belt, held it close enough to my mouth to trigger the automatic VOX switch, and asked Detective Salazar if he was listening.

"You just missed me. Left the office about five minutes ago."

"Question about the teenagers at the cattle guard. You learn anything from them?"

"Only where to get the best burger in town. Eden Junction Bar and Grill. Order the Both Barrels Double Meat Cheeseburger. And be sure to ask for caramelized onions."

"No wonder you made detective so fast."

"Anything I can help you with?"

"The name of the driver."

"Jude the Dude."

"S'cuse me?"

"Said that's what he's called on the Flagler High School football team. He'll start at right tackle this fall. Sucker tips the scales at three hundred fifteen pounds."

"A lot of Both Barrels cheeseburgers."

"Nice guy. Very polite. Seemed above the average in the IQ department."

"I thought so too. He has a real name?"

"He does. Hold on a minute. Got to get out my notebook to get it right the way he said it. Here it is. Judson Thomas Mayes the One, Two, Three."

"Really? He actually said it that way?"

"He did. I don't think he likes 'the Third' much. Probably the only kid in school with a Roman numeral after his name."

"Comes with being a doctor's son, I suspect."

"He did say that. You going to talk with him?"

"If he's not out bagging rabbits with his buddies."

Judson Mayes III wasn't out rabbit hunting. He answered the phone at his house. When he volunteered to come to the courthouse for a chat, I asked if he could bring his mother or father. This time, I knew he needed to be accompanied by an adult.

I sensed some nervousness in his reply. "My mom doesn't come with me to appointments much anymore."

I wanted him to be at ease. "Would it be a problem for you if she did?"

His pause lasted only an instant. "Only if she started correcting my grammar."

Once again, I found myself liking the guy.

Jude the Dude and his mother arrived within an hour, and I seated them where I thought we'd all be most comfortable — in one of our interrogation rooms.

I thanked her for coming. "May I call you Ms. Mayes?"

Her eyes flashed. "No, you may not."

"So how should I address you?"

"With some respect, I would hope. I'm also a physician. A psychiatrist, to be precise. Referring to me as Dr. Simpson-Mayes would be appropriate."

Dr. Simpson-Mayes was gristle in the stew pot from the start. "This is an interrogation room." She was still standing, ramrod straight, her pricey leather purse dangling from one hand. She looked dressed for a business meeting. Maybe she'd come here from one. Beige patent work pumps. White pants. Navy blue jacket. Light tan ribbed blouse. A string of pearls.

"Yes, ma'am, it is. But this isn't an interrogation."

"So why aren't we meeting in your office?"

"I'll be totally honest with you —"

"That would be nice."

She walked to the other side of the table. Parked her purse in one of the empty chairs. Pulled one out for herself. And sat down without invitation. She appeared not to care if I finished my sentence, so I didn't. I'd been about to explain that my small office would not easily accommodate her strapping son.

That giant of a young man did what I had been about to invite him to do. He pulled out a stout metal bench we kept shoved up against the wall for overflow visitors and lowered his immense heft onto it.

His mom didn't let up. "All this because my son and his friends took a few potshots at some buzzards."

"Judson and I have already talked about the buzzards. We're good on that."

"So he's done something else?"

"Not that I'm aware of."

"It's because of what he saw at the Huntgardner house?"

"In and around the Huntgardner house, yes."

"Well, he tells me and his dad that he saw very little."

"Sometimes, it's those little things that help us in law enforcement the most."

Halfway through this tit-for-tat conversation, her son had lowered his head into his massive hands and started shaking his head. Without warning, he straightened up and slammed those sauce-pan-sized hands flat onto the table top. If we'd had a Richter scale in the office, I'd have expected it to register at least a 4.0. "Mom, I saw something."

The two adults in the room let this simple admission reverberate off the walls. His mother because she was speechless, and me because I wanted to see where he intended to take this. If he started waffling or fabricating events, I'd correct him. Or at least that was the plan.

But as the silence in the room grew, it became obvious to all three of us that he was going to need help. And that was going to make this sound more like an interrogation than I'd intended. I'd have to see how his mother reacted. I didn't want her asking for a lawyer for her boy. To my knowledge, he'd done nothing beyond violating a fish and game regulation about shooting at turkey vultures. I didn't think he'd need a lawyer.

But I sensed more than ever that I needed to know what he knew.

I ventured a question. "You saw something after you left the Sweetwater cutoff?"

"Well, a long way past that. We'd just made the turn to go down to the professor's house from the back road that runs to the ridge when we almost got run over."

"Run over by what?"

"Somebody hauling construction stuff."

"Like a big semi? Heavy equipment hauler, that kind of thing?"

"No, not that. A pickup, pulling a trailer. With a piece of machinery on it."

"Machinery for doing what?"

"We talked about that. Had a scoop on the front end — on an arm. Like they dig ditches with. A claw."

"Any markings on the truck?"

"You mean signs?"

"Yes, signs, logos, addresses, phone numbers?"

"Not that we saw. Plain white pickup. One of those big four-door jobs, though. With dual rear wheels."

"And they were driving recklessly?"

"Careening all over the road. I thought the digging machine was going to bounce off the trailer as they went by. Could've been bad news if it had. Might have landed right in our laps."

I chanced a glance at Judson's mother. One look at her face was enough to know she'd known none of this. And, now that she did, she was alarmed by it.

"So you don't know who was driving the truck?"

"Really don't."

"And that's all you saw?"

"Really is."

I don't know if his mother had detected the extra half-tick that occurred before he replied. But to my trained ear, it might as well have been an air raid siren going off. Plus, he'd said he really didn't know who they were.

"Really" was a word that stirred the interest of any alert interrogator. That's because it was forever showing up around claims of what had been said or imagined to be true — and weren't. Like when someone said, "Okay, what *really* happened is this." Didn't always mean someone was lying. But many times, it meant something was being left unsaid.

I'd have let it go this time if it hadn't kept reappearing in Judson's and my exchanges like a Whac-A-Mole.

Dr. Simpson-Mayes glanced at the door. The expression on her face suggested that she thought they'd be leaving soon.

But Judson had that other tell. His intriguing eyes. And those eyes were betraying him again.

So I did what I had a habit of doing when I didn't think people were leveling with me. I leaned back in my chair.

Maybe it was an old cowboy move — or cowboy *movie* move. I'd thought about bringing a piece of straw with me to questioning sessions so when I leaned back in my chair, I could start picking my teeth with it. I might do that some day.

But with Judson, I sensed my follow-up move should be the reverse of my usual wait-them-out move. I lowered my chair to the floor. Leaned across the table. And got as close to him as my supporting elbows would allow.

"Judson, I think you saw something else."

CHAPTER 23

As I listened to what Judson said next, I was already reviewing my options. I could do what Judson and his friends had done: take a drive over the prairie. But that was too slow, and it limited what I could view. I wanted to see everything that might be important, and I wanted to see it as soon as possible. That meant from the air.

We didn't have a helicopter — far too expensive for a department of our size. I could rent a chopper and pilot at Flagler Regional Airport, but I knew that after I paid the bill, I'd have trouble affording toilet paper for the office for the next year.

I could also request the Texas Highway Patrol helicopter from Midland. But who knew when it might be available.

Or I could do what I tended to do most times when I needed to view something from the air. Ask my friend Miles Cayden to crank up his eighty-one-year-old Piper J-3 Cub. "The Balcony Seat," I called it. The little airplane was cheap, but it allowed you to see what you needed to see, provided what you wanted to look at couldn't outrun you.

Problem was, I couldn't take Judson up with me.

The J-3 Cub only had two seats, one behind the other. Besides, its useful load was 450 pounds. Even if Judson managed to squeeze his massive frame into either seat, we'd have needed a malnourished dwarf for a pilot.

I tut-tutted myself for that thought. *Not very politically correct, bud.*

So I said as little as possible as I listened to the articulate man-child in my interrogation room.

He was fidgety. To an extreme. Didn't look straight at me again as he talked for several minutes. "I think they were spooked by something. Like they were fleeing, you know. Escaping."

"That would be a good observation."

"Scottie and Dennis wanted to go back to town. But I wanted to see if maybe we couldn't find where they'd been digging. I'm curious like that — gets me in trouble sometimes." He glanced at his mom. She offered him a wisp of a smile, but it dissolved as soon as he looked away.

He kept going. "Went all the way to the professor's house, kind of slow-like."

"You didn't see anything else?"

"Just some buzzards. Flying. The bodies — they were around front, right?"

I gave him a head tilt.

"So we went back to the ridge road. Saw some tire tracks pointing west. Toward that finger of the hills you can see veering off to the north from the main ridge. So that's where we headed."

I offered him another encouraging nod. His mother and I were proving rapt listeners — as attentive as any I could remember being in the room since we'd had a baby killer confess.

Besides, I sensed there was no need to ask any questions. Judson was getting there on his own.

"There was something else. Puzzled us, you know. Especially the first one we saw. But then we saw another one. And another. Wooden stakes, with strips of cloth tied to them. Bright yellow cloth things. It was a trail being marked."

CHAPTER 24

Forty-five minutes after I called him, Miles and I were bouncing around the thermals west of town like buzzards.

Well, not quite like buzzards. More like we were on an amusement park attraction being operated with no pity. But then, yes, like buzzards too. Up and down. Bounce and tilt. Circle and bob. Like a tiny cork on the ocean blue. Yes, like buzzards. I hoped we didn't meet the fate of a certain poor buzzard that came to mind.

Miles dropped the plane to near treetop level as we neared the ridge, and I almost lost my cookies.

Again.

I was sitting up front. That was normal when the Piper carried passengers. The plane balanced better if the pilot sat in the rear seat, even if flying solo.

We were low enough that spotting the trail wasn't a problem. We could see the tire tracks in the grasses. And the yellow markers. Both headed north. Judson had said the trail continued for five miles.

At seventy-five miles per hour, covering five miles takes four minutes. I know, because I timed it as we approached the geographic anomaly that Judson had called a finger of hills running perpendicular from the ridge. That's when I saw it.

Saw *something*. Hard to recognize what it was with the terrain whizzing past so quickly.

The wind noise in an uninsulated cabin and the roar of a sixty-five-horsepower engine almost in your lap made speaking difficult. I turned to look at my flying buddy and went through the motion of pressing the air down with my hand. Could he slow down?

He misunderstood. Took us out over the prairie in a tight turn. And brought us in even lower. Our turbulence whipped the grass blades like a violent storm was passing.

The plane had a bare-bones instrument panel — only five dials. I reached out and tapped the airspeed gauge. Pointed to the main needle. And moved my finger a fraction. Could he *slow* it down?

We were soon waddling in the air like a fat duck. The needle on the airspeed indicator pointed to forty — knots per hour, not miles. Compared to before, we were crawling through the air. And from my balcony seat, I started to absorb what lay at the end of the trail of yellow markers.

By our third pass, I had begun assigning things to categories. This seemed to make what I was seeing more — what? — investigable.

There was the realtor's benchmark. Location, location, location. Category number one.

In some ways, the tableau below us was picture-perfect. In western Abbot County's often uncharitable terrain, that was a departure. An anomaly. We had pretty views but few that you would want to reproduce on a color postcard. Whatever *this* was, its location was no accident. The choice had been a careful one.

We flew back and forth over it again and again. A tiny plain. The size of, say, three or four football fields arranged in a square. Three acres at most. Little more than a good-sized plot for the family horse. You could drive within a few yards of the area and never know it was there.

It was hidden, cuddled by its surroundings — encircled by an escarpment of eroded crags and rocks. I was curious about why I'd never known about this extraordinary setting before. It was so out of sync with our usual western Abbot County landscape that I'd have remembered it. But then, I'd never flown over this exact spot before. Or, for that matter, because of its isolation, even driven by it.

Another reason it was so well hidden? Before you reached it, you had to navigate a thicket of trees.

The moment I saw them, I knew that they were aristocrat pear. In the spring, they would produce brilliant white flowers. In the fall, stunning deep red leaves. In between, the trees made stately green sentinels, which was the case at the moment. They weren't native to Abbot County. Moreover, the circle they made at the edges of the clearing was too perfect. They had been carefully placed when they were planted. They had to have been growing for a decade, probably more.

And there were four features in the clearing that I categorized as symbols.

First, there were the two large, gleaming white oval shapes dominating the center of the clearing. I was only guessing, but I thought both designs had been formed with rock. White decorative rock. The kind people in Flagler sometimes used to landscape their yards so they wouldn't have to mow the grass.

Viewed from the air, the ovals conveyed the feeling that they were meant to be considered a pair. One was positioned above the other, almost but not quite touching. They were identical in size and arranged in perfect vertical alignment.

The second feature in the clearing was a phrase in Latin. It curved in an arc that aligned with the tree line. I got my ballpoint pen and notepad out of my shirt pocket, braced the pad against my leg, and wrote what I was seeing in block letters:

"UNUS MUNDUS."

I'd double-check what that meant as soon as I got back on the ground. But I remembered enough from my college classes in the classics to do an impromptu translation: "One world."

Even from the air, the Latin words sprang out at you. That was because each of the letters was tall — eight feet or more. Tall and a brilliant white, like the two ovals. You'd need a reconnaissance satellite to see them from space, but I doubted this was the point. I had the same feeling about the line of characters that was the third feature: "*E TENEBRIS.*"

More Latin. That one I'd have to look up. But like the letters in the Latin phrase above it, these had been created with obvious care. Again, the characters were sizable. They too were placed in an arc, though this one was at the bottom of the circle of trees. It bent in perfect symmetry to the curve of the tree line.

My feeling was that none of the designs — the ovals, the letters — had been there long.

I felt the same way about a large pile of red dirt that lay beyond the trees close to where the tire tracks ended. It was almost sure to be left over from the large hole that had been dug above the bottom sequence of letters.

This was my fourth feature. It had destroyed the careful symmetry and placement and beauty of everything else because it didn't fit with the artful surroundings. If anything, it looked like an afterthought. The empty chamber was almost certain to be a cavity into which any number of body bags could be lowered.

On the flight home, I brooded over my growing confusion. I'd been hoping what Judson Mayes had belatedly confessed to seeing would offer us a firm leg up on identifying our killer or killers.

But what kind of murderous mentality went to all this trouble? Especially, if the "trouble" had required many years of planning and preparation?

I had a hunch the county assessor's office could point me in the right direction. As soon as I got back to the office, I planned to ask Helen to call him and find out. I needed to know who owned the most unusual swatch of landscaping I'd ever seen in Abbot County. And the only one I'd ever seen with what I guessed was an open grave dug amid trappings that were otherwise beguiling and beautiful.

There was more on my mind. I realized I'd not bothered to ask Judson a crucial question: had he noticed any damage to the front end of the pickup truck that had almost run him and his buddies down?

We were going to have to talk again soon.

CHAPTER 25

Angie and I took turns cooking on Thursday nights. Why that night? Because Thursday nights were as close as we could come to a regular date night. Other nights belonged to other priorities.

On weekends, I could get busy helping my deputies manage Saturday and Sunday night misbehavior at Abbot County's honky-tonks. And frequently on weekdays, Angie got called out to one of her other counties. On these occasions, she might get home late. Or not at all.

Some Thursday nights weren't promising, either. I thought this might be one of them. On the phone, I suggested we could eat out. But she wouldn't hear of it. "I've got fresh salmon. And fresh asparagus. And key lime pie."

She'd subleased a patio apartment not far from downtown and was already home. And she had a plan. *You're a pretty lucky stiff, sheriff — don't disappoint the lass.* I wasn't going to, but I needed this to be a "working" date night.

It went well.

Had a nice rhythm.

Proceeded as I'd hoped.

For a while.

Beautiful, flaky salmon fillets, pan-seared to perfection. Crunchy asparagus, baked how I liked it — to the precise point of becoming tender. The key lime pie was ambrosial, and not only because it was my favorite dessert.

I used my linen napkin to blot my mouth. "I'm so happy you're probably the most stubborn person I've ever met."

Angie glanced over her shoulder at my notepad, resting by her phone at the end of the bar. "And now I'm going to earn my keep."

"Not yet."

I leaned across the table as far as I could reach without toppling into my plate and kissed her. She kept her lips pressed to mine longer than simple courtesy required. It gave me more hope that this was going to work out fine.

When she pulled back, she launched an impish look in my direction. "Heard you booked a flight without taking me."

"It was only a two-seater."

"I could have sat in your lap."

"And I'd not have gotten any work done."

This time, she leaned over to kiss me, and I knew it was time to get to the serious side of our working date night.

I walked to the end of the bar. Retrieved my notepad. And her phone. It was one of the FBI's smartphones. She could do everything on it I did on my laptop, she being a phone person and me an old-fashioned laptop person. I handed the phone to her and asked her to search something. I read out the first row of letters I'd copied during the flyovers at the clearing.

"That's Latin." She'd studied the language too, first at Texas Christian University and then at the University of Iowa. "Means one world."

"Thought so too. But what about these."

I gave her the letters at the bottom of the circle of trees.
E TENEBRIS.

She frowned. "'Out of' something, I think." She punched it into a translation site on her phone. "'Out of the dark.' Now, what else can I do to help the brilliant Yale Divinity School graduate with? That *was* an advanced degree, wasn't it?"

I threw my napkin at her. "Well, brainy gumshoe that you are, type that in."

She giggled. "Type what in?"

"'Out of the dark.'"

She gave me that little half-smirk that signaled she was about to have some fun at my expense. "You want all five billion Google results or just those on the first page?"

"What are the ones on the first page about?"

"A supernatural thriller film about a Spanish family that moves into a haunted house in Colombia."

"Try '*E tenebris*.'"

"At your service, Great Swami."

She said the first entry was a poem by Oscar Wilde. So were the next three entries. Then she quoted from an entry in the Masonic Dictionary. It noted that in early mythology and the primitive ages, darkness preceded light. "That means the sun is the child of night or darkness, Oh Learned One."

On that note, we abandoned our scholarly research.

CHAPTER 26

Angie was up and gone before I raised an eyelid. She'd be dodging armadillos and tortoises all day. Fielding a lot of "Howdy, how yah doins." And not be back until after sundown. She was on one of her goodwill day trips to sheriff and police departments in her northernmost tier of counties. She'd had a 250-mile drive ahead.

By the time I'd showered and shaved, I realized what my first official action of the day would be. Call Helen and ask her to set up a meeting in the Conference Room Corner.

My plan was to summon all available deputies. Tell them everything we knew. See if I could instill a heightened sense of urgency. Give out specific assignments. And send them off on what might be one of the most challenging quests in their law enforcement careers. And mine.

We needed to identify one or more missing people who had been in Abbot County.

We had ten sets of bones plus assorted tissues, and we still needed to find ten personal histories — ten identities — to go with them.

Knowing who they were should help us know why they were at the Huntgardner house. Until we knew why they were there, we shouldn't expect to understand their deaths. If we could understand their deaths, we'd have a much better chance of determining if all of them had been murdered. It wasn't likely, but the deaths could have been accidental.

And I'd have done all this pretty much as planned had I not glanced in the back seat of my patrol car as I left Angie's house.

My eye flitted across a cardboard box that should have been delivered days ago. One crammed with books.

Obviously, there was no great urgency surrounding the books or they wouldn't still be sitting back there. They were mostly paperbacks, a few new but most of them used, books about anything and everything and sometimes little of nothing. I'd been intending to drop them off at an abandoned warehouse next to the Flagler Shorthaul Railway's switching yard. My homeless friend, the Count, maintained his library there. On a dilapidated bookshelf he'd scrounged from a dumpster.

I'd first known him as Mason, last name, origins and intervening history all unknown. To me, at least.

I realized that by heading in Mason's direction, I could fulfill two goals with a single trip. A jewelry store whose engagement and wedding rings I'd been wanting to check out was close by. That sealed the deal. First, inspect more rings. Then, take my homeless friend his books. Or at least leave the box sitting by his bookshelf.

It'd been three years since I'd given him the bad news. That he couldn't spread his grubby sleeping bag in our local laundromats every night.

That night, he'd declined a ride to our county homeless shelter. But he'd later taken a liking to living in a tent. He never explained to me where he got his lodgings. All I knew was the tent appeared one day staked under a live oak tree in the abandoned community gardens known as "The Acres." Other homeless folks had soon joined him, bringing their own tents. The old two-story warehouse containing his library was across the street.

His name change had come shortly after I started bringing him boxes of discarded paperbacks. That was because I'd learned how much he liked to read. One of those well-thumbed books had been Alexandre Dumas's *The Count of Monte Cristo*. This was when he'd started calling himself the Count.

000

When I pushed on the partially unhinged door of the former Bartlett Machine Shop building, it pushed back. So I pushed harder, generating a tortured screech as the battered door dragged on the scarred concrete floor.

The Count was sitting on the floor underneath a window. Using the light coming through the window to read. Fresca, his mongrel pooch, was there too. Observing. The dog already knew who had come calling. And that all she had to do to get me to scratch her tummy was amble over and flop on her back at my feet.

You could see she was considering it.

"Yo, Count!"

"Sheriff!"

"You're reading something."

"Yup."

As I approached, he tilted the book so I could see the cover. I bent for a closer look of the shopworn green cover. It was a copy of Michelin's annual camping and caravanning guide — for 2001. "You're going camping?"

"Gonna be an expert."

"In camping?"

"Tent cities. France is full of 'em. Good as motels — cheaper too."

I gave him a thumbs-up. "Good to know."

"But you'll need to go to the patty-series every day. For breakfast goodies."

"Patty-series?"

He showed me the word. *Pâtisseries.*

"Right. Bakeries. The French have wonderful bakeries."

"You have to pay to put up a tent, though. Not like the Acres."

"Well, their customs must be different."

"And give 'em your passport every night. If you don't have an international camping car net."

He showed me the word. *Carnet.* French for book. "Carnay, right."

"That's what I said."

"Yass'um."

He changed the subject. "Bring me something to read?"

"I did." He already knew that. Why else had I lugged a box into the building?

Then the Count went quiet.

I was wondering if he had decided to exercise his constitutional right to remain silent. But I think he was searching for the right words. "I had big teeth on it, you know."

"What did?"

"The thingamajig on the trailer. They backed it into the building across the street a couple of days ago."

I reached down and scratched Fresca's stretched-out tummy, knowing she was about to be short-changed.

But I needed to get to the office and have Helen file for a search warrant for Flagler's old Cromwell Company warehouse. I'd been told there's a thingamajig parked inside it that the local sheriff needed to see.

CHAPTER 27

Helen reminded me that cranky old Judge Kincannon over in District Court would want to know the owner of the warehouse before he'd give us a search warrant. The county tax office gave her that. I heard her ask the clerk to spell the name again. She said thanks and started typing it into her computer.

Before long, I heard my first "Mmm."

I could have said, "Mmm, what?" but I knew she'd say what as soon as she knew.

"Lots of stuff about him on the net." Another pause followed, and I knew to expect another "Mmm." It arrived not long after. After more keyboard clicking.

At that point, Helen leaned toward her computer screen. Tracked something with her finger. And launched another "Mmm." "Meersman. That's *Doctor* Worley Meersman to the great unwashed public. He moved to Flagler three years ago to teach at the University of the Hills. Says here he's an assistant professor of physics."

I signaled my enthusiasm at her discovery. "Bingo."

"Started the U's first class in astrophysics, in fact."

"Bingo."

"Wrote a dissertation at one of the California universities on the impact of scientific discoveries on people's belief systems."

That revelation didn't get a "bingo" because I didn't know if it had anything to do with our suspicious deaths. But it was a factoid-of-interest. I flagged it as such. "Bingo-possible."

"He spends his summers cataloging Professor Huntgardner's papers in the Hills-U library. He's writing a book about them."

"Double bingo with a cherry on top!"

I asked Helen to call the university. If she was in, speak to the head of security. See if Dr. Meersman had done anything this summer to warrant their attention.

I returned from a quick trip to the men's facilities to find Helen holding a phone to each ear. She'd talk for a moment on one phone while holding the other one away from her mouth. Then she'd change the phones' positions and talk into the other one. Her conversations produced quick results.

The officer in charge of Hills-U's security force didn't seem surprised we were looking for Dr. Meersman. He'd failed to show up at a summer seminar twice in six days. They'd checked his house and found his yard full of newspapers and his mailbox jammed full. They had no clue where he was but were now checking his house twice a day.

His home phone was unlisted, but the university's alumni office provided a private email address. When Helen tried sending an email, she got a notice back saying that his inbox was full.

More to mark our turn of luck than commemorate our victim, I jotted one down on my desk blotter. *R.I.P. Friend of the Professor's.* I didn't mean to be cruel, but it was a habit I had. When things have been falling apart and then reverse themselves, it's hard for me to suppress an epitaph befitting the moment.

My feeling was growing that my epitaph was going to work for a bunch of unfortunate folks.

For the first time, I felt okay about giving the media more specifics.

I dictated what I thought a press release should say to Helen. Knew she'd turn my words into passable officialese. The gist of it was how much we'd welcome hearing from anyone who thought they knew a physicist or astrophysicist or physics professor or physics researcher or secondary school teacher of physics or a science writer whose whereabouts might be in doubt and had been for several days.

A CNN reporter was the first to respond. I stood listening to Detective Moody as she fielded the phone call. "Yes, this in connection with our ten unexplained deaths in Abbot County."

She extended her phone receiver almost straight up and away from her ear, then lowered it somewhat. "Yes, there is a reason we are particularly interested in people with training in physics who might be missing . . . From where? From anywhere."

My deputy was now whirling her pen on her desk blotter. "Yes, we have a tentative identification for a possible victim."

She gave an opposite twist to the pen. "No, I'm not able to give you a name or tell you more at this time . . . Yes, I can confirm that this person is a physicist . . . No, I can't tell you where they lived or were employed."

She picked up the pen and began doodling on her blotter. "No, at this time, we haven't developed possible identifications for any others. But we'd like to."

CNN must have rushed out a news ticker bulletin because our first call came within minutes. It was from a worried wife in Ashtabula, Ohio. After Detective Moody hung up with her, she shared the woman's details.

Her husband taught physics at one of the area's Kent State University campuses. He'd gotten a late-night email more than a week ago and left for the airport early the next morning. Said he would call her later about when he'd be coming home. But he hadn't called. And he hadn't returned. "Weird."

I was lingering at the end of Rashada's desk. "Weird how?"

"Well, he just didn't tell her *anything*. He got an email message. Erased it. Immediately booked a plane somewhere. Left the next morning and told his wife he'd be in touch. And disappeared."

"Didn't tell her *anything*?"

"Tried to joke with her. Said he had to go see a man about a flying teacup."

"Has she ever heard of Flagler?"

"Said her husband talked about it all the time. Got his undergraduate degree here."

That ended my conversation with Detective Moody. All four lines on her phone console were flashing.

I reached for her notes from the first call and pointed to Conference Room Corner to show her I was taking them. But she was so involved with the phone she didn't notice I'd left.

Other deputies had started fielding calls too. I moved to the writable wall in the far corner of our situation room. Dr. Meersman's name went up first. The missing Ohio professor's name, age, and location was next. The other deputies noticed what I was doing and began bringing me their notes as they hung up with a caller.

As the minute hand on our department wall clock neared straight up noon, the wall was filling up:

Worley Meersman, 40, assistant professor of physics, Flagler.

Parnell Sethridge, 46, physics professor, Ohio.

Will Lemsberg, 61, high school physics teacher, North Carolina.

Rodd Desjarlais, 55, science teacher, Chicago area.

Kieffer Bahn, 29, biomedical science writer, Baltimore.

Nathan Harmeling, 45, associate physics professor,
Bay Area, California.

I took a couple of steps back and counted them to be certain. There were six. When I'd left the Count and Fresca three hours before, we'd had none.

That's when I remembered one of my favorite Yogi Berra quotes. It had described something as "too coincidental to be a coincidence." I didn't know what Yogi was referring to, but it must have been something like what was happening on our suspicious deaths case.

Then I got a phone call that confirmed it.

CHAPTER 28

I had thought about asking Deputy Chief Tanner or Detective Moody or Detective Salazar to join me for my chat with Judson Mayes's mother, but I couldn't see any of them at their desks.

As for Dr. Simpson-Mayes, once again, she was dressed to the nines. "Professionally attired" was a phrase that came to my mind.

In our interrogation room, she didn't wait for an invitation to sit down. She went straight to the same chair she'd used before. And placed her purse in almost the exact same spot on the other chair and sat a cloth grocery bag she was carrying beside it.

This time, the purse looked like something out of the 1930s — gold mesh, gold tone metal frame, gold chain carrying strap. I doubted that any of it was real gold, although I wouldn't have bet the farm on it. But the purse radiated a vintage authenticity, so it could have been made in the '30s.

I saw something in her face I was not expecting — embarrassment, perhaps. Couldn't imagine about what.

Her first comment cleared it up. "I don't typically eat lunch at sports bars. But then, I don't have lunch that often with my ravenous son."

I wanted to put her at ease, so I gave her my reelection

photo smile. "Let me guess. You went to the Eden Junction Bar and Grill."

This seemed to have the desired effect. "So you know about the Both Barrels Double Meat Cheeseburger."

"With caramelized onions."

"I've already gone through half a roll of breath mints. But that's not what I need to talk with you about. They had CNN playing on one of their big-screen TVs. I saw the news bulletin."

I knew which one, but I wanted to appear as congenial as possible. "About missing physicists?"

She gave no indication at all that she'd heard me. No "yes," no nod of the head, no nothing. Only a curt bit of instruction. "You will need to understand something."

I was already understanding why Judson displayed confidence beyond his years. *The apple doesn't fall far from the tree!* "You have my undivided attention."

"You were so intent on questioning Judson the other day that you failed to include me."

I felt my smile edging toward a look of neutrality, and that's not where I had wanted this to go.

"In fact, you kept trying to intimidate both of us. That juvenile move you made leaning back in your chair and spreading your legs? I teach my women clients that when a man emphasizes his pelvis, he's trying to establish authority over you. Manspreading. Male apes have been doing that for eons. And it does convey a strong message, because . . . because a woman can't do that — especially in a business setting."

Okie-dokie, Sheriff, you've got a wildcat on your hands. Keep your legs close together this time, son. "Not sure I'd ever thought about that. Good to know, for sure."

"I'm a psychotherapist. I spend a lot of time talking with people myself. Therapy is a kind of interrogation. But we have more rules to follow than you law enforcement people do. And that's why you're going to have to let me do this my way" — she raised both hands, palms up — "or it's the highway."

This was a first for me. I couldn't remember someone pushing so hard in my interrogation room to make it their own territory. But new experiences can be good. "We'd appreciate any help you can give us."

Again, not so much as a head nod. I was beginning to feel like an extra in the school play.

"What I'm about to do can be dangerous under our rules of ethics. With rare exceptions, our clients are entitled to think that we'll say" — she scooted her pressed thumb and forefinger along her lips — "zip, about what they share with us."

I blinked twice and clasped my hands in my lap.

"But there are exceptions. We can disclose private information without consent if we are trying to protect the patient or the public from serious harm. I think that's what I'm doing here. And I'm going to leave it to you to decide what, if anything, it means."

Had she glanced at me, she'd have noticed I was blushing. Not because of anything I'd said. But because I'd spread my legs pretty wide in maneuvering my chair closer to the table. She appeared not to have noticed. And what she said next banished any concern I had about whether my pelvis was too exposed.

"I've been doing a lot of distance therapy lately — mostly on Skype. This allows me to accept a client from anywhere in the country. In the world, actually. But the clients on this list are all from the United States."

She had taken a piece of paper from her purse when she first sat down but had forgotten about it. I had noticed that it was letter-sized, creased once. Now, she reached for it. Pressed it flat against the tabletop. Used her fingertips to pivot it so I could read it. And gave it a gentle shove in my direction. "These names may be useful to you."

But before I could look at it, she reached over to retrieve the green tote bag sitting beside her purse.

She needed both hands to do it, but she moved the bag from the chair to the table. Spread the mouth of it open so I could have a good look at what was inside. And voiced another opinion. "There may be items in here that will be helpful to you too."

I pulled the bag closer, surprised at how heavy it was. Opened it wider. Let my eye range over what I could see without emptying everything onto the tabletop.

I recognized what I was seeing, but it took me a moment to understand why the bag contained so many small items you would expect men to carry — wallets, watches, money clips, eyeglasses, car key rings, nail clippers, mobile phones. Then I did understand, at least in part. "These came from our victims, I'm assuming."

"They gave them to me before they left for the professor's house. Asked me to keep them."

I gave her a keen stare. "Because?"

She gave me what I'd come to regard as the Judson look. Took another moment to think about it. "Because . . ." Took another moment. "You know, I don't really know. They told me it was for safekeeping. But somehow, I felt like it was more complicated than that."

"Do you have their clothes and their everyday shoes too?"

"Those I don't have. Have you checked their motel rooms?"

"Didn't know where they were staying. Until now, we didn't know who any of them were." I closed the green tote bag. Sat it on the floor. And slid the sheet that she'd unfolded to where I could read it. "So, yes, I think this will be helpful."

The sheet had several names written on it. They weren't in the same order as the list I'd created on the white wall in our situation room. And there were no details about the people named. No ages, no places of residence. No titles or job descriptions.

But I didn't need that information for six of the people on the list because I already had it. It was the other three names I knew nothing about:

Niall Taylor-Haskell

Hayden Derek Walcott

Robert Earle Morrow

I counted them to make sure. Nine. Not ten. So we didn't have possible identifications for all ten of our suspicious deaths. But nine was enough to speed up my heartbeat. "I take it these are all physicists of one job description or another."

"That's correct."

"And they — I'm going to take a guess here — are all graduates of the University of the Hills."

"They are, yes."

"And that they are all acquainted with Professor Thaddeus Huntgardner."

"You may ask that, but I can't reply. It would impinge on their confidentiality."

I sensed that the dance she had warned about had begun. "These folks sought you out because you live and work in Flagler?"

"You can assume that, but I can't say."

"And they had issues that required a therapist from Flagler?"

"I can't answer that for reasons of confidentiality."

"Can I ask if they had issues that were similar in nature?"

It was several seconds before she responded. "I don't think you should assume that, but you could."

We were settling into a rhythm, so I took my time formulating my next question. "Could some other therapist in Flagler have helped them — or were you the only one?"

I was expecting a quick reply, even if she couldn't answer, but she seemed to struggle with the question. My respect for her was growing. She intended to be truthful within the bounds that her legal and ethical limits allowed. "Possibly."

"Possibly someone else could have helped them? Or possibly that you were the only one?

"Possibly I was the only one."

"I assume that you've brought me this list because you are concerned that ill has befallen the people listed here."

She seemed a bit vexed at the question. Or maybe it was my wording. "Certainly, being found dead should be considered an ill that has befallen."

I apologized to her, as I should have. "Forgive me, I still sometimes lapse into divinity school speak." I quickly added, "You've brought me this list because you think these individuals are dead?"

"That's my fear."

"And there's nothing that they told you in your therapy sessions with them that might explain this?"

Her face tightened. I could see that the tension within her was growing. My suspicion was that she wanted to answer the question in detail. But I knew what was coming. "I can't answer that because it would violate their confidences."

"Do you think you have other clients whose lives may be in danger?"

"I have reason to hope not."

"And what would that reason be?"

I don't think she had anticipated the question in quite this form. After all, the question went to the heart of what she had been trying to conceal. And yet it put no specific individual's confidential information in jeopardy.

She answered before her cautious side could prevent it. "I don't have any other clients who knew Professor Huntgardner's secret."

She was aghast at her professional error. Aghast and beaten at a game she'd trained for all her career. She reached for her purse and shoved her chair backwards with her legs so hard that it toppled over. And fled from my interrogation room.

I had an acute interest in Professor Huntgardner's secret. But what I needed at the earliest possible moment was evidence of Professor Huntgardner's corporeality. There I went again. That was another divinity school word. But what word should I have used? His "realness." His "extant-ness"? No, I liked "corporeality" best.

Where was he?

Full as my plate was, I was going to have to take the time to do what any good tracker does. Go to where the trail starts. And follow it until it ends or at least begins to yield results.

I needed to see what Garrick Drasher at Pecan Mountain Nursing Home could tell me about Professor Huntgardner and hidden things.

CHAPTER 29

I'd asked Detective Coltrane to run point on Professor Huntgardner's disappearance. Again, it was an intuitive call — one based on a hunch that productive information was going to be hard to come by. That's to say, we were going to be running up against a lot of — to use Dr. Simpson-Mayes's concept — zipped-lip-ness.

Detective Coltrane had a low tolerance for zipped-lip-ness. The ex-military policeman made no apology for what he called his "bad puppy" style of investigation.

The scrappy pup allusion fit him well. He could come across as a sweet, cuddly ball of fur one moment. But if he thought people were playing games with him, they could find him erupting like a pet dog shaking the stuffing out of its toy. The anger seemed genuine. He didn't like being misled or ignored. And he could erupt at any time.

I'd passed him in the hall earlier in the day and learned that he'd already had a couple of dust-ups with the nursing home staff.

They'd started hiding behind "Mr. Drasher's rules" instead of answering his questions. His suggestion was that I visit Drasher without him. But as I was preparing to leave the court-house parking lot, he walked up to my patrol car. Knocked on the window. Slipped into my passenger seat. And briefed me on what he'd found so far.

The vividness of his commentary surprised me. "The place is about as chaotic as a county fair midway on Saturday night. The mystery isn't that they'd lose a client. The miracle is that they can keep track of any of them."

That information whetted my curiosity. "And the reason for that?"

"Too much and too few. Too much going on, and too few personnel to make it work well. Nobody seems to know that much about running a nursing home that operates like a bazaar. You know that it's more than an old-folks home, right?"

"Yeah, I was out there the other night. Looked like a busy place."

"The seniors are getting short shrift, I know that."

"So where the professor's disappearance is concerned, that tells us — what?"

He started digging under his thumb nail with one of his upper incisors. It was a habit I'd long since learned to watch for because of what it signaled. Useful insights were on the way. Either that or an eruption.

This time, though, it was neither. He shared his puzzlement.

"From what I can tell, everything that happened with the professor the other morning was according to Hoyle. The floor attendant remembers wheeling him to a van. She showed me where she'd checked his name off on a floor roster they used in emergency evacuations. They had to check off a box when they took a resident out of their room and check another box when they were loaded for transport. And there was another box for when they were unloaded. The professor seems to have made it to the school gymnasium. But then they lost track of him."

"And what is your opinion of Pecan Mountain's developer and manager?"

"In a word?"

"Sure."

"Cocky. Leaves you with the impression that anything you'd want to know about him or his operation is probably above your job description."

◦◦◦

At the nursing home, I got this same perception merely from watching Garrick Drasher walk toward me in the lobby. Only my one-word impression was different from my deputy's.

Hunk.

Garrick Drasher might or might not be too complicated for Flagler's laid-back atmosphere, but he was almost certainly too pretty. *Lordy, this dude should have gone to Hollywood, not Flagler.*

Before we'd exchanged a single word, I was picturing him on a campaign poster. This was the exact kind of look I'd sought from my photographer. Rugged. Vigilant. Virile. Easy, confident smile. Perfect white teeth. The clean-shaven chin dimple, broad lips, broad cheeks, broad brow, broad cowlick, the right boyish flair to his whiskey-brown hair — he'd have turned heads on any street in America.

His sartorial taste matched his physical features to a tee. Tan suit, perfectly fit. Light blue slim-fit dress shirt with a spread collar. Red-striped four-in-hand tie tucked inside his buttoned coat. U.S. flag lapel pin. Nothing missing or out of place. He gave me a once-over that seemed to leave him reassured. It involved a toe-to-head sweep of his eyes that was so practiced it was intended to go unnoticed. I felt it might be the missing eye that had triggered that, but I was probably being hyper-sensitive.

His segue was a smooth as his haircut. "Let's have coffee in the Oasis on the Prairie."

My agreement wasn't necessary. He led the way. Chose us a table. Flashed two fingers at a waitress. And, not bothering to look my way once, raised both arms and gestured around the big room. "You're probably wondering what all this is."

Garrick Drasher's grin suggested I should be wondering that, whether or not I was. But I disappointed him. "No, actually, I was wondering if you could shed any light on Professor Huntgardner's disappearance."

That worked. He looked straight at me for the first time without my thinking that he was looking through me. I was now an official participant in this conversation. "I'd certainly like to. I'm exceedingly fond of the old gent. But I can't imagine what I could tell you that I haven't already told your detective."

"About your chats?"

"What chats are those?"

I wasn't here to be a straight man to his coyness. "Your chats with Dr. Huntgardner. All those talks about hidden things."

He recovered in an instant, but I knew from his double take that I was now being reevaluated. "Oh, you know about those?"

I didn't intend to admit to more than I knew. "Only that he liked to talk about hidden things."

"Well, actually, one of our consulting psychologists suggested it. The professor's like most dementia sufferers — losing his working memory. Can't hang onto information much at all in the short term."

"I experienced that in my brief visit with him."

I saw it again. People can't control micro expressions of surprise in their face. Often, they are followed by signs of fear. But since I'd not been around Drasher enough to have developed a baseline, I couldn't say for sure what I was seeing. But I could have suspicions. His retort was a nothing answer. "Oh, so you met him?"

"'Met' is a bit strong, as you can imagine. But, yes, I paid him a brief visit the other evening."

"And you talked about hidden things?"

"It was your receptionist who passed that information along. I don't think she knew any more than that."

"Well, I like to take the professor things on my visits. Things I thought he'd be interested in. And hide them while he shielded his eyes. And he'd try to remember what they were."

"Do you think this is something his abductor or abductors might have known about?"

"Ordinarily, I'd have said no. But then I wasn't aware you knew about our little game either."

"What kinds of things did you hide?"

Drasher shrugged and looked away. He seemed to be weighing how much he should reveal. But then he apparently decided to be transparent. "Piddling things. Like his door key."

"Door key?"

"To his house."

"He has the door key to his house?

"In his keepsake box — again, something the therapist suggested. And not long ago I gave him a piece of trinitite. You know what that is?"

"From the Trinity blast."

"Yes, you probably know that Dr. Huntgardner lived about a hundred miles from the test site as a young lad. Just over the mountains. He saw the tremendous light from the explosion. Supposedly it changed his life. I thought that it might help him reconnect with something important. Something he'd be able to recall."

Trinitite was fused sand from the nuclear blast. No more than twenty-four hours ago, I'd looked out of curiosity to see if it could be purchased on the internet.

It could be. A piece the size of my big toe was available from a minerals dealer in Telluride, Colorado, for $10 plus shipping.

I put the question to Drasher. "You bought this on the internet, perhaps?"

He tried to hide his impatience, but it showed in his eyes. "I'd carried it around for years. Bought it when I was stationed for a few weeks in New Mexico in the Air Force."

"You were in the Air Force before you came to Flagler?"

"ISR Agency. Intelligence, Surveillance and Reconnaissance Agency."

"And you came to Flagler because we are one of the business capitals of the world?"

He laughed with what I'm sure he thought was appropriate mirth. "I spent a bunch of money on consultants before I decided that Flagler would be a good destination."

But I found myself paraphrasing Hamlet — *the gentleman doth chuckle too much* — and decided to press the issue, this time with a more pointed irony. "A good destination because we are badly in need of former Air Force intelligence agents here?"

The chuckling was over. In fact, the interview was over. He stood up. Because my chair was on casters, he was able to push it around about thirty degrees with me still in it. Then he reached for me, half-lifting and half-tugging me out of the chair, indicating that we'd be moving elsewhere. "Bet you'd like to see his room."

"I can remove the crime scene tape, yes."

I thanked him for the coffee and told him I knew the way. This time, it was my turn to be imperious. Never looked back to see if he would try to follow.

I was already wondering if I'd find the piece of trinitite among the professor's belongings.

I didn't.

I'd have considered my search of the room a waste if not for something else I found.

It was in one of the dozen or so books arranged between book ends on a small chest of drawers near the head of the professor's bed. The book was *Fundamentals of Physics* by Thaddeus Johans Huntgardner, PhD. The item that widened my eyes was a bookmark. At least, that appeared to be its current function.

But not how it had begun its life.

It was a receipt for two orders of fries, two large Cokes, and three Both Barrels Double Meat Cheeseburgers from the Eden Junction Bar and Grill.

CHAPTER 30

This time, I wanted to talk to Judson Mayes without his mother around. You could think of it as wanting a man-to-man discussion. But I was thinking of it as more an inquiring-mind-to-inquiring-mind kind of chat. One off the record.

I'd tell him he wasn't suspected of anything. And he wasn't. Not anything illegal that I knew of.

But every time I'd found myself in the company of this sharp-eyed, sharp-eared, sharp-witted young man, I'd been treated to unexpected information that had reordered my world in some way. Although in each instance, I'd left his presence feeling that he hadn't told me everything he could and should have.

I'd thought he wasn't going to answer his phone. But he did on the sixth or seventh ring. Said he was sorry about that, but he couldn't get his phone out of his pocket.

When I asked where he was, he said out behind the Eden Junction Bar and Grill. I asked what he was doing. He said he was trying out the camera on his new mini-drone. I asked if some refreshment sounded good. He said he could meet me at the restaurant in five. I told him I'd need twenty. When I arrived, he was waiting in the parking lot in his sporty jeep.

I wasn't sure whether we should try sitting at a booth — didn't know whether he could get in one. The first one we stopped at, he rejected, saying it was too small. So, I let him pick a booth. The one he chose accommodated him. But as he worked his way along the bench, it reminded me of a dog trying to squeeze through a fence hole.

I wasn't going to eat. But if he wanted another Both Barrels cheeseburger, or two, or three, in the middle of the afternoon, he could have them courtesy of the Abbot County sheriff.

He ordered two. With caramelized onions. A large order of fries. And a jumbo Coke.

I held up the receipt. "Found this in a book at the nursing home."

He reached for the slip of paper and rubbed it back and forth between his fingers. "Thermal paper. It's what they use now in a lot of cash registers. It changes color when heat hits it. That's what they have here. A cash register with a thermal printer."

"The date on it is Monday, a week ago."

He gave it a closer look. "Three burgers. I never order three. So if this is mine, I was with somebody." He flicked the front of his chin with his forefinger a couple of times. "Yes, it probably is mine. I was here that day with Scottie."

"And you have a habit of saving your receipts?" It seemed unusual for a seventeen-year-old.

"I have a habit of sticking them in my shirt pocket and forgetting about them. Mum hates to find them, especially if they go through the washing machine first. She thinks the receipts are dangerous. Something about high levels of bisphenol A in the thermal paper. Chemically, BPA is kind of like estrogen, you know."

I told him I didn't know that. But that the receipt hadn't interested me not because of what it was made of but because I'd not expected to find it in Professor Huntgardner's room.

"Oh, that." He reached for another potato stick. "I'm trying to get into Harvard. Mum thinks volunteering at the nursing home will look good on my application."

"So you've been doing it for a while?"

"Since school let out. I try to do it at least twice a week. Read to the old folks. Or chat. Sometimes play games. Or with the professor, just sit. He's usually asleep. I'd probably not stay around when he's napping, but I found that old physics textbook he wrote on his shelf. Pretty Gucci. Sitting there reading it with the author only a few feet away."

"Pretty Gucci?"

He grinned and gave me a tolerant look. "That's the new 'cool.' The new 'awesome.'"

Gucci, indeed. I hoped he got into Harvard. But that was a year off. I needed something now. I needed one of the brightest minds of Flagler's current generation to wade with me once again into the deep waters of our community's secrets. "You knew there was a bomb scare at Pecan Mountain before dawn Wednesday."

"Yeah, Mum told me about it. She wasn't sure it was okay for me to do my volunteering thing Wednesday afternoon. She called, and they said it was okay to show up."

"You had to have done more than just shoot the bull with the oldsters or read Professor Huntgardner's textbook on all those visits. What's it like living at Pecan Mountain Nursing Home?"

He didn't need to think about it. "Like living in the last orphanage on the road to hell."

"You really mean that?"

"Got a 'for instance,' for you. All those call buttons? The ones on the head board under the little sign that says, 'Love without limits. Just push'? I pushed one for the professor on at least five visits. Every single time, instead of a nurse's aide, somebody on the kitchen staff showed up — in a dirty apron. It's all part of that whack job Drasher's 'be all the talent you are' philosophy. Everybody has at least two or three jobs. The nursing aides also peel potatoes and mop the freaking floors."

I don't know what surprised me most — the audacity of what he was describing or the ease with which this clever teenager had seen through the veneer of Garrick Drasher's con job. Either way, I knew the perfect reply for my audience. "Not Gucci."

"This isn't either."

He reached for his phone and started cycling through his visuals. "I was playing around with my drone camera the other day after I finished up at the nursing home. Launched it in the front parking lot and did a 360 degree sweep all the way around the place. Now, you tell me — you ever seen anything like this at a nursing home?"

He handed me his phone. He was showing me an entrance at the back of the building. I'd never noticed it before because it had been camouflaged by a high fence. A fence, I was thinking, that had been placed there for the exact purpose of keeping people from seeing what was on the other side.

The door was an industrial-sized double-garage-type door, and it was up. Open. This allowed me to see inside the loading area served by the door.

Twice, I used my fingers to enlarge the images on the screen. Even so, I wasn't sure I understood everything I was looking at. One thing in particular. The intended use of the vehicle parked in the back of the unloading area.

The lighting over the truck wasn't the best, but I had ample reason to suspect that I was staring at an armored transport of some kind. A SWAT team–like van? An armored cash-in-transit car? A military fighting vehicle? One thing I did know. It wasn't a necessary conveyance for taking old folks to their dental appointments.

The other thing I noticed there could be no question about. It was an elevator door. The door was open, and two people could be seen waiting for it to close and the elevator to move. The Pecan Mountain Nursing Home building had another floor. A basement.

I gave Judson back his phone. "What'd you think when you saw this?"

His answer was quick and mature. "That it was something I needed to show the local sheriff at the first opportunity."

"So why didn't you show it to me at the office Wednesday?"

"Just forgot it. Lots going on that day, if you'll remember."

I asked if he had talked with anyone else about all that he'd seen at the nursing home. "Your mom, perhaps?"

"Not my mom. My dad. It bothered him too. Really, really bothered him. I know because I overheard him a little later talking on the phone."

"Talking to whom?"

"Somebody who knew what he meant when he said they'd waited too long. They should have gone ahead and initiated action when they first talked about it."

I didn't expect Judson to be able to answer my next question, but I had to ask it. "Do you know what kind of action they were talking about?"

When he shrugged his massive shoulders, I moved on to a question I knew he could answer. "When was this?"

"When they first talked about it?"

"No, when you showed your dad this video."

He thought for a moment. "Monday night, after I got back from . . . well, from meeting you."

"Do you know where I can find your dad?"

"Somewhere on Galveston Bay."

That's when I saw the look again. I knew he was lying about his dad. He saw the doubt in my face and decided to embellish his lie. "He's a licensed commercial pilot. He flew down yesterday — he has his own plane. Said he wanted to see if the speckled trout and flounder were biting. We keep a boat at Kemah."

I decided to play along. "Do you know when he'll be back?'

"Monday or Tuesday, I'd guess. He's got a medical practice to run."

"What kind of medicine does he practice?"

"General. But then he does a lot of geriatrics too. He's Professor Huntgardner's visiting physician at the nursing home."

I held my expression steady so that Judson couldn't see the surprise. One more realization that this conversation had produced. I should have spoken with the good doctor long before now.

I had one more question for my guest. "Any thoughts on what might have happened to the professor? Where he might be? Who might have taken him?"

For the fourth time since we'd met, I was certain that he wasn't going to tell me everything he knew about something that mattered. And I still didn't understand why.

Not Gucci.

CHAPTER 31

Fridays are wind-down days in most offices, and ours was no exception. Normally, the fact that we still had serious crimes to solve and were willing to keep our noses to the grindstone didn't earn us any reprieves from other people's habits. We were still slaves to their itch to leave early for the weekend cottage or fishing hole. I didn't object when my own staff left early, but I tended to stay late. And my weekends were different from most of my people's.

Sometimes I'd thought that my head's approach to work was like that of the young widow Ruth in the Old Testament. The "whither thou goest, I will go" Ruth. Where my head went, my work went too. That meant home on the weekends.

I'd waved goodbye again to young Mayes in the burger joint's parking lot. Then called Helen to see if she minded waiting a few more minutes. I was headed in to check on the status of a few things.

First, I needed to know if cranky old Judge Kincannon had issued our search warrant for the warehouse. Second, see how our efforts to collect personal histories, DNA, and dental and medical records on the nine victims we thought we'd identi-fied were going. Third, check if our BOLOs on our growing menagerie of suspicious vehicles had produced any sightings. Fourth, find out when Doc Konnie expected to have a report on the victims' blood work. Fifth, learn if any analysis had been done on the sliver of plastic she'd found in victim number ten's pelvis. Sixth, check if there was anything new about who that tenth victim might be.

But I never got around to asking about any of this. The box sitting on my desk was the reason.

I hadn't seen a box like this in a while. From the odors it was giving off, it had been a long spell since anyone had seen it. Or bothered to open it. The musty-smelling cardboard had absorbed mold from somewhere. And cigarette smoke. And other sundry odors donated by the march of time. The whole thing had a long-ago smell.

I turned the storage carton over so I could see how it was marked. At minimum, it should have a category and a year. Like "DUI Cases — 1988." Instead, my eyes were treated to a designation I'd never seen on our records shelves before. For certain, I'd have remembered anything that outlandish. The box was labeled "The No Cock Crowed Cases." The final "s" had been added later using a different colored marker. Along with an arrow showing where it went.

Another thing I'd not seen before was the way the box was dated. The year "1973" was centered beneath the main description. You'd have thought this was the only year for which the box was intended to hold records. But then, a string of later years had been added.

Each time, the marking pen had to have been different. You could tell from the color and the variations in the width of the felt tip. The dates on the box were "1973–1974–1975–1976." Since it started in the middle of the box, the line of dates was getting close to the box's edge.

I knew enough about how the department's records had been kept over the years to know this box dated to my granddad's era. Luther Haines "Sheriff Luke" McWhorter, the man whose first name I bore, had been sheriff from 1972 to 1988. He'd been the first of us keep-hanging-around McWhorters to pin on the star.

For whoever had put it there, lugging the box to my office must have been a pain.

It had to have come from the wire security cage in the basement of the old county records building two blocks away. The aging structure had no elevator. The only way to get boxes and files down into — or up from — the basement was to hand-carry them or use a hand truck to transport them one step at a time. For a single box, provided it wasn't too heavy, hand-carrying was a lot less trouble.

But it was still trouble. So my first question was who'd have bothered. The next question was why they'd placed the box in the exact center of my desk blotter. The geometry was as precise as a place setting at The Ritz. Taken together, the questions made me confident statements were being made. Possibly, statements of some importance. Given what else had been going on in Abbot County this week, they could be ominous statements.

Helen had kept hawk's eyes on me through the glass wall between our offices, so I had a pretty good idea where to start pursuing answers.

I waved at her to join me. Waited until she found herself a seat. Let her arrange the geometry of her physical presence as she wished. And gave her no choice but to join with me in staring at the box. She sat still as a watched worm for a time. Then pincered a transient thread off her blouse. Her first sound was an attempt to clear her throat.

The phlegm failed to cooperate, so she did it again.

Then a third time.

Watching her, I could see that she had grown emotional. I'd been watching her with such concentration that I'd become a captive to her rhythms. I was breathing harder myself. This encounter was assuming a greater intensity than I'd had any reason to expect. It felt like we had already passed the ominous point and were approaching an "end of the world as we have known it" fork in the road.

"I promised your daddy that I'd never show you the contents of this box."

"Mercy's sake. What's in it?"

She seemed to choose that moment to revisit some scene in the past. When she answered, I decided this was exactly what she'd been doing.

"That's just it, your father would never tell me. He'd give me file folders or notebooks or photographs or whatever and tell me to take them down to the storage room and put them in this box or one of the others. There's more down there like this, you know. Five more, at least — hidden behind regular file boxes at the very far end of the stacks. But I had strict orders never to rummage through them. Or examine what I put in them."

"But this is from my grandfather's time in office, not Sheriff John Aubrey's. You never worked for my grandfather. And didn't work for my father all that long. What was it? Six years?"

"Can't tell you more than that. I was a good girl. Just did what I was told."

"So why break your promise now?"

Helen shifted in her chair. "I know you're looking hard for answers these days. I'd never forgive myself if I could have helped and hadn't done it. Besides, there's the other thing." She looked around the room like she was searching for the right words. She was, I knew. I'd give her time to find them. It was only a few seconds, but it seemed like forever and a day before she decided what else she was going to say. When she spoke again, she said nothing all that profound; it wasn't even that original. But her meaning was clear.

"Both your daddy and your granddaddy knew this, but they could never figure out what it was. At least, I don't think they did. But there's something rotten in Flagler." Her eyes dropped to the box again. "Has been for a long time. And this time, it's gone too far."

CHAPTER 32

Angie knew about my penchant for working on Saturdays but had insisted on honoring a ritual. She called it Little Piggies Come to Dine. I had no idea why. The name sounded cute and seemed to make her happy, and it was something private to the two of us, so I'd not objected. We'd been doing it for months now — and it *was* a ritual.

Little Piggies Come to Dine always happened at my house. We'd never talked about the reason for that either. It could have been that I had more kitchen utensils. Or a bigger refrigerator. Or a bigger kitchen in general. Or this was where Little Piggies Come to Dine had happened the first time, and it had become a habit.

Since I was an early riser, I was assigned to get fresh donuts. This meant a trip to the Donut Shoppe, sometimes before the sun was up.

By the time I returned, she would be in the kitchen making Bloody Marys or mimosas. I hadn't imagined how good warm donuts went with a Bloody Mary. Or, if it was during what Angie called the "Orange You Glad You Met Me" months, she'd be extracting fresh citrus with my electric juicer, then I'd fry bacon or sausage and get out my omelet pan. She'd make waffles.

As we cooked, we'd tell jokes. Or whoppers. Trade playful squeezes in front of the stove. Tug each other's apron string loose, then turn retieing it into a romp and a hug. But that wasn't happening much today because of the gorilla in the next room.

Six gorillas, to be exact.

They were the five cartons Helen had steered me to in the old records building basement plus the one she'd put on my desk. I'd brought them home. Carried them one at a time into my dining room. Parked them on the floor against the dining room's far wall. And arranged them single file.

As we ate, Angie could see me glancing at them through the door. "If they could talk, what do you think they'd say?"

I borrowed Helen's line. "That something's rotten in Flagler."

Angie thought that was funny. "Besides ten near-fleshless corpses lying in the medical examiner's autopsy cooler?"

"Those too — for sure."

"Then let the humble special agent for the FBI you seduce so regularly assist you with her remarkable nose for finding the truth."

"I'd be much obliged."

We cleared away the dishes on my bar, then moved to my dining room where I put away the artificial flower arrangements on my dining table. "Makes sense to take them in chronological order. You want the first box or the second?"

She slumped against the arm of her chair and deliberated for a moment. The voice she answered with was her on-the-job voice. "You need to know how all this started. You go first."

She scurried out of her chair and grabbed the second box in the row and placed it on the table facing where she'd be sitting. So I'd gone second anyway. I didn't comment. It'd be awhile before I became conscious of it, but those were the last words either of us would say for long minutes. The voice breaking the silence was Angie's. As was customary, she started with a question. One with a tinge of one-upmanship. That was habitual too. Some of her friends shrugged and said that it went with the job. I'd told them, no, it went with the person. "Did your grandfather always put dumb names on his records boxes?"

The end of my box was facing her.

I turned the box end with the writing toward me. "Figured that out. My granddad always loved Sherlock Holmes stories. Used to read them to me when I was a boy. One of his favorites was called 'The Adventure of Silver Blaze.' It was about —"

"The dog that didn't bark in the night."

I gave her a thumbs-up. "So I think early on my granddad suspected the strange goings-on in Abbot County had more to do with things that hadn't happened than the things that had. The old boy had a weird sense of humor. Instead of labeling the box 'The No Dog Barked Case,' he went barnyard and wrote 'The No Cock —'"

There was admiration in her voice. "'The No Cock Crowed Case.'"

"Right. And when the dead-end evidence kept growing, he added, or had somebody add, the *s* and the additional years."

I patted one of the growing piles I'd been creating on the tabletop. "Don't know what you're finding, but to me, this seems like our own local version of *The X-Files*. Endless paranoia. And horseplay that doesn't amount to much."

My comment sent her rummaging through one of her own piles. "That would explain this letter. From the head of the Texas Rangers, if you can believe it."

She slid the document in my direction. The underlined headline read: "An Official Notice to the Sheriff of Abbot County to Forward No Further Requests for Undercover Assistance without Sufficient Reason."

She chased it with her conclusion. "The Rangers got tired of listening for the cock to crow."

I couldn't argue the point.

CHAPTER 33

We got tired of listening for the cock to crow too. The shadows outside my hilltop house were growing. So was Angie's and my eye fatigue.

We'd talked about quitting, but if there was a smoking gun in the boxes, I wanted to find it now. Not later.

We'd agreed to skip to the final box and divide the contents between us. Angie would take a document, then I'd take the next one, peat and repeat, back and forth, until we were finished. And we'd renewed our commitment to give everything a careful look, tired eyes or not.

The mix of materials hadn't changed much.

In every box, there had been letters, clippings, and documents. File folder after file folder, often with meager contents.

Interview notes and interview transcriptions, sometimes paper-clipped, sometimes stapled, sometimes sitting loose. Memos dictated or handwritten by a sheriff or a deputy or unknown parties. And lots of photos: snapshots, Polaroids, dark-room-produced 8x10s. Some of them showed people who had some connection to events that had happened in Abbot County. Others had people I didn't recognize. I couldn't understand why a lot of the images had been included in the file boxes.

And, in the final box, one of my father's reelection campaign posters. It was folded into quarters. When I opened it up, my eyes were drawn immediately to the crude block letters someone had written below his picture: "GIVE IT UP OR DIE!"

Neurons crackled somewhere in my head. My blinders disappeared. And my perspective moved 180 degrees.

My realization was this: *We'd all been wrong!*

During all the years that the other two McWhorter sheriffs had served, the county had indeed harbored crowing cocks — very skillful ones. They had crowed and crowed and crowed. Sometimes in the daytime, sometimes at night — but *always* in the dark. The problem had been that neither of my predecessors had understood what they needed to notice. I'd missed it too. The sights and sounds — the signs — that we were dealing with cocks of a very different kind.

Angie hadn't noticed it, but my body had responded to my new insights with a jerk.

And my hands.

They wanted to go another ten rounds with the flotsam of information we'd stacked on my dining room table. Start by shuffling the pieces like playing cards. Pick and re-pick. Think and rethink. I wanted Angie's reaction and the benefit of her razor-sharp mind and her skill at peering into the shadows and zeroing in on developments that I'd missed. And I wanted her blessing for my bombshell insight.

Not until I reached for my dad's campaign poster again and held it up for her to see did I have any inkling how unlikely that was going to be.

She took one glance at the poster and sneered. "Dumb and dumber! Has to be college kids."

I felt sandbagged. "College kids? Surely, you jest."

Her head did that pivot I'd learned to expect when she was digging in. "No, some of the shenanigans were brilliant

— they were! But they were the kind of stuff that you'd expect from fraternity types who were acting out."

I was trying not to sound incredulous but losing the battle. "For the better part of two decades? They must have set world records for hanging around the campus."

But she was off and running. "Take these other posters . . . *please!* Ridiculous! I mean, as if something called 'Templars of a Deeper Sky' would have been taken seriously. Or 'Annunaki — The New Chronicles.' Here's my favorite: 'The Flaglerati Forever.'" She was just getting started. "And that stunt with the Heaven's Gate lookalikes? That was clever. But it wasn't meant to be taken seriously. I mean, it was a bunch of clowns. No way they were actually associated with Marshall Applewhite. And making the Abbot County Sheriff's Department look like fools — that could have been a challenge passed on from class to class."

"Heaven's Gate lookalikes" was Angie's description. The words hadn't appeared in the deputy's memo about the visitors that I'd found near the bottom of my first box. The deputy had called them hobos in one place, hippie types in another, vagrants in a third. Whatever they were, a half dozen had hit town one day in September 1975 and stayed for about a week. They'd slept in tents and sleeping bags and begged on the streets. Said they were awaiting word from higher powers named Bo and Peep.

My granddad — the Sheriff McWhorter one — had tried to send someone undercover with them, but they hadn't stayed around long enough. After a few days, they'd disappeared with no more warning than came with their arrival.

There was no need for Angie to explain who Marshall Applewhite was. Marshall Herff Applewhite Jr. was the founder of the Heaven's Gate religious cult. "Bo," as he sometimes called himself, was a native of Texas, but most of his deadly mischief had happened in California. His claim to fame was that he'd orchestrated a mass suicide in 1997 that had taken thirty-nine lives.

Angie and I were simpatico on the veracity, or lack thereof, of the visitors being members of the cult, and I told her so. "Their story sounds bogus. I'm not even sure that Granddad Luke would have heard of Marshall Applewhite and company anyway. And the mass suicide in California was almost twenty years later. So, I'd put that one in the category of deception and disinformation. Fact is, there are a lot of circumstances in these boxes I'd categorize that way."

This time, Angie looked triumphant, not disdainful. I was surprised. Not at her. Well, yes, at her too. But more at myself. Something had offended me.

I let my mind revisit the conversation. Then I realized what it was: her comment about the sheriff's department looking like fools. The thought brought its own instant self-reproof. *Your skin needs thickening, McWhorter.*

I decided to tell her what I considered disinformation and strategic deception in our boxes and what I considered something else, but she got there first. "Write these down."

She held her own pen upright and started tapping it against the tabletop, point by point.

First tap. "The silly magazine story mock-ups we've found, none of which were ever printed so far as I can see."

Second tap. "The rumor that Flagler's rich and powerful were going to be invited to a bull testicle roast out on Horseshoe Creek."

Third tap. "All those strange holes that got poked in the ground around the county. Even your deputies got the giggles at the thought of 'the digger' being at work again."

Fourth tap. "The anonymous complaints to the Texas Commission on Jail Standards that your Abbot County jail was filthy. Regular as clockwork. Every three years. The commission found it amusing until they didn't. Always said your jail was clean enough to starve a cockroach."

Fifth tap. "The break-ins at the local mortuaries. With nothing ever taken or damaged and no idea at all how the perpetrators got in. The only leave-behinds were all those silly notes left in caskets."

There was that triumphant look again. "Had to have been college horseplay. Couldn't have been anything else."

She sounded light-hearted and dismissive. But if she'd bothered to glance at me, she'd be blind not to notice the way my face tightened around my eyes. I kept hearing the cock crow. If we ignored it, the life's work of two men I had adored might be discredited. Either that or I was being selfish about my family's reputation.

I concluded that what we'd been seeing in the boxes was bigger than the McWhorters. My grandfather's intuition hadn't been far off the mark. For years after he'd started collecting evidence, confusing as it was, the cock had been crowing.

Then the crowing had changed.

Changed in pitch and in frequency.

The sounds, the signs — they'd all *changed*. They were more serious, but until now, they were still the kind of circumstances that would not have caused my father or grandfather to detect the switchover.

And then, for reasons I didn't understand, they'd quit trying to detect the crowing at all.

I wasn't sure when it had happened. But it had to have been before I was appointed to fill out my ailing father's final term. That was in June of 2002.

And the ten victims at Professor Huntgardner's house?

They were signs that the cocks were crowing again.

The two people best equipped to discover why were sitting in my dining room. Angie and I couldn't afford to miss the meaning of these six boxes. The meaning and the clues. If we did, the cocks would continue to crow. And I feared with every fiber of my crime-fighting being that there were going to be more victims in Abbot County.

By bequeathing us the records in these boxes, my two predecessors had done more than open my eyes. They'd given me a chance to set my people free.

But from what?

I still didn't know. Tomfoolery that had gone on for decades? That, for certain. But I was willing to bet my career that it was something more serious.

I knew only one way to get through to Angie when she was in the grip of one of her Charge-of-the-Light-Brigade tirades. Deprive her of the means and opportunity to browbeat me.

I pushed my notepad to the side of where I was sitting and placed my pen in the middle of it.

I reached over and took her pen from her hand and laid it beside my own.

I entered her space again and slipped my fingers underneath the pile of materials she'd been building. Being as gentle as I could, I moved the pile away from her and sat it off to one side.

I used the same motion to move my own pile to the same end of the table.

Then I reached for the box from where it had been resting at the other end of the table and moved it to the floor.

Now there was nothing else to move.

Nothing else was separating us.

No files, no boxes, no writing implements, no personal paraphernalia, no guns, no badges, no unidentified objects, no buffers, no armor.

The only things that Angie had in front of her were the total seriousness of my look, the unyielding urgency in my voice, and a naked persona intent on pushing the current discussion in a different direction.

I'd never seen the look on Angie's face before. It wasn't a look I'd seen on anyone's face before. I'd heard it described in novels. Talked to myself about people looking that way when I was being melodramatic. But I'd never seen a person go bug-eyed.

Until now.

The gravity in my voice was matched only by the solemnity of my gaze. "We're sitting on a powder keg in Flagler, and you are caught up in the juvenile games you think you are seeing in these boxes. I have to go in another direction. Can you go with me?"

I hadn't the slightest doubt that we both understood how high-voltage this moment was. How we'd gotten to this point, and why it has come at this instant, and whether the way it had arrived was wise or necessary — all that was beside the point. We were staring into the looking glass.

She made a fist and moved it up and down. American Sign Language for yes.

And we were through it.

CHAPTER 34

I turned off the floodlights and stepped down onto my flag-stone patio, in need of a stretch after hours of rifling through boxes. Daylight had disappeared.

With no moon out, it was a proceed-at-your-own-risk night. I'd wanted the clearest possible view of the hills along the ridge tops to the west. My backyard offered a front-row seat.

What I found myself watching came from somewhere else. You've heard of people screening a movie on the inside of their eyeballs? I was doing that now, with startling clarity. While it wasn't a regular event, I'd had such episodes before. The images would always burst into my awareness with no warning, hang around at their own pace, and then dissolve, never to be seen again. Only wondered about.

This time, I was envisioning a young Thaddeus Huntgardner slouched against his parent's ranch house, hands thrust deep into his pockets. He was waiting for the desert's tarry darkness to give way to the dawn. Waiting, observing, reflecting on the mysteries of life — with great patience. Or so it appeared. But then I wondered if I had it wrong. What if he wasn't waiting for the sun to rise. Instead, what if he was daring it not to appear?

I could only imagine what had triggered this little drama in my mind. Curiosity? Anxiety? Premonition? I kept waiting for the next scene. For movement, for a clue, for a reason. It never came, and I knew it wouldn't. But my mind seemed reluctant to see its brief one-scene movie fade away.

And it hadn't been dramatic. No plot. No climactic ending. No earthshaking insights. Only questions, gnawing at the edges.

It might have lingered longer if not for Angie's touch. She'd slipped an arm through mine and pulled me tighter. I understood. We were both still shaken by how close we had come at the dining table. To what? A bottomless abyss in our relationship? An annihilating collision? A primal flaming out of our shared attraction?

She leaned a cheek against my shoulder. "You're checking for the Saturday Night Lights."

"You suppose they were real?"

"As real as the Marfa Lights."

The Marfa Lights were a phenomenon often spotted midway between the desert floor and the mountaintops in deep West Texas. Witnesses said the mysterious orbs sometimes remain stationary as they pulse on and off at a wide range of intensities. Usually, they're a yellowish-orange but sometimes they'd take on other hues. Reds, greens, blues. And sometimes they split into fragments, then recombine over the desert.

Angie's reference to the Marfa Lights was a wise crack. I found it encouraging. She trusted me enough to risk kidding again. I used the opening to get back in the conversation. "Some people say they can see the Marfa Lights."

"Exactly. The other sheriffs in your family said they could see the Saturday Night Lights too. And about half the rest of Flagler's citizens. They just never found out what was causing them — or, maybe, who."

This time, I disengaged from her arm and stretched mine around her. Pivoted her so that we both faced the hills in the western ridge. Plenty of shimmering lights. But they were recognizable. Street lights, a few car headlights, backyard floodlights.

But no sign of the Saturday Night Lights that had so mystified both my predecessors and a townful of witnesses off and on year after year.

Abbot County's lights were mentioned several times in the boxes. Always in the same context. And always without explanation. No cause had ever been found. Then they quit appearing. There had been no mention of them, at least to my knowledge, in years.

Angie slapped at a mosquito. I'd already felt a bite on the back of my neck. She reached for my hand and tugged me toward the house. "You still haven't told me what you think you should do about the boxes."

We returned to the dining room once again, and Angie sat down at the table.

I had a question ready.

"Doesn't it strike you as strange that the FBI has never descended on Flagler? Not once in all this. I mean, the whole tenor of the bureau changed after J. Edgar. Organized crime, watch out — here come the Feds. And, to me, what the sheriffs were up against during the time of the boxes was nothing if not organized."

There was a flicker of defensiveness in Angie's look, and then, with a single swift blink, it disappeared. "Look, can we just cut to the chase? You see something. The other McWhorter sheriffs saw *something*. They had to — else why go to all the trouble of accumulating what's in the boxes and preserving it for the ages? Kindly spell it out for the local FBI lady, will you? I mean, if you've been wanting the bureau to show up, well, she's here."

I went to the kitchen and returned to the dining room with a different notepad. Legal-sized, not letter-sized. White, not yellow. With unmarked pages, not lined. When I squared it longways in the center of my dining table, it gave me more room for sketching. I intended to work on it upside down so Angie could follow. This was a skill that I'd mastered to save time in interviews and instructing my deputies, and I'd gotten good at it.

I gave Angie a little context. "Don't know much about what happened prior to seventy-two. No McWhorters on the scene back then. We could look for crime patterns in the earlier sheriffs' records, such as they are, I suppose. But don't think it's necessary. Look at this."

I drew a horizontal line about a third of the way from the top of the now-elongated page.

Writing upside down, I began to enter dates along it, starting on Angie's left. Each time, I stopped to let her know what I was thinking.

The first entry was 1972. "That's when our No Cock Crowed boxes begin."

Farther down the line to her right, I placed 1988. "The year my granddaddy retired. Nineteen seventy-two to nineteen seventy-eight — that was the span covered by the first two boxes. I agree with you in part about what they documented. To use your words, it was goofy stuff. Fake emergency calls. Holes dug in the ground for no apparent reason. False complaints. Silly vandalism. Nuisance stuff by the bushel. But I don't think it was mostly schoolboy pranks. I'll explain why in a sec."

Angie didn't look up. Her eyes remained glued to my pad.

I moved farther down my line and added another date. 2002. "Sheriff John Aubrey McWhorter's term of office was from 1988 to 2002. During which, serious crimes in Flagler quit being faked and started getting real.

"Three major downtown fires — all thought to be arson. But nothing was proven.

"Cattle rustled and butchered on crude stone altars out in isolated pastures. Numerous times. The case was never solved.

"The break-ins at our mortuaries. No major damage but constant fear that bodies were going to be mutilated or stolen. Again nothing proven.

"Dr. Wilson Carmichael, one of my Bible professors at the University of the Hills, disappears, never to be seen again. Never solved.

"Signs of secret encampments that didn't get noticed until the campfire ashes had cooled. Telephone threats to people who were clueless about why they were singled out. The Saturday Night Lights — clearly staged, if you ask me — but for what?

"A lot of mischief, if that's what you want to call it. A lot of felonies too. But nothing, *nothing*, ever solved. And it wasn't for lack of trying. Sheriff John Audrey and his deputies ran themselves ragged. We've seen the evidence for that in the boxes."

Angie took her eyes off the pad for the first time and gave me an affirming nod. "So the cock was crowing."

"The cock was crowing. Again and again."

"And then —"

I pointed to the date closest to the end of my line. 2002.

My companion did the honors. "And then, you took office."

I tapped the date again. "And the serious crime stuff stopped almost on a dime. There have been a few major incidents of criminal behavior during my term, and we've found the culprits for most. Put the perpetrators through the system — a lot of them in jail. Kept a lid for the most part on Flagler's proclivity for nastiness and mayhem. Until last Friday." I extended my line to within an inch of the right-hand edge of the sheet. Then added a single word. "Now."

I had the total attention of the FBI special agent sitting across from me. "When the cock started crowing again with a vengeance."

"That seems to be the case."

Angie was fingering the edges of my pad. "What are you thinking?"

"Several things." I started drawing and writing on the pad again. "Please don't be offended, but I don't think our local college students have ever contributed significantly to the crime in Flagler. These are Bible colleges — quote, unquote. Most of the kids that go there are rule-followers, real straight-laced. We don't get many bad apples in the first place, certainly not serial offenders willing to stay and muck around with the campus and the community year after year."

I used my pen to point to the line between two of my entries. 1972 and 2002.

"During this span, I think Flagler and its sheriff's department was whipsawed by one or more groups intent on strategic misinformation. Or disinformation — whatever you want to call it. It's used in warfare a lot. The idea is to confuse the enemy. Make them think they need to be focused on one thing. Surveil this particular location. Shadow this group or person. Watch for particular consequences. Which is exactly the wrong thing to do if what matters is something else entirely."

I laid my pen to one side of my pad. Rested my case, you might say. Felt a little hubris. Thought that I'd argued my theory well.

This moment of self-congratulation lasted about as long as a firefly's blink.

CHAPTER 35

I never saw it coming.

Angie reached a hand toward my pad. Used her thumb to tease up the page where I'd been sketching. Slipped her other hand beneath it and pressed the pad to the table. Grasped my page with her free hand and tore the page off the pad. Didn't crumple or damage the page in any way. But laid it aside.

Removed it from contention, you might say.

And drew her own line on the blank page now staring at both of us. "What if we start a lot earlier?"

I knew her question was a claim to ownership and not one she expected to be answered. So I took instructions from the Psalmist: "This is the day the Lord has made; We will rejoice and be glad in it." *I mean, what else can we do, Lord?*

I repeated her question. "So, what *if* we started a lot earlier?"

The room grew quiet. Angie had reached around and dragged her long ponytail over her shoulder. That way, she could stuff a wad of hair into her mouth and nibble. She'd done this before, and I'd asked if her hair was that nutritious. But I accepted that she did this sometimes when her mind went on an adventure of its own. She'd be back when it decided the trip was over.

It consumed so much time that I did some fiddling of my own. Stuck an index finger inside the collar of my golf shirt.

Traced the seam down to the backing that held the buttons and button holes. Explored a button hole. Wondered where the shirt was made. If I reached behind my neck, tugged the brand tag into view, I could find the answer. China, in all likelihood. Or Indonesia. Didn't matter. I liked the shirt.

When Angie's mind returned, she started writing dates on her line. The first one went at the beginning.

"Nineteen forty-five. A bomb goes off in the Huntgardner kid's head, not to mention on the Alamogordo bombing range. I mean, both were world-changing events, don't you think? His world was never the same after that. And —" She wrote another date a little farther down her line. 1947. "Roswell, of course. And Huntgardner enrolling at the University of the Hills that fall. Flagler's world was never the same after that."

Angie wasn't as skilled at upside down sketching as I was. I laid a hand flat in the center of her page. "Got a suggestion. You come around to this side of the table."

The brilliance of the idea became apparent the moment she lowered herself into her new chair. Now, we were no longer in opposition. We were partners again.

She added another date. Her handwriting was much steadier this time. 1951. "You're going to have to help me a lot from now on."

"Always a pleasure."

"Well, you know things I don't know."

"'Sometimes I am a fox and sometimes a lion. The whole secret of relationships lies in knowing when to be one or the other.'"

"Who said that?'

"Napoleon Bonaparte. Almost. I changed a couple of words."

She gave me her boys-will-be-boys look. "I meant you know more about Professor Huntgardner than I do. I assume he graduated from the university in 1951. Do you know when he joined the physics faculty?"

I lowered the last two fingers of my right hand and tapped my thumb with the other two. Since it had drained tension once before, this time I was resorting to American Sign Language. My signal meant no. "But I'm guessing it was in the mid-'60s. I think he became chairman of the department about the time they opened the new science building."

"Which was when?"

"Nineteen sixty-eight."

She wrote 1968 at the end of her line. And reached for the page she had removed without ceremony from the pad. *My* page. She aligned the two sheets end to end so that my line started where her line stopped. Hers quit at 1968. Mine started at 1972.

"Three things. First, the contents of the No Cock Crowed boxes aren't the end-all and be-all of everything. I think we should assume that Flagler's craziness commenced years before the McWhorters invaded the sheriff's office.

"Second, timelines work best with a good beginning." She looked pleased. "Did I just say that? Write that down. Sounds Napoleon-ish." She laughed at her own joke, then she got serious again. "It all begins with young Huntgardner. Strange, isn't it?" She went quiet again for so long that I turned to her with a puzzled look. "The atomic bomb blast. We haven't begun to connect the dots on what it meant for Flagler."

That's when she began tapping my page from the pad with a steady one-two rhythm using the middle finger of each hand. The movements were coordinated, but I don't think she noticed. One finger was doing a two-step tattoo over the first date I'd entered — 1972. The other was connecting in similar fashion with the final mark. Where I'd written "Now."

"Third, you're right. Our murders aren't going to be solved until somebody can tell who's wearing Pinocchio's nose. This quaint little city's problem isn't so much that it's a house of cards. It's a house of lies. But then, that's what you've been telling me. Right, Mr. Bonaparte?"

This was when I noticed my own middle fingers had been keeping time with hers. "So, where would you start?"

I don't know if she'd been thinking about it or if the answer came to her in a flash, but she didn't hesitate. "I'd start by seeing if we can find Dr. Huntgardner."

I could have reminded her that it was not for lack of trying that we hadn't located Huntgardner. I'd given that assignment to others, but I knew the drill. My detectives had reached out to the professor's acquaintances, his colleagues, and his immediate family and friends. Registered him with the National Missing and Unidentified Persons System (NamUs). Checked hospitals in case he was injured. Checked churches in case he was troubled and wandered in. Checked jails in case he'd somehow run afoul of the law. Checked out social media and created a fast website.

I'd have asked for updates on all those activities as soon as I got to the office the next morning if the cock hadn't chosen to crow again much sooner.

CHAPTER 36

I didn't learn anything about the predawn fire until the phone call. It arrived during my Sunday morning breakfast. I was eating alone. Angie had needed to leave before the sun rose to drive to the Dallas/Fort Worth airport. She was catching an early morning flight to D.C., and our local feeder airline didn't have a flight scheduled until later in the day. So she hadn't stayed the night.

The caller was the Flagler Fire Department's assistant arson investigator. I kept chewing my food and listened to him hem and haw. He said he knew it was Sunday. Thought I might have been in church. Said he hoped he wasn't interrupting anything important. Could always call back later if I preferred. Should he be talking to one of my deputies instead of me? Wasn't sure how urgent all this was, anyway.

At first, I found his diffidence amusing. Then something to tolerate. In the end, it was annoying. He was going to need help getting to the point.

"Marshal Burrows, the fact you consider it important works for me."

"Call me Delbert, Sheriff."

"Delbert, I'm going to take a wild guess. You're at the

scene of a fire, and you've seen something you think I should know about."

"Yes, sir. I've got a whole crowd of people hoping you can come tell us what it is."

That's how I learned of the fire at the former Cromwell Company warehouse close to the Flagler Shorthaul Railway's switching yard at the south edge of downtown I'd had a special interest in for more than a day now. That news alone motivated me to carry my plate of scrambled eggs and link sausage to the refrigerator. Eating had lost its place on my priority list.

I hadn't dressed for going out since I had nothing scheduled.

A quick call to my dispatcher let him know that the sheriff was about to be on the move. As I dressed, my brain stayed busy. A search warrant was no longer going to be needed from cranky old Judge Kincannon. The pickup of interest and its trailer-mounted backhoe should now be available for viewing.

I also had a growing suspicion. One that began vague and unsettling, then began to spread in my awareness like incoming fog. One or more malefactors in Abbot County had started abandoning their tactics again. For almost two decades, their MO had been to go to any lengths not to be noticed.

So much for that.

Leaving ten bodies moldering for the buzzards didn't fit that approach. Neither did strapping a bomb to the sheriff's car or torching a massive downtown building. An arson investigator was already probing, and no doubt other examiners would follow. The local sheriff would soon be on the scene. Media headlines were certain to follow.

It felt like a mistake. A bad mistake. A compoundable mistake. A mistake that was going to help the current sheriff dig deeper into the underbelly of his community's most malevolent secrets.

Maybe I was leaping to conclusions.

But Delbert Burrow's excitement had been fueled to the point where he'd become almost incoherent. I doubted that a blackened truck and trailer with a backhoe smoldering on it could be the full explanation.

As I walked toward the old Cromwell building, what surprised me was that fire apparatuses hadn't been moved. Engines and ladder trucks were still parked where they'd arrived. No hoses had been rewound that I could see. Firefighters were standing around, a cluster here, a cluster there.

Gawking.

This happens at most fire scenes after the fire is extinguished. Personnel are letting the adrenaline settle. Savoring the excitement. Reliving the battle. Getting their energies back. When you've conquered dreaded fire, you are entitled to do that. But Assistant Marshal Burrows had said this fire had happened before dawn. Hours ago.

Then I noticed the yellow crime scene tape that had put the entire building off-limits. Including the fire hoses that snaked through some of its doors.

Stringing crime scene tape was something arson investigators often did. But I'd never seen them do it before their firefighting colleagues could gather up their gear and return to their firehouses. And that seemed to be the skinny here.

The voice boomed at me like a wrecking ball. "Sheriff, sir! Molotov cocktail. Nothing fancy. Half gasoline, half motor oil. Went through a side window."

Delbert Burrows's face looked like it had been drawn by a kindergartner for an art project. Nothing fit. Seeing it for the first time, I struggled to sound like the adult in the conversation. "You have a nose for sniffing around, do you, Marshal Burrows?"

I winced at my clumsiness.

He had a nose that looked like two mismatched woodpecker

holes in a warped barn board. He could have taken instant offense but appeared not to have noticed. "My sniffer does most of my sniffing. You know how they work, don't you?"

I grabbed at the chance to change the subject like it was the last free pass to heaven. "You need to tell me."

He explained how the nozzle drew in vapors. The targeted gas molecules and applied reagents in the vapors reacted with each other. This produced electric currents, which the sniffer measured. And, voilà (the actual word he used), you could tell if you have combustible and hazardous vapors, which ones and how much of each.

"Um-hmmm."

That was me, signaling admiration. Buzz-cut-wearing Assistant Fire Marshal Delbert Burrows might be able to scare a stuck eighteen-wheeler out of the mud with that face, but his head housed an excellent brain.

I quizzed him while I got my protective gear out of my car trunk and started slipping it over my street clothes. "You're in charge of the fire scene here?"

He grinned a broad grin. I somehow knew it was coming. He had a diastema — a gap between his two front teeth. A large one. Thank God he was bright. Mother Nature hadn't cut him any slack in the looks department.

"Oh, hell, no. I'm just in charge of you." Another grin, but one followed by a moment of searching my face. "You don't remember me, do you?"

I turned to gaze into the earnest countenance anchored by two gigantic jug ears and ransacked my memory. Nothing.

"You taught me how to cheat at marbles." He was enjoying this. "When you lived on Willows Street, I lived next door. I've never forgotten. You showed me how to fudge over the line — get a little closer to the target with your agate. I'd never thought of that before. 'Course, I was only a snot-nosed kid. Seven or eight, I think."

I expressed chagrin that I'd not been a healthier influence. He chose that moment to bushwhack me again. "Providential, I think."

If there was one thing I hadn't expected to burst out of the mouth of the unsophisticated-looking assistant fire marshal of Flagler, this would have been it. I wondered if he'd meant to use it, so I asked him what he was thinking.

"Providential — your living next door to me. This way, I could tell my boss that I know you and convince him that you should investigate this case. Except I had a case of nerves when I called you. Weren't sure you'd want to come."

"But this is a fire scene, Mr. Burrows. Fire marshal's domain, not mine."

"Truth is, Sheriff, I'm not sure whose domain it's going to turn out to be."

We were walking up to the yellow crime scene tape at the front of the warehouse. The triple-wide rolling steel door that had been installed during the warehouse's remodeling had a gaping hole close to its center. A firefighter's carbide-tipped circular sawblade had made three connecting slices in the door.

Then the fire crew had kicked the severed metal aside and voilà — to use Delbert's word — a new opening. One big enough to walk through.

I reached out to stop Delbert before we stepped inside. "But why keep your firefighters from gathering up their gear and returning to quarters? The fire's obviously out."

What happened next I'd be able to replay in my mind in faithful fidelity for the rest of my days.

My long-lost marble-playing acolyte went still. Bent to lay his sniffer device and his krypton-gas-bulbed flashlight on the concrete driveway. Turned toward me and took a short step. Reached out and grasped my arms not far above the elbows. Turned my body until it faced his square-on. Looked in both directions over my shoulders. Put his massive nose within half a foot of mine. And spoke in a sotto voce voice that was so soft I had to strain to hear him.

"Sheriff, what you are about to see inside . . . if it is what I think it is, I don't know how Flagler will ever explain it. Or live it down."

"So you decided to call me."

"Not at first. Didn't think of you right away."

"Where'd the idea come from?"

"I remembered . . ." He was still hedging. "Remembered what else you told me that day."

"The day we were playing marbles?"

"Um-hmmm."

"Okay, what else did I tell you?"

He cleared his throat. It sounded awkward because there was nothing in it that needed clearing. "You told me it was easy to cheat at marbles. But that you'd still have to live with yourself after. You told me to stay away from easy."

Well, good for me. "What does that have to do with this?" I asked.

"I decided to call you because if I was about to stay away from easy, you were the guy I wanted to do it with."

CHAPTER 37

The fire from the Molotov cocktail had darkened the interior of the warehouse, especially toward the back window, but hadn't interfered with what we could see when we entered the warehouse.

The big dual rear wheeled pickup truck, Ford F-350, and the trailer carrying the backhoe were parked to our left. That was the Count's thingamajig. To our right, a creepy bus glared down at us like a replica of one of Arthur C. Clark's monoliths. Not the vertical ones — the elongated one in *2061: Odyssey Three*.

The assistant fire marshal pushed the door open and stepped up into the bus first. I followed. We both realized about the same time we were going no farther.

We were stuck on the half-a-card-table-sized landing that was supposed to deliver you to the aisle running through the center of the bus. And it would have if not for an elaborate door of metal bars that blocked our path. I flicked one of the bars with an index fingernail. Didn't get a ding back. Clang was more accurate. Stainless steel made such sounds. These bars were serious. To keep people from getting on? Not in the main, although they did that too.

The door had a deadbolt lock. But you'd need more than a

key. Above the lock was a touchscreen. You'd likely need the code *and* the key before you could enter.

I struck my hand through the opening closest to the lock and ran my fingers along the opposite side. I felt what I was expecting to feel. You'd need to navigate the same setup — a lock and a touchscreen — *to get out*.

I shined my light beam on Assistant Fire Marshal Burrows's face. "You've already seen the door?"

"That was my first clue. I saw that and started wondering if this might be more than a remodeled warehouse where Nevermore's Metal Works was planning to make cattle guards and windmills — like the sign out front says."

"Pretty bizarre, I agree. But then I've seen arrangements like this on prisoner transporters, for example."

"Like I say, the real peach pits in the pudding are upstairs."

"And we get up there how?"

"There's an elevator, but the power's off. So we'll have to take the stairs. Circular and a bit steep. Goes through a hole in the ceiling at the back of the garage."

"You made your way up there with this place still full of smoke?"

"The building had been cleared. The ladder crew always does that in a building this big, even with a small blaze. You don't want fire sneaking up walls or getting into the attic. So they'll pull down some ceiling tiles, go up on the roof, maybe cut a hole. Got something to show you there too."

He asked for a minute. Said he wanted to get some bigger torches.

"Some of the things you're about to see, you'll need more light to get the full impact."

He returned with standard-issue firehouse lanterns. One for each of us.

▫▫▫

We followed our light beams up the circular staircase and found another of those stainless-steel-barred entrances, similar to the one in the bus. The assistant fire marshal gave the door a slight nudge and watched it swing open with the precision of a fine watch movement. It stopped about two-thirds of the way open. He nudged it again, sending it wide open. Since he was in front, he walked through first.

He stopped after a few steps. Then, he switched his light from diffused to focus and sent the beam penetrating straight down the lengthy hallway like the headlights on a car. More steel-barred openings. Maybe a dozen on each side. Placed at identical intervals so that each one had a matching partner across the hall.

The effect was like the infinite reflections you get from facing mirrors. Do they ever stop? Physicists and philosophers say they never start, that it's all an optical illusion. My younger colleague and I knew the barred doors didn't go on forever, but the way our torches played with them, it seemed like they could.

Burrows noted as much. Said it looked like turtles all the way down.

I agreed with him. "You've been in the rooms?"

"Nope. Doors locked."

"But can we —"

"Yep, we can see in. They don't change that much. What you see in one, you pretty much see in the rest of them. For a while."

"For how long?"

"First four on each side. One door to a room for those. Then the rooms get bigger. Each one gets two doors. And the contents inside change."

We both pressed up against the bars in the first door and flooded the cubicle with light.

I asked him what he'd noticed first.

Don't think he'd been expecting the question and had to think about it. "Uh . . . the pull-down bed."

"How can you tell it's a bed?"

"Maybe not a bed — but it's got a thick pad on it. Could be an examining table, I suppose. Couple of interesting things about it."

Burrows did it again. Stopped dead in the middle of an explanation. But I was learning to read him; he was thinking, so I waited.

"See, you can adjust the height. Those two tracks on the wall? That has to be what they're there for."

"And the other thing?"

"I think they restrain people on it. Look at where the cinch-strap buckles are."

I'd noticed the short Velcro-equipped contraptions. One at each corner of the long cushion and one in the middle on each side lengthwise. Each of the ends opposite the buckle appeared to be riveted to the shelf frame, if that's what it was.

I felt a little chagrined that I'd not yet made the connection. Of course, they're restraints.

"What else?"

"The flooring."

"What about the flooring?"

"It's seamless. Edges curve up the wall. Extremely easy cleanup. I know about this stuff because we study how it burns. Made to keep bacteria from getting underneath it. Through it too. I'm pretty sure the floors were designed at the factory and delivered in one piece."

"That would be expensive."

"Sure would be. But then this whole place is expensive."

"Why worry about bacteria?"

"Maybe it's not just that. Maybe it's something else they want to keep control of. Clean up easily."

"Like what?"

"Like DNA."

CHAPTER 38

There wasn't a whisper of air movement, and my protective clothing had never felt so icky, so we gave the remaining rooms only a cursory look.

The control room was behind the fifth set of barred doors on the right side of the hallway.

Simple enough setup. And yet, elaborate.

Two rows of four surveillance monitors on each of two long walls, and two rows of three surveillance monitors on the far wall.

Behind another set of bars were crew quarters. Had a small kitchen, an eating area, a lounging area, a wall lined with bunk beds for four persons, and a door I assumed led to a toilet and showers.

Then came areas that were a total puzzle to me. Burrows didn't seem to have any ideas either. Or if he did, he kept them to himself.

One had placards of all the letters of the alphabet strung along two of the walls at eye level. A collage of the numbers from one to ten was arranged inside a large black frame running along the third wall. The rug had square designs, each overprinted with a single simple English word — *the* or *and* or

174

go or *get*. None of the words was more than three letters long. And none was repeated.

Another room looked like a research laboratory on one side and a hospital operating room on the other. The effect was so morbid, I had to suppress a shudder. If we'd been investigating a Nazi concentration camp, I'd have thought we stumbled across Josef Mengele's personal torture and experimentation chamber.

The room was even weirder. The tables and chairs were ordinary enough. Had there been nothing else in the room, I'd have dismissed it as a classroom. But plopped all around the room — sometimes on chairs, sometimes lying flat on a table, sometimes stacked atop each other in a corner — were . . . what? Mannequins? Stuffed dummies? Maybe half the size of the average adult.

I couldn't tell much more, since I couldn't get close to any of them. From what I could see, they all had arms, legs, and a head shape where arms, legs, and head shapes should go. But no eyes, noses, mouths, fingers, or toes.

To his credit, Assistant Fire Marshal Burrows understood my growing impatience and discomfort. "Got time for one more bit of weirdness?"

"We've come this far —"

"It's on the roof."

"Wouldn't you know it?"

"Follow me."

Two short stair flights later, we were standing on the roof of the old Cromwell Company warehouse.

Burrows tugged a heavy canvas cover off something flat and circular and at least fifteen or twenty feet across.

It looked to me like a heliport. A landing pad for helicopters. That wasn't what stunned me. The design painted on the pad did that.

I'd seen it before.

It was a carbon copy, on a smaller scale, of the layout in the clearing that Judson Mayes III had discovered.

Delbert Burrows hadn't recognized it, but he'd assumed its meanings were sinister. "What do you think this is?"

He wasn't referring only to the chopper pad, if that's what it was. He meant all the bizarreness we'd been observing for the better part of the past hour.

I didn't need to think about how to answer.

"Something unspeakably perverse. I think last night somebody threw a Molotov cocktail into a facility tailor-made for torture and mass murder."

The look on his face had many parts. But satisfaction was foremost among them. "So, I was right?"

"Yes, it seems so."

▫▫▫

Surreal?

When you surveyed everything that had happened in Abbot County in the past nine days, that was one word for it. Surreal, and getting more so by the hour. First, ten deaths — almost certain to be homicides — at Professor Huntgardner's old house, far out in the county's western boonies. An abandoned house whose insides had been ripped apart like a lion savoring a wildebeest. Next, the discovery of a baffling shrine or piece of land art a few miles to the west that seemed to be hiding, or being prepared to hide, its own secrets.

Then, the disappearance of the professor himself. Followed by an attempt to blow the local sheriff's car — and the sheriff — to smithereens. A chance observation by a homeless person that pointed to all the corpses at the Huntgardner house belonging to physicists. An arsonist's attack on a remodeled downtown warehouse owned by one of those physicists that may have concealed something beyond belief — an assembly-line torture and murder chamber in the middle of downtown Flagler.

I had questions. I had puzzles. I had suspicions. I had unspeakable possibilities to consider, rule out, or act on.

And I had very little to go on.

Because, at the moment, no illegal actors were in law enforcement's crosshairs, and there was a desperate need to put some there.

My phone buzzed.

The text message was from Angie. She'd arrived in the nation's capital. She hoped to return by late Tuesday night. Said I should keep an eye peeled for crowing cocks. She'd added in parentheses: "No smiley face intended — serious."

Angie was gone.

So should I gather my most trusted deputies and do a brain dump? They'd be supportive. Mirror my mood. Suggest things they hoped would be helpful. Offer their own ideas on a game plan. Offer to work extra time on the case.

But that would be disruptive. And unfair. Each was already dealing with a piece of the puzzle. Or several pieces. They'd been focused on one or another of Abbot County's mysteries for days.

Not a good idea, Sheriff.

I was still the go-to guy on this one. *So where do I start?*

Goaded by my analytical left brain, my loosey-goosey right brain lost no time providing an answer.

Cadaver dog.

CHAPTER 39

I wanted a cadaver dog because I didn't want to make another serious misjudgment. The first error had been confirmed not long after Delbert Burrows and I exited the warehouse.

There was no damage to the front end of the big dual rear wheeled pickup truck parked in the warehouse to the side of the creepy bus. Or anywhere else. None to the trailer or the machinery on it, either.

I lost no time running the two license plates.

I'd expected both to be registered to one Worley Meersman of Flagler. The Worley Meersman, PhD, we were assuming to be one of our ten bodies at the professor's house. The missing physics professor and the owner of the remodeled warehouse. And who I was now suspecting might be a serial killer. One of a well-heeled pack of serial killers, all of whom had ties to one of Flagler's church colleges.

But the truck and trailer were not registered to the late Dr. Meersman. They were registered to one Judson Thomas Mayes II. Jude the Dude's father. The physician. The professor's personal doctor. Who was supposed to be on Galveston Bay this weekend, bending his fishing rod. I strongly suspected he wasn't.

I wanted the cadaver dog because of what I already knew about the secret society or whatever it was — sect, cult, fraternal organization, organized crime syndicate? — of physicists in Flagler. My growing fear? That they had been burying murder victims within the circle of aristocrat pear trees north of Professor Huntgardner's house.

The nearest cadaver-sniffing dog I knew about was in Austin, 225 miles to the southeast.

His name was Reverend. He was called that because of a habit. When he made a "find," he would cram both paws together and position his head atop them so it looked like he was praying. Or begging. And a cute beggar, or supplicant, he was. I'd been around Reverend a couple of times when he was working. Friendly. Eager. Smart. The sandy-haired, long-legged golden retriever seemed to like me.

It could have been because I got along so well with his partner.

Most search and rescue types I knew were rough-edged. The kind of personalities that enjoyed traipsing through the brambles more than chatting about the world's great unsolved mysteries.

I recalled some of my discussions with the head of Texas Volunteer Searchers of Austin. Topics such as why more woolly mammoth skeletons hadn't been found in Texas. Or why the human sense of direction is so much less precise than that of many animals. Or what the benefits to oral health would have been if dental floss had been invented sooner. Or why prime numbers are so weird. I'd learned a lot on a variety of subjects from listening to Reverend's partner. Lady luck would be smiling on me if Bronson "Boots" Blakley and Reverend could respond on such short notice.

Boots answered on the second ring. He and Reverend could leave in thirty minutes. The drive would take four hours.

That would give us three hours of daylight. How could you ask more of Lady Luck than that?

CHAPTER 40

I'd expected to see Reverend riding loose in his handler's SUV. After all, he wasn't a police dog, trained to attack on command. He was a cadaver dog, trained to sniff out human remains. But he arrived in a stout cage, peering at me through the metal slats that allowed him to see out but advance no farther.

"Thought you'd let Reverend ride up front."

My friend, Boots, reached out to shake my hand. "Wish I could. But if he got excited, he could tear up my ride. And if we rolled up on another dog working — game's over."

I'd never heard this before. "He could hurt himself?"

"The other dog too. And, maybe, hurt me."

"So he can get mean?"

"Not in a vicious sense. He gets so excited. These are high-drive animals, you know."

We had a time-consuming ride ahead. Some of it on a bumpy dirt road. Some of it on the bare prairie. And not a lot of daylight left. I put a backpack with a flashlight, two bottles of water, three energy bars, and a pair of binoculars next to Reverend's cage. Three minutes later, we were gone.

Boots steered with his left hand and played with his bushy mahogany beard with the other.

And listened.

I cycled through the litany of woes that had rained down on my county in a little more than a week. The only question he asked came at the end was "What, exactly, makes you think a bunch of bodies may be buried where we're headed?"

"Most of all, the helipad we found on top of the remodeled warehouse. It has symbols painted on it."

"And you say they're the same as what you saw in this clearing where we're headed?"

"To a T."

"Tell me again what it looks like."

"It's not complicated. Two big ovals and two Latin phrases. One of the phrases is '*unus mundus*.' It means 'one world.' It goes all the way back to the thirteenth century. The other phrase is '*e tenebris*.' It means 'out of the dark.'"

I stopped to see if my listener wanted to respond, but he stayed silent. He did dip his chin a couple of times, so I took that as a sign to keep going. "Everything, including the ovals and the Latin words, has been shaped with white pebbles."

He looked puzzled.

"Stones — like you'd use to decorate your yard. I'm guessing they made forms and filled them with rock. Went to a lot of trouble."

His silence got heavy. I'd seen slow traffic lights change quicker. But he'd say something soon. And did.

"Don't know about the Latin phrases. Leave that to you. But the ovals? Hermes Trismegistus."

I had to think about who that was. "The learned ancient?"

"That's the one. He said God is a circle. Center's everywhere and circumference is nowhere. And you've got a circle."

"I know. The trees."

"Yep. And then there's the matter of the eyes."

"You think that's what the ovals are meant to signify — eyes?"

"Could be. Very popular symbol down through the ages. The all-seeing eye."

I'd already flipped my pocket notebook open to the drawing I'd made in the Piper Cub. "Okay, let's say they're meant to be eyes. We've got two of them. But they're positioned funny." I held up my drawing. "Like this. One sits on top of the other. Not like a face. On a face, they'd be — you know — side by side. These ovals aren't."

Another pause. "I've been thinking about that. What if we have two all-seeing symbolic eyes, not two human eyes? What could that say?"

"To whom?"

Boots drummed a hand on the steering wheel. "Well, whoever's looking. You've got some sort of signaling going on here, don't you think?"

"Signaling to whom?"

He glanced at me then back at the road. "By the way you tell it, anyone looking down."

"Looking down from where?"

"Well, in your case, from an aircraft."

"And what's the message?"

"Isn't that the sixty-four-thousand-dollar question? But I can think of one possibility."

I rested my notebook on my leg, reached for my ballpoint, and got ready to write.

Boots saw this and chuckled. But I wasn't being cute. This self-taught search and rescue expert had given me more new ideas twenty-five minutes into our drive than I'd had in three days of puzzling over the peculiar exhibit on the prairie. "One might be enough."

He laughed again. "Isn't every day I get the undivided attention of one of the Ivy League's finest."

"Just a humble Texas boy who wanted a change of scenery, thanks. But you're right, you've got my attention."

Boots returned to his serious face.

"Remember the seventies? And that *I'm Okay — You're Okay* book that set off such a craze in pop psychology? Maybe this is that kind of message — two kinds of okayness. Two all-seeing eyes. Not in competition. And not paired together. But coexisting in the circle of God, so to speak. Look at the circle one way, and one is on top. Turn it over and look at it the opposite way, the other one's on top. Doesn't matter. Both are okay. You think?"

Looking over at me, saw the intent look on my face, then served up his best imitation of a hillbilly Texas twang. "Howse 'bout 'em apples?"

Indeed. Here was a professional dog handler explaining how the world was working in terms that would have sounded right at home in one of my Yale Divinity School graduate seminars. I considered joking that "such apples" were hard for a one-eyed person to spot. But instead, I left the subject dangling, and we devoted the remainder of our drive to chit-chat.

Reverend might find nothing at the circle of trees. But if he didn't, I sensed that I'd not be needing to apologize to my friend Boots for dragging him and his dog all this way. Abbot County's descent into craziness was intriguing him. And his keen observational skills were rekindling my own confidence that breakthroughs could be had.

As he'd reminded me with little effort, my challenge was deciding where to look for them.

CHAPTER 41

Reverend's deep barks filled the SUV. Somehow, he knew that we'd arrived.

Boots raised the rear door. Cracked the door to Reverend's cage open wide enough to reach inside and grab his collar. Let him take a short jump to the ground. Told him to sit. Then did something that surprised me. He let go of his cadaver dog and told him to "go find Johnny."

Boots knew he'd need to explain this. "I could say, 'Go find the corpse,' but 'Go find Johnny' sounds better. Friends and family are usually around during a body search. Or the general public."

I wondered about something else. "What if he sees a rabbit?"

"Wouldn't give it a second glance. Maybe not even a first."

Reverend's boss pointed to a plastic grocery bag in the back of his vehicle. "He doesn't get chews for chasing rabbits. His chase target is odors from a human body. And he knows that."

"What if it's a dead rabbit?"

"Same difference. He's trained to find human remains, not animal."

Boots and Reverend had another surprise for me. About ten minutes into our search, Boots tossed a scarred yellow tennis ball out into the clearing. You'd have thought they were back home on the lawn. Reverend tore after it. Clamped his jaws around it. Squeezed it a couple of times and trotted back to return it to his partner. Ready for another round of ball-retrieval.

This went on for about five minutes. Then Reverend got a drink of water and returned to work.

I watched to see if I could spot a pattern to his movements around the clearing. There wasn't one. All I could detect was unpredictable lopes and quick veers and abrupt stops. Always directed by his nose.

He wielded it like Assistant Fire Marshal Burrows did his sniffer. Back and forth. Up and down. Wide swath, then a pinched one. If he couldn't get close enough to the ground to suit himself, he tried to dig a hole. The dirt was so hard he wasn't having much success, but he'd sent a fair amount of white rock flying.

Then I saw there *was* a pattern to the dog's movements. I'd been looking for the wrong thing.

My friend Boots had been moving across the clearing a dozen steps at a time. Each time he moved, Reverend made a corresponding shift. When I noticed this, he was nearing the center of the clearing.

I walked over to Boots. "How much longer can Reverend do this?"

"Not much longer. I'm going to give him another drink. Then we might get another ten minutes."

"Can he check outside the trees?"

"Not today, I don't think. I'm concerned about the heat. We can come back tomorrow. Early, maybe. Be cooler then."

The surrounding trees were throwing longer and longer shadows. The summer sun had started to set, but the heat wouldn't dissipate. My thoughts were wandering.

Not the right word.

Migrating. Better word.

Reconstituting. Best word yet.

My fear over finding bodies in the clearing was lessening. They might be somewhere else. But that required a new theory, and this was what my mind wanted to work on. Tomorrow was another day, and my theory was going to need reconstituting.

Or so I assumed.

Then Reverend decided on his own to search outside the tree line. Not tomorrow when it was cooler.

Now.

That was clear from the beeline he made for what mariners in the Middle Ages called "Potente." Due west. The point on the compass that gathers in the setting sun.

He stopped in the deepening shadows, a few steps beyond the tree line. And began to scratch the packed dirt again with his front paws. Scratch and sniff. Raise more dust, and sniff. Move a few inches away, disturb the surface with those sharp claws.

And sniff.

Until he stopped. Laid his head on his paws. He continued to move his bushy tail nonstop. Barked. Checked to see if his handler was paying attention.

Boots was on the move but not toward his dog. He was returning to his SUV. I headed for Reverend, walking slow. When my friend caught up with me, he was holding a narrow, pipe-like affair with a wooden handle at one end. He held it out so I could get a closer look. "Best fifty-dollar investment I ever made. Called a Paul Brown probe — don't know why. Beats shoveling where Reverend's located all to hell."

"A soil corer?"

"Yeah, you can call it that. Reverend and I use it to take sniffing samples. He's going to go nuts when I get there with it. He knows what it's for."

Boots was soon perspiring like he'd been eating chili peppers.

The dirt was more than hard. It was rocklike. He'd put as much force on the device's coring rod as he could without bending it. That had sent it about half an inch into the dirt. "This red clay gunk of yours is harder than the bottom of Satan's cistern."

I had an idea. "What if we poured water around your hole?"

"I've tried that before in soil this hard. The first inch or so of dirt says 'thank you very much' and soaks it all up. Nothing much changes."

Another thirty minutes of daylight remained, and I didn't want to quit. "You have a hammer?"

He was about to shake his head in defeat when he had a light-bulb moment. Or half of one. "What I've got is an old croquet mallet that I've cut the handle down on. I use it to drive stakes. But you can't hammer on a Paul Brown — you'll crimp it in the middle."

"How long are the stakes?"

"Couple of feet."

"Have any with you?"

"One, maybe."

"One might do it."

Boots dropped the probe on the ground, told Reverend to stay, and started in a brisk walk for his vehicle.

Halfway to the SUV, he stopped. Shook his head. Turned to look back at me. "Too bad you don't have Reverend's nose. You got a head for this."

The stake and the mallet helped us extend our hole to two feet. We fed enough water into it to start growing tomatoes. The probe found softer soil, and Boots sent it deeper and deeper. He dropped to his knees, so he could still push on the handle. About six inches of the rod was still visible when we all heard the thud.

We'd hit something solid. Something the corer wasn't going to penetrate.

Boots started withdrawing the Paul Brown. "Let's see what Reverend makes of this."

The dog was beside himself at the prospect. If Boots needed me to control him, we had a problem. I told Boots that. "Don't think he knows me well enough for me to grab his collar when he's like this."

Boots had the coring device free of the ground. "No need to do that. He knows the drill."

He turned the grip ring until we could view the soil sample inside it and held the instrument out to the dog, allowing Reverend to sniff it at the opening. One more time, he told him to go find Johnny.

Reverend dropped to the ground. Pushed his nose flat against the slit that displayed the soil in the corer. Sniffed once. Withdrew his nose as if to clear his sinuses. Pushed his nose up against the pipe-like device again. Sniffed again. And began to pray. He considered Johnny found.

The resounding thump had dissolved any optimism I'd been feeling about not finding signs of any bodies buried in the circle of trees. Now, dread was flooding in — fear that Reverend had found more than one Johnny.

Boots tossed the coring device a few feet away and left it where it landed. "I think we've at least got a suspicious wooden box. If you want to find out what's in it tonight, we're going to need a shovel crew and some floodlight stands."

I was already adding to the list. "And a CSI team. And the medical examiner's people. And a consignment from one of Flagler's all-night diners. What does Reverend eat?"

His owner's grin telegraphed how fond he was of the talented canine. "Scrambled eggs. Hot dogs. Three or four hamburger patties would be nice. Or a couple of liverwurst sandwiches. But he's headed back into his cage. Look at him. He's tuckered."

CHAPTER 42

The food never arrived. My mistake. I'd forgotten to ask anybody headed out to bring it. That was a shame. Everyone in the sheriff's department — Deputy Tanner, Detective Moody, Detective Salazar, Detective Coltrane, all of them — knew the closing hours of every café, burger joint, and bar kitchen in town. Knew the best cooks to place late-night or early morning orders with. And they welcomed a chance to rustle up grub for colleagues because they'd get a chance to order something for themselves.

From the sounds coming from the back of the SUV, Reverend didn't consider food an issue. Or anything else. The snores had kicked in about thirty seconds after Boots put him back in his cage. Ever since, they'd rolled through the vehicle, regular as high-tide ocean waves, and about as loud.

"I take it Reverend doesn't share your bedroom."

"Uh-uh. No way."

I told him I had one more location where I wanted Reverend's assistance. The remodeled Cromwell Company warehouse. To get in all the rooms, we were going to need machinery — and machinists — capable of cutting through hardened steel. But we could give Reverend's nose enough to sample that we'd at least know if this was a high-tech slaughterhouse.

Boots said he'd like to see the structure himself. Told me where he planned to stay the night. Said he wouldn't mind a chance to sleep in and a late breakfast. I suggested meeting at the Eden Junction Bar and Grill. Told him we could get Reverend a couple of double meat cheeseburgers. We humans could have something more sensible like their whipped-eggs breakfast pie, hash browns, biscuits and gravy, and home-made strawberry preserves. He said he wished I'd not been so specific. Now he'd lie awake all night in anticipation.

Boots and his devoted sidekick headed back to town not long after the first of my department's vehicles arrived. A CSI team. Only a couple of guys — and I was lucky to get those. All my crime evidence folks were young, and late Saturday night wasn't the best time to try to round up a crew, even if they did wear their phones around the clock.

Soon afterwards, we got occasional glimpses of a parade of vehicle lights making their needle-prick approaches through the darkness.

They seemed to be taking forever as they crept toward the ridge. That was because the crappy road between us and the Sweetwater cutoff wouldn't let them come any faster.

After thinking about it, I got the road equipment manager for the county out of bed. Apologized. Told him our predica-ment. Rock-hard ground. A probable hit by cadaver dog four feet below the surface. I was thinking a casket or at least a large box. We needed help excavating it.

That explained one set of headlights. He'd rounded up a work crew and sent us a backhoe.

My CSI youngsters had hand shovels. The driver for the ME office's van didn't look like he knew how to use one. The two night-shift deputies who'd responded did. Better yet, they'd brought one for me.

The powerful steel teeth of the backhoe's digging bucket needed less than a dozen hefty bites before I heard the thump again. Same solid reverberation as before. I wasn't sure what to compare it to. My grandmother's old cedar chest popped into my mind, not that I'd ever heard it make that kind of a sound.

I gave the operator a go-easy signal. Two more partial scoops, and I shut him down.

I was about to lead the way into the hole when the machinery operator shouted a warning. Too dangerous to do that, he indicated. Gestured to let his machine have another go at it. I did. He didn't need long to uncover the rest of the box lid with his digging bucket. Then he maneuvered his machine so it could reach sideways into the expanding hole.

I had to watch him work for a time before I understood. He was sloping the sides — all four sides. Making their angle more and more shallow. He didn't want us climbing into the excavation until he had minimized the risk of a trench collapse.

For this reason, it was deep in the night before we made our way into the hole with our shovels.

I doubted that any of us had experienced a night quite like this. I hadn't — not once in sixteen years on the job. The raspy mating sounds of the male katydids in the trees had provided us with background music. There hadn't been a lot of talking. I'd noticed a lot of yawning. I was sure that every single one of us wished the night to be over.

The box looked to be a cedar chest. Longer than most computer tables and about as wide and deep. Dirty as it was, the richness of the red wood grain still shone through. Both my grandmothers had had one.

I decided we should try and remove the lid before we extricated the entire box. If it contained nothing of interest, we might leave it in place. Fill the hole back up. And go home. To bed.

Our digging crew moved enough of the surrounding soil to keep it from piling in when I asked them to remove the lid. That turned out to be a shrewd idea. Otherwise, it would have tumbled down on the box's contents. I didn't want the body disturbed. Nor the Bible that had been buried with the individual.

One glance suggested that this was an adult's body — what was left of it.

The skeleton was resting on its side, with both arms drawn behind its back. Another oddity was the belt. It was wrapped round the victim's neck.

I had a potential name for the owner within moments of our lifting the lid free. That was because of what was written inside the Bible: "Property of Wilson W. Carmichael."

This might not actually be Wilson W. Carmichael, of course. It could be someone else. But I wasn't expecting that. I was suspecting that this was Dr. Wilson W. Carmichael, Bible faculty member at the University of the Hills, who had been missing for more than twenty years. No Cock Crowed Box No. 6 had a file devoted to his disappearance. I hadn't looked at it all that close, but I remembered a few details. Mainly how Dr. Carmichael had left his friends one spring night in 1997 and was never seen or heard from again.

As I stared at the frontispiece entry in the old Bible, I couldn't resist repeating aloud a snippet of "Amazing Grace": "I once was lost, but now I'm found."

My next thought I kept to myself. *Welcome back, Dr. Carmichael. You need to tell us why you went away.*

I'd think about it some more once I'd had some sleep.

CHAPTER 43

The first time my phone let loose with one of the musical tones I'd set it up to play, the LED display on my digital clock said 8:09 a.m. This time, it was the Spanish guitar ringtone.

My initial impulse was to ignore it. I'd been in bed less than two hours. Couldn't the universe let a dedicated public servant who'd been up all night get a few hours' sleep?

Then I saw the 512 area code — Austin's area code. Had to be my friend Boots. Wasn't going to be good news. No doubt my plans for the day were already falling apart.

He said he and Reverend were headed back to the Hill Country. A gas explosion near Houston had collapsed most of a café filled with people. Rescuers were asking for Reverend's help. He apologized. If I needed them back, they'd return as soon as they could.

I said I'd let him know. Wished them safe travels. Tossed my phone back on the top of my nightstand and rolled over on my side. I was asleep in seconds.

The next time my Spanish guitarists started striking up golpes, the LED display said 8:59 a.m.

My dispatcher, Jeff Sanders, apologized. Wouldn't quit, in fact. Sounded worse than Delbert Burrows. But Doc Konnie had called a couple of times insistent that she'd discovered something that I'd want to know about the remains in the cedar box. I told him not to worry, that Doc Konnie would do enough of that for both of us. Told him that I'd call her. And I meant to do that as soon as I hung up — and would have if I'd been able to stay awake that long.

I couldn't.

My next view of the LED display was at 10:05 a.m.

The managing editor of the local newspaper said he wouldn't have called me at home, but the Associated Press wouldn't leave him alone. The AP guy was bugging him for confirmation about the discovery of another professor's body. Said the AP was planning to suggest that anyone who knew about professors disappearing call their local police department or the Abbot County Sheriff's Department.

I told him we did have a new active investigation, but I couldn't say anything more. I stumbled to my bathroom. Got a drink of water. Refused to glance at the mirror. And burrowed back into my bed.

Have no idea where the next hour and twenty-eight minutes went. Or where I went.

Can remember only what my LED display was showing when my phone rang again. 11:33 a.m.

Assistant Fire Marshal Delbert Burrows said he'd been waiting at the old Cromwell Company warehouse since eleven. Was I coming?

I cursed.

I'd texted him on the way back to town six hours earlier and asked if he could join Boots, Reverend, and me in taking another look at the place at 11. I began to apologize. Profusely. All the while thinking, *Oh, Lordy, I'm beginning to sound like Delbert Burrows.* I told him I'd call him the first chance I got and bring him up-to-date. He said no problem. Said I sounded sleepy. Said he understood. Said it must have been a long night. Said he was sorry he had disturbed me but wanted to be sure he had the time right for our meeting.

This time, I was the one who said no problem. And again, I was so sorry. Did Flagler have Apologizers Anonymous meetings? If so, Delbert and I both needed to go.

Angie called at 12:23 p.m. Our conversation felt more than a little familiar. I told her that I loved her but that she'd done it again — called me when I was having an official daft day. She asked me where I was. I answered in a single word. "Tripping." She asked for another word. "Hallucinating."

She did what she always did. Looked for serious meanings first, before considering alternatives. "Sheriff Luther Stephens McWhorter, have you taken something you shouldn't have?"

"No, no, although I'm about ready to. Just can't get people to leave me alone. Up nearly all night. No sooner did I get to bed than the phone started ringing. Happening about every hour. Nonstop. I'm beginning to feel, well, stoned."

Angie, ever the problem-solver, was on the job with specific instructions. "Okay, turn the damned phone off. Turn the damned clock to the wall. Call me when you wake up."

She said she still expected to be home early Tuesday evening. Planned to catch a late-morning flight to DFW. Had a seat reserved on the late afternoon flight to Flagler. Wanted her favorite sheriff well rested when she arrived. That meant I had to do as I was told.

I did. It helped that my phone went quiet and stayed that way for what seemed like the rest of my life.

I felt like a new man when I reached for it at 5:46 p.m.

The feeling lasted for, oh, a fraction of a second. The time I needed to tilt the phone into view and see who was calling.

My phone screen didn't say who.

It said what.

The White House. The White House was calling.

CHAPTER 44

It was not the POTUS on the line.

It was the POTUS's switchboard operator.

Not the one, I soon concluded, you get when you call the White House. Not that I'd ever spoken with that one, either.

I'd wondered a few times what I'd do if I ever needed to contact President Jim Bob Fletcher. I'd found a phone number on the internet. It was the one any ordinary citizen could use. Would the president take my call if I used it? I thought he might. We didn't belong to the same political party, but before he'd become Abbot County's most famous resident, I'd ridden with him a few times in a convertible at the head of parades. Sheriffs do courtesy things like that, no matter what political party the others in the car belong to.

Fletcher had a politician's leak-tight memory for faces and names. I knew he'd remember who I was, and at least what the back of my head looked like. I'd never called him because I figured I'd only get one free pass. I didn't want to use it unless and until I had a good reason to.

The voice on the line said she was calling on behalf of the president. "Behalf"? Her use of the word puzzled me. Jim Bob Fletcher had only been in office six months. Wasn't it a little early to be flacking for reelection contributions?

But it wasn't money that she was "behalfing" about. She wanted the number for a secure phone connection in the Abbot County Sheriff's Department.

I told my caller that we'd never had enough to be secretive about to need a secure number. "Best I can offer the president is the number you've just used."

She asked if I could please hold.

I swung my legs off the bed and located my flip flops. Thought about getting up and putting on my bath robe, but how I was dressed wasn't going to matter the slightest to the president of the United States. Neither would how I'd been doing lately. Or how the weather's been in Flagler. He wasn't calling to chat. Truth be told, I couldn't begin to guess why he was calling.

Fletcher had mastered the vocal tricks that good politicians use. The ones that make them sound like leaders. Different tones for different zones. At least, that's how one researcher had put it in an article I'd read.

So the first thing I listened for when the president came on the line was how his voice sounded.

My judgment was instantaneous. President Jim Bob Fletcher's tone fell somewhere between long-lost-best-friend and let's-do-serious-business-together.

The best-friend zone didn't survive long. Jim Bob went from ingratiating to jittery in two sentences. It was as if he was afraid for both of us if the wrong words were used.

"This office I occupy opens a lot of doors and a lot of filing cabinet drawers. And, on occasion, it loosens tongues."

I knew he was setting the stage for something if he didn't get lost en route. The less I said, the better. "Yes."

"I've seen some things, read some things. Been told some things."

"All right."

"I can't talk about this on the phone — just not safe. Not wise, let us say."

I was beginning to feel like an equal to the other party in this conversation, so much so that I thought I could at least state the obvious. "Then it needs to be done face to face."

"It does — but in Flagler, not here."

"Can I ask if this is about the crime spree we're up to our necks in?"

"It is, but there's so much more to it. That's why I called. I know you'll find the perpetrators and all that without my help. But what's happening in Flagler has a national security aspect to it. Possibly, an international security aspect." President Jim Bob Fletcher had abandoned any pretext of trying to project charisma. I could hear fear in his voice. "I need you to get on top of this. And I can't help you from here."

"What's preventing the president of the United States from helping a lowly Texas sheriff?"

"I don't know who I can trust."

"So what do you need from me?"

"I'm going to send you someone with that information."

"All right."

"A secret source of information — a Deep Throat, like in Watergate, remember? He'll be there in a day or two."

"Okay."

"I'm going to give him this phone number. He'll say he's collecting donations for the Overwatch Group when he calls. And when you actually meet, the code word is Gideon's Trumpet."

I wasn't quite sure what I was feeling as I listened to all this. Curiosity? Concern? All with a bit of amusement thrown in? "Overwatch Group and Gideon's Trumpet — got it."

"You're going to need a place to meet and talk totally removed from the public. You can't be seen together, and you can't be overheard. Just can't be. Too dangerous. You need to maintain total privacy, or this might not turn out well. And he'll give you the passwords when he calls."

My mind went to the basement of the parking garage where Woodward and Bernstein and their mole met in the movie *All the President's Men*. I told the president I'd be ready for the contact.

There was no reply.

I'd already been reassigned — to the over-and-done-with-that zone.

Silence was the new tone.

CHAPTER 45

I was born in October 1976, so I wasn't even a gleam in my father's eye when President Nixon's "Plumbers" burglarized the National Democratic Committee's headquarters at the Watergate complex in Washington, D.C. The five guys who brought the house tumbling down on the Nixon administration were arrested on June 17, 1972.

This meant my knowledge of Watergate had come from history classes. And occasional news stories.

Like the one in 2005 naming former FBI associate director Mark Felt as Deep Throat. For some reason, I remembered that the journalist, Woodward, had signaled Felt when he wanted a meeting by moving a flower pot with a red flag on the balcony of his apartment. The POTUS wanted me to participate in a similar kind of arrangement. One that was already approaching Kafkaesque dimensions — or maybe I should be saying Nixonian dimensions — and I'd only just gotten my first assignment.

So what the best place in Abbot County for a mysterious visitor to whisper secrets in my ear? Dangerous secrets, from what the president had said.

And besides that, did I have to go along with all this?

Well, at this point, I didn't know enough not to go along. A matter of curiosity — yes, there was that. But it was more.

I suspected I was nowhere close to understanding Flagler's turmoil. Not enough to get ahead of it. Each time I seemed to be closing in on possible culprits and believable theories, reality had opened a new door. Produced new crimes. Claimed new victims. Loosened new atrocities.

And then there was this: I'd told the world's most powerful leader that I'd play ball. So, yes, it did feel like I was already committed to going along.

We had several large parking garages in Flagler. But none had basements. If anything, their bottom floors were the busiest parts of the structures. You could go in the other direction and have clandestine meetings on the roofs. But if you did, you'd run the risk of being photographed from neighboring buildings.

Another was one of the old missile bases.

During the '60s, we had twelve deep silos for ICBM missiles and their nuclear warheads scattered around West Central Texas. Their deadly missiles had been controlled from Burford DeBlanc Air Force Base north of town. Four of the silos had been in Abbot County. The sites were remote, and all were fenced. The chance of being overheard inside their fences was close to zero — nil, in fact, if you were down in the silo.

Which was the problem.

Any time the fundraiser for the Overwatch Group and I wanted to have a conversation, we'd have to hie away to the county's hinterlands. Hope we didn't run into a cow or a hay trailer. Force open a weather-encrusted lock on a chain-link fence. Raise a heavy lid on a big hunk of concrete sitting in the middle of the prairie. And park ourselves on some rusty metal steps underground while we trafficked in presidential secrets.

I thought not. But as fast as my imagination could conjure up other locations, my no-not-that analytical mind slammed the door shut.

Abandoned buildings? Too iffy. You never knew who you'd meet in them — kids, pot smokers, teenaged lovers, squatters, owners, more cops. Church bell towers? Flagler only had a few and none that would be suitable. Football stadium press boxes? Too many authorizations to get, and too high a likelihood that the schools' security people would show up.

My house, my office, my car parked in a dark alley? In some ways, I was the most surveilled individual in town. Before long, someone was going to ask, "Who's the guy in the black Homburg the sheriff keeps meeting with?"

It had to be a place that was easy to get to. Where nobody came, where nobody cared, where I could find my way around like it was my backyard. That's when I knew where the Overwatch representative and I were going to have our chats about getting Abbot County away from the brink of the abyss without endangering national or international security. We'd meet in the tumbled-down old tin shack in the far back corner of the BewaretheJunkyardDogs Company's abandoned wrecking yard.

For years, various members of the sheriff's department had used the unremarkable old shack to meet with confidential informers and street snitches. The wrecking yard's owner had honored my request for a key to the padlock on the gate with no questions asked. And the name on the signs kept out trespassers and thieves. That was the owner's brilliant little joke. If you named your salvage business BewaretheJunkyardDogs Company, you didn't need the dogs.

I was ready for Deep Throat Number Two when he called. I could only hope his reason for coming was to tell me about more than just nefarious acts. I was up to my kiester in nefarious acts.

What I needed most was a workable theory about why a bunch of physicists been so intent on shouting "unus mundus" to the skies. And why they may have paid for their audacity with their lives.

CHAPTER 46

It was after-hours, so the answering machine at the office of the Abbot County medical examiner gave me three choices. If my call was an emergency, it gave me another number to call. Or I could leave a message. Or I could call back any time between 9 a.m. and 5 p.m. Monday through Friday.

I left a message. And knew as soon as I hung up that I didn't want to delay knowing what was happening with the ME's investigations.

I placed a call to my chief deputy. Sawyers skipped the small talk. "Rat poison."

I started machine-gunning pared-down questions at him. "Doc Konnie knows this how?"

I got pared-down answers back. "Victims crapped their pants."

"Rat poisons make people's bowels move?"

"This one did."

"Does she know how rat poison got in their bowels?" But I didn't wait for him to answer. I had another question. "She think they drank it or eat it?"

"Her guess is drank it. She thinks this may be the largest mass murder in history where aldicarb was the poison."

"What's aldicarb —?" And answered my own question. "Rat poison."

He told me more. "Comes in little brown grains that look like food. This appears to have been a really insidious form of aldicarb. She's guessing it was slipped into their coffee."

"What makes her think that?"

"The drinking cups in that garbage bag we found not far from the Huntgardner house."

"It's easy to acquire — this aldicarb stuff?"

"Not in the United States. It's so dangerous it's been banned for years. One teaspoonful will kill a rhino. If you want to stock up on Tres Pasitos, you'll have to order it from one of the Latin American countries. You'll get the best price from suppliers in the Dominican Republic."

I repeated the name he'd used. "Tres Pasitos?"

"That's the commercial name of the poison. Means 'three little steps' in Spanish. That's about how far a rat can walk after eating it. A human will begin to asphyxiate within minutes. It attacks your muscles. You can't move, so you can't breathe."

"So our victims died horrible deaths?"

"Like the ME says, it's nasty stuff. I'd guess they went crazy. Started fighting to get out of the house. Blood pressures dropping. Hearts pounding and fluttering. Not a pleasant way to go, for sure."

That explained the tortured position of the body we'd found on the front porch, the one I'd first seen after following the buzzard. "And what do you suggest we do with this information?"

"Tell as many people in Flagler about it as we can. Ask them to be alert for plastic sandwich bags with little brown grains in them." He thought for a moment. "Maybe ask them if they've drunk any coffee lately that tasted funny."

"That wasn't funny, Sawyers."

"Wasn't, was it?"

I asked him to put the ME's report on my desk. Then had two more quick thoughts. One was reflective; the other, motivational.

The reflective one left me feeling guilty. I thought how much simpler it would have been if the killer or killers of the Huntgardner victims had shot them. Bullets, we understood; poisons, not well at all.

The other one was more constructive.

I thought we were going to have an answer for singer Johnny Cash's question, "Will the circle be unbroken?" And breaking it open wasn't going to lead to a better home for a bunch of folks in the sky.

Knowing the cause of death for the nine physicists in Professor Huntgardner's house had triggered an emotion I'd not felt a lot in recent days. Optimism. It lasted until I walked into Doc Konnie's industrial kitchen at exactly nine o'clock the next morning.

Then it evaporated.

CHAPTER 47

"**Y**ou have come, my dear sheriff."

"I always come when my favorite pathologist summons me."

"Well, I save you trips sometimes, ὀχι?"

"Yes, you do. And I thank you. But I gathered you wanted me here for this."

I got no answer. Her abrupt departure was reply enough. She was headed for one of her caster-equipped metal tables. I expected to see her pick something up off the table, but instead, she began rearranging an object lying on it.

A man's belt. Coiled tight around the buckle. Seeing it sent my mind back to my first glimpse of the skeleton when we removed the cedar chest lid at the circle of trees. I'd noticed a belt wound numerous times around the victim's neck.

Now that I was seeing it again, I could tell that it was a long belt — one that had been worn hard. Its surface was so distressed that I wasn't sure about the original color. I was guessing black, but it could have been a dark gray. The surface still had that bumpy leather look in the places where it wasn't worn smooth. It seemed wider than most men's belts.

As Doc Konnie fiddled with it, I was reminded of something I already knew. Women don't tend to treat things like men do. If I'd reached for the belt on the table, I'd have grasped the buckle and dragged the rest off until it dropped toward the floor. Folded it a couple of times to make it more manageable. Only then would I have invited my onlooker to examine it.

Doc Konnie treated the belt like a pastry in the making. She left it lying on the table surface. Cleared away anything that might impede it. Then unwound it slowly the length of a belt loop or two at a time. Almost like she was kneading it. Taking care all the while to protect its position on the tabletop. She was arranging it so that the belt surface was facing me.

Not until the beat-up strip of leather extended along most of the table did she step back. Then she reached for another pair of latex gloves. Waited for me to slip my hands into them. And gestured that I was free to reach for the belt and examine it close-up.

My intention was to start with the buckle and do the man's thing — let the rest of the belt hang free, double it up, and examine it a few inches at a time. First on one side, then on the other.

But that never happened.

As I stepped toward the table, I realized several things. Any one of them would have shocked me. Taken together, they left my knees close to buckling.

I realized that the belt had been personalized. The letters carved or stamped — I couldn't tell which — in the center of the belt were clear enough from a few inches away. Worn or not, they spelled "Sheriff John."

The buckle removed all doubt. The initials etched in it had long since lost their sparkle but not their power to identify. "JAM."

I'd seen that belt before. Many times. It had belonged to my father, Sheriff John Aubrey McWhorter. A few seconds earlier, if someone had asked me where it was, after thinking about it, I'd have said, "Probably in his casket."

From the look on Doc Konnie's face, I'd gotten the casket part right.

I searched her visage for the slightest sign that my fear was misplaced. But the look in her eyes wasn't changing.

"You found this belt in the box containing the professor's corpse?"

Her chin dipped twice in confirmation. Then she reached out and grasped my wrist. I recognized the gesture as one offering to join in my consternation. When she didn't let go, I realized the worst was yet to come. I'd never seen those Greek eyes look as sad as they did as she shared what came next. "The dead man, I'm thinking he was strangled with the belt, neh."

■ ■ ■

The skin oils that form fingerprints are nonvolatile, meaning they don't vaporize. If left undisturbed, they can stay around a long time. Would a near-water-tight cedar box buried four feet underground in dry soil for twenty years be disturbance-free enough?

Doc Konnie was reading my thoughts. "No prints I have found. Wiped? — could be. Deteriorated, maybe. Maybe not ever there. Don't know. Just, όχι. No prints I find."

"Other things in the cedar box?"

"Only the Holy Scriptures. Same again, όχι." No, she was saying.

"And the cause of death?"

"I do tests more. But for now, I listen to the bones. The hyoid in the neck, it is broken."

"A homicide, then?"

"Neh." Yes, she was saying.

I turned the subject to the other homicides. Told her that I'd read her report on the rat poison and asked her if that discovery had surprised her.

She said it had been no surprise that the nine victims found in the house had been poisoned — the absence of other possibilities pointed to that. But she hadn't suspected it had been done with an aldicarb-based pesticide. She'd never had a case like this before. Said finding Tres Pasitos responsible for homicides in America was almost unheard of. She'd done a search and found only one attempted Tres Pasitos homicide on record. Someone had put the deadly pellets in a couple's coffee. An alert hospital lab had detected the chemical traces and saved their lives.

"I will drink no Abbot County coffees for now. You will not drink the coffees, neh?"

"I've always been a tea drinker. So, no, no coffee for me."

"And you will look to find who serves this coffee to rats and physicists in Abbot County?"

"My best people are already lifting the lid on every coffee pot we can find."

When she headed for the door that led to her office, I knew we were moving on. The discussion about lethal coffee had been adjourned sine die.

I followed her like an obedient puppy.

She swept behind her desk. Plowed through a pile of file folders. Came up with the one she was seeking.

Said she had more news for me.

It was about the tangerine-colored fragment of plastic she'd found embedded in the hip bone of our tenth victim. She said it was from the front grill assembly of a Ford F-150 pickup. Which side, she didn't know. The model year — that wasn't so definite either. Anywhere from 1997 to 2003. The assemblies for those models had all been the same.

"You will ask LoCash Cowboys to change their Madisonville Ford truck song, όχι?"

I had no idea who the LoCash Cowboys were, but what Abbot County's ME did next left me with little doubt.

Doc Konnie dropped into an Elvis Presley crouch and began to mimic thrumming a guitar then let loose a ridiculous takeoff on a C&W-type song about an F-150 pickup.

> We'd all get along better in a F-150 pickup,
> But don't order coffee, darlin',
> Especially the three-step kind.
> The coffee, it's no start up, it's a hiccup,
> And you quickly run out of time.

A number of things amazed me about her performance. But what startled me most was her pronunciation. It was perfect when she was singing.

She shot me a glance. Not the mischievous look I expected, but a stoic and resigned one.

"Humor. To it we go when our sanity needs a cover."

Her mangling of the English language was back, but she was right.

I nodded. "Good place for our humanity to hunker down."

She stepped around her desk. Shoved the file folder with the report on the headlight deep into my midriff. Gave me a hug.

But I had another folder to look at first. And I hoped that it had a clue. I was desperate to know how and why my father's beloved belt had ended up around the neck of Abbot County's most well-known missing person.

CHAPTER 48

Finding the large rust-colored accordion-type folder wasn't going to require any searching. I saw it the moment I entered my dining room. The folder took up a quarter of the space in the last box in line along the far wall — No Cock Crowed Box No. 6. Its tab read, in letters bunched close together, "Dr. Wilson Carmichael, Missing Person."

In our marathon sweep through the boxes on Saturday, Angie and I had paid little attention to the folder. Main reason? The folder had intimidated us. It was jam-packed, and we knew if we started removing its contents, they were going to become the kudzu on the table. Spread everywhere. They would defy any effort to organize them. Plus, after scanning the first few documents, we hadn't seen much of interest. They did nothing at all to explain why Dr. Wilson Carmichael had gone missing. Or where. Or who might be involved. My father and his investigators seemed clueless.

A professor missing for more than twenty years wasn't a priority, just another puzzling circumstance involving local college professors. And Flagler was drowning in weirdnesses involving local college professors. Seeing no answers, we'd soon lost interest.

But things had changed.

These excuses for ignoring the folder in Box No. 6 no longer seemed valid. Acknowledging that seemed to blast a hole in the dam holding back my memories of my father. Now they flooded in.

I remembered how I used to sit on his lap as a youngster and he would let me play with his gun. It didn't matter that the gun wasn't loaded. The very idea drove my mother to conniption fits. But then my dad allowed me to do a lot of things.

On weekends and during summers, I often took the prisoners in our spartan little jail their two-a-days. I slipped their food trays under the door and handed them their drinks through the bars. In the field, I accompanied my dad to many a crime scene. He didn't allow me to help cover bodies of the deceased, but I stood close to more than a few upturned cowboys boots while he or one of his deputies did the draping. I went with him to target shoot, using the sheriff department's high-powered patrol rifles. At first, he positioned his large frame behind me so the gun's recoil wouldn't knock me backwards. But as I grew older, I could shoot them without him anchoring me.

As I reflected on these memories, most of them treasured, I realized that these experiences were in large measure the reason I'd become a law officer myself. They also reminded me of something else. My father had been a very private man. There was a lot about him I'd never known. Now it looked like I was about to learn more than a few of his secrets.

I carried the bulky container to my kitchen. Sat it in a bar chair. Moved some of its contents to the counter to make the box — and the chair — more stable. I made myself a glass of iced tea, perched on a stool, and began to read. I intended to skip nothing. Look at every piece of paper — typed or handwritten. Every newspaper clipping. Every receipt, every business card, every photocopy. And absorb every possible meaning in every image I came across. That's what I intended.

But it didn't happen that way.

The reason was the letters.

They were in the first manila folder I removed from the accordion folder. A substantial file, crammed with numerous pieces of monarch-sized white stationery, each with a matching envelope stapled to it. The envelopes were all addressed to "The Honorable John Aubrey McWhorter, Sheriff of Abbot County, County Courthouse, Flagler, Texas." In the lower left-hand corner of each was the word "Personal." Underlined.

The penmanship of the sender was ruler-straight. And not only the written lines. The cursive letters on the envelopes and the letters had an upright primness. You'd have thought they'd been to etiquette class.

On the other hand, the writer had a penmanship style that struck me as giddy. Or bouncy. All the *e*'s were capitalized — and shaped backwards. The prongs flowed from the right, not the left. The descender on a capital *Q* had a short dash through it so that it looked like the Venus symbol for female. In letters like lowercase *g*'s, *d*'s, and *p*'s, the loops were larger than they needed to be. And descenders on the lowercase *y*'s looked like fish hooks and pushed the next line lower than it otherwise would have been.

It pointed to a woman's handwriting. But all this became insignificant the moment I began to read.

From the beginning, it was clear that the world I'd woken up in this morning was not going to survive to the end of this file.

Perhaps I'd feel a sense of psychological devastation later on. Maybe I was going to need a therapist to help me sort it all out. At the moment, my greatest hunger wasn't for a shrink but for Angie's presence. For her steady *Cool Hand Luke* counsel. But I wasn't going to wait for it. When you are seeing lies in the landscape of your life being stripped away one by one, you want it sorted and done. At least, this was the way I was feeling.

So much so that I lost all track of time.

The letters were arranged by date beginning with September 26, 1997. Most were only a single page. Most contained only a few lines. The salutation was the same on all of them: "My dear sheriff." And all were signed the same way: "Faithfully yours, The Prairie Canary."

The first line of the first letter read, "Question for you: do you favor power or principle?"

The second line read, "I think you are a person of principle. And they're setting you up That's why I want to tell you how to find Wilson Carmichael."

Only the letter didn't tell my father how to find Professor Carmichael. Its few sentences read like a manifesto. A run-on manifesto; there wasn't much punctuation. But each new sentence started with a capital letter and had a tiny measure of separation from the sentence preceding it. The meaning was not hard to follow.

She said Abbot County had been taken over by people of power.

This had confused people of principle. They couldn't tell which lies and which liars in Abbot County warranted a close look and which were a waste of time. Unless these judgments were made soon, Flagler's underbelly was about to be ripped open like it had been sliced by a samurai sword.

She said this had gone on long enough. She could help it end. She'd write again soon.

She did on October 8.

The next letter took its cue from an interview my dad had given the local paper two days earlier. The Prairie Canary said he had been wrong to suggest that Carmichael's disappearance might stem from a midlife crisis.

"You said you based this view on what the wife has told you. But again, you were told lies."

She — and again, I was just guessing at the writer's gender — said Carmichael's problems at home had begun long before he reached middle age. But that these hadn't led to his disappearance.

She closed, "He got sucked into the conflict. You need to discover who is at war in Abbot County."

She promised to write again soon.

But she didn't. Not until March 12 of the next year.

My dear sheriff,

Forgive me for pulling a Professor Carmichael. For disappearing myself.

You could say that I've been at war too.

It's especially difficult when your child

1) doesn't know who his real father is.

2) has a father who doesn't want him to know.

3) has a mother who isn't his father's wife.

4) has been told that someone is his mother when she isn't.

I then am one of the liars.

I also know things that may not be lies. But you're going to have to decide which is which.

She promised to begin spilling Flagler's secrets in her next letter.

She did and she didn't. She seemed to be offering an important clue, but it was enigmatic.

The next letter was dated March 20. It was brief. Only three sentences.

Have you ever wondered why crime in Flagler seems so well organized?

And yet, we have no organized criminals in clear view.

Is it because the crimes are something else or is it the criminals who aren't what they seem?

There was no promise to write again, soon or otherwise. But the winds move at a brisk pace on the West Central Texas prairies in March, and so did the Prairie Canary's imagination. The next letter was dated a mere two days later.

I hope my letter the day before yesterday didn't confuse you.
    Usually when we think of organized crime, we think of the Italian Mafia.
    Flagler's organized criminals are too genteel for that.
    But it's the same old, same old. The defenders against the adventurers.
    Since biblical times, it's been a fearful thing to get caught between them. As Professor Carmichael found out.

She added,

More to come soon.

"More" was dated March 26. As usual, the letter was short.

I know you know a thing or two about religion. But to unravel Flagler's mysteries and crimes, you'll need to know more than your Sunday-school-shaped under-standing of religion can provide. So don't worry about the bookish issues. Focus on practicalities. And on people.

She'd say more about which people and which practicalities in her next writing.
She did so in a letter dated April 2.

Even twenty-plus years later, reading it caused the muscles around my eyes to tighten. My father's reaction must have been similar.

The Prairie Canary said she had gone sleepless for several nights wondering what to do with the information she was about to reveal. She was going to trust my father's judgment. And his sense of discretion.

Discovering the fate of Wilson Carmichael was all about uncovering secrets. Helping my father uncover secrets was why she'd started writing. But she hadn't anticipated that she'd need to reveal secrets so personal.

He'd have to keep the secret she was about to share with him or there would be no hope of uncovering the others.

But she never said what that secret was. At least, not in that letter or any of those that followed. Over the next five months, she wrote nine more letters to my father. There were numerous references to Thaddeus Huntgardner. She said Huntgardner had let his life passions cause him to retreat from the rational. He genuinely believed that the piece of space junk he'd brought to Flagler harbored the potential to change the world. He believed the aliens who had manufactured his fragment were returning for it. And when they came — to Flagler, of all places — all the technological and spiritual systems of thinking that had preceded them in history would be antiquated.

This was why Huntgardner had selected the few members of his "Mafiosi" with great care. First, they had to be physicists who had trained with him at the University of the Hills. And they had to share his curiosities and passions. None was permitted to take a job outside the United States. This was so they could assemble on short notice.

And they all had to accept that their membership in Huntgardner's secret society was for life. They'd also had to acknowledge that the penalty for betraying its secrets was death. She wrote:

The name of the professor's mysterious group is the Unus Mundus Masters, or "the Masters."

I've never been able to learn how many "few" amounted to or the full extent of their crimes and machinations. But I've had reason to think there is something extraordinary about them. Why else would another secret society in Flagler have felt the need to mobilize to oppose them?

The Society of Ezekiel's Wheel is every bit as secretive and deadly as its physics-oriented counter-part. I know little about its founder, but he was a Bible professor at the University of the Hills. He specialized in the Old Testament's Book of Ezekiel. And, in partic-ular, Ezekiel 1 where Ezekiel describes his vision of a wheeled chariot descending from the skies.

The Bible professor viewed Ezekiel's vision as a warning. Aliens had tried to plant a bogus Messiah on Earth once before. He claimed that Ezekiel, the prophet, had caught them in the act. Blown the whistle. And destroyed the infidels. The Society of Ezekiel's Wheel planned to do that again if it found anyone trying to plant a bogus Messiah on Earth again.

She went on to note that the Ezekiel's Wheel group, like the Masters, had operated from a series of hush-hush locations in town over the decades.

Sometimes, their physical headquarters had been hidden away in churches, sometimes not. Both groups, she said, were accomplished at doing what secret societies down through history have done: keep their memberships, their presence, and their operations secret.

She admitted that she lacked a shred of hard proof. But she was staunch in her belief about this: these groups had been at the root of Flagler's ongoing outbreaks of civic disorder, vandalism, and occasional serious criminal acts for the past thirty or forty years. Each and every time, their actions were a response to something they feared the other group was doing or might muster the resources to do.

And she'd had no doubt that was what motivated their members most.

Fear.

The fear of each other.

Each group believed its counterpart to be devious and destructive. And dangerous. Not only to Flagler. To the entire world. And perhaps beyond.

I read that far in her voluminous missive without encountering anything that I felt actually touched on my own life. At least not yet. Then, with no warning, all of that changed with a single word.

My subconscious eye spotted it coming a few words in advance. So when my reading voice reached it, my imagination had already begun to race.

Roswell.

What flashed from my memory was the image of that note I'd found on my living room table. The one that read, "DON'T MAKE ROSWELL'S MISTAKE!"

To the best of her understanding, the Prairie Canary said what Huntgardner's Masters feared was that Flagler would repeat the mistake made at Roswell: destroying the aliens without making any attempt to welcome them, honor them, listen to them, learn from them.

On the other hand, the Ezekiel's Wheel group was rabidly opposed to greeting them. Its fear was that if this was done, the aliens would destroy Christianity. Install their own Messiah. And displace the very idea that humankind was the only model of intelligent thinking the universe was meant to emulate.

She told Sheriff John to watch his back — that double-cross was in the air. And that, more than he realized, he was in the crosshairs. The authority of his badge was one reason. Both groups had wanted him in their pocket. Neutrality had worked, she'd observed. Until he'd gone beyond it.

She promised to suggest a course of action for him based on her revelations. But she never did. At least I was not able to find any mention of strategies or tactics in the rust-colored folder with the accordion ends.

There were no further letters from the Prairie Canary.

CHAPTER 49

Thinking about it as I showered and ran my electric razor over my clefted chin, I had three very good reasons to expect a challenging day.

The three women on my schedule were the reasons. Before the day was over, I could expect all of them to be annoyed with me, if they weren't already.

Annoyed?

Too docile a descriptor.

Furious?

More in the ballpark.

The person I most dreaded confronting was the one I cared about the most. Angie still wasn't back in town. Her flight from Ronald Reagan Washington National Airport to Dallas/Fort Worth International Airport had been late last night, and she'd missed the last flight to Flagler. She'd called from the airport hotel, travel-weary and homesick. Said she'd clutch a pillow to her breasts in bed and pretend it was a certain virile, rugged, cleft-chinned, one-eyed sheriff she knew.

I'm not sure whose need for a good cuddle had been most acute.

I'd asked her to send me a photo of what her pillow would see in a cuddle. Her laughter had lasted so long that I knew she was considering it. But better judgment won out. "Not a good thing for a special agent of the FB of I to do."

She'd land midmorning but had to go straight to her office.

Said she'd pick up green-chili enchiladas from Casa Mariachi for dinner. Said she'd arrive at my place eager to display what an FBI special agent dared not feature in photos sent into the public ether.

I told her I was eager for an unveiling. Which I was. But I wasn't optimistic it was going to happen. Not right away. We had too much to talk about.

Or to avoid talking about.

It was the latter that was most likely to bring me grief.

But the encounter of the day that I felt the most uncertain about was going to be the first one. I'd decided to show Helen the letters my father had forbid her to look at.

In a way, she was entitled to see them.

I'd said nothing to her yet about the contents of the six boxes of old records. Six boxes I would never have seen had she not edged aside her devotion and broken a promise to a man she'd adored.

She'd been a girl fresh off the farm, "greener than the last watermelon in heaven," as she liked to put it, and he'd given her a job. A good one. And she'd thrived in it in no small part because of her shrewd handling of other people's secrets and confidences.

When you get stung because you kicked the hornet's nest, you have only yourself to blame. But she knew things I needed to know, so I had to do this. She was not going to be happy being asked to reveal still more secrets.

The other strong-minded woman I hoped to converse with at length before the sun went down, I wasn't sure I could find. If I did find her, I wasn't sure she'd even return my hello.

The last time we'd talked, she'd stormed out of my interrogation room hotter than a firebox on a steam train.

But Dr. Magdalena Simpson-Mayes might be the one person in Flagler who could put all the pieces together. Or at least enough of them to give me a real sense of how Thaddeus Huntgardner's mind worked.

Not because she was going to talk to me about the professor. She wasn't. But because she'd helped her clients explore what allowing Professor Huntgardner's ego to affect your own could do to you.

She could talk about those minds under the rules that therapists went by because all their owners were dead.

◦ ◦ ◦

I handed Helen the manila file folder with the letters without saying so much as "good morning." She reached for it. Took it in her hand. But kept her arm outstretched, as if she wanted me to take it back.

Instead, I continued to my office.

I hung my hat on the usual peg on my hat tree. Reached for the pile of call slips on my desk. And entered into a charade of pondering who I'd be calling back.

At no time did I allow Helen out of my field of vision. What she did with the letters had everything to do with what I did next. Not so much with my morning but with my investigation into Flagler's morass of deadly mysteries. As I'd hoped, she'd opened the file, picked up the letter on top, and started to read.

I'd thought that we might play eye tag. Take furtive glances over our reading glasses at each other. Then slide our gazes elsewhere so as not to be caught spying. But after a couple of minutes, I quit the game. Helen wasn't looking up, so I never took my eyes off her. I leaned back in my chair and monitored her every action.

There weren't many. Except for the times when she re-arranged herself in her chair, they were confined to managing the letters. She advanced through the first few letters at a brisk pace.

She'd read one, then turn it upside down and place it on the stack she started at one side of her desk blotter. Each time she added a letter, she'd take a moment to tidy the stack so that it remained square and trim. Then she reached for another one.

As the stack grew, her advance through the letters slowed. Several times, she stared at a letter before discarding it. Once, she laid a letter she'd read to the side of her discard stack as if to begin a second stack. But halfway through the new letter, she reached for the orphaned letter and placed it in the regular stack.

When she'd read all of them, she reached for the pile she'd made. Turned the letters right side up. Placed them back in the file folder. Closed it and looked up at me for the first time. She looked hollowed. Emptied. Carved out.

My training as a counselor said to go sit with her. Then be silent. Give her time to process. Let her know she wasn't alone. Wait for her to make the next move. My training as a lawman said don't squander the moment. Start the dialogue before the opportunity escapes. She needs to talk. She wants to talk. Go grease the wheels.

But this was Helen, not some stranger I'd brought in for interrogation. I was starting to doubt the wisdom of showing her the letters to begin with when she made my decision for me.

She motioned me into her office. Pointed to the hallway door. Indicated she wanted it shut and locked. Reached around to her credenza. Opened it. Took out a bottle of mineral water. Unscrewed it. Took a deep swig. Put the cap back on the bottle. And swiveled her chair to face me square-on.

"Now I know what the bank safety deposit box was all about."

This time, both my counseling and interrogation training were screaming the same caution: *Let her take the lead*. I combined a slight head tilt and a quick head dip of understanding and said nothing.

She laid her hand on the file folder. Spread her fingers. Kept them in place. Kind of a maternal act. "I always wondered. The county paid for it, you see. But the letters . . . the envelopes . . . they always said 'personal.'"

Say something supportive, Luke! "They did." I gestured toward them. "They still do."

"But I never knew what they were about. Only that once they started arriving, he tried to be here when the mail was due. If there was a letter like these, he'd take it to his office, close the door. Open it. Read it. Refold it and tuck it away somewhere in his clothing. Usually, he'd leave soon after."

"So you never knew what was in the letters?"

"No, they were a mystery to me. I was a little embarrassed by them, you know. They were marked 'personal.' Your dad, a married man. Family man. Big man in the church. Pillar of the community. Getting letters from what was obviously a lady. Reading them and then rushing off."

My mind was racing. How much more did Helen know? Was it possible that she knew too much? If so, I needed to think long and hard before I asked the question that revealed that. Because there'd be no going back. "Did you ever have suspicions about who the letter writer might be?"

"Not until after they quit coming."

I reached for the file folder. "August 29, 1998. That's the date on the last letter in the file."

Helen tapped the air with her palm out like she was urging someone to go further. "It wasn't that soon. When did your mother go into the nursing home? The late fall of '98, wasn't it?"

I pursed my lips. Thought about it. Dipped my chin several

times after a spell. "Yes, and she was sick for a long time before that. After her stroke, she was pretty much incapacitated."

"You'll have to chalk this up to a woman's intuition, but I always thought your dad figured out who this woman was. And this was why the letters stopped."

"So you think he started meeting with her?"

"I was never sure, but I think I saw him with her once."

People drop their jaw when they are surprised for one reason: opening your mouth wide is the quickest way to get a massive load of oxygen into your lungs.

So my jaw dropped. And I inhaled.

Helen knew I'd want to hear every detail, so she hastened to dampen my expectations. "Can't tell you much. They were standing by a car in front of a restaurant. She reached for him, hugged him. No kissing or anything like that. Got in her car and left. I could be wrong about it all, you know."

"Or you could be right. It would explain a lot of things."

My dad was in no sense a lady's man. I'd always had suspicions that my mom was the only woman he'd ever bedded. But my mom's illness had changed him. He didn't withdraw. He became needful. Vulnerable. Clinging, almost. And then all that needfulness had seemed to go away. I'd realized it even back then but had no idea what was happening.

"There's one more thing. Or it may be nothing at all. But I wondered at the time."

Helen looked into the distance. In our offices, gazing at the painting of ponies racing on the prairie that I had hanging on my far wall was about as far away as you could gaze. She had her eyes locked on the picture. Like she was revisiting a long-ago scene in her mind.

It turned out this was the case.

"Hadn't thought of this in years. But your dad did something right before your mother died that I felt was odd. He'd never done it before. He'd always left such tasks to his deputies."

Helen told me how my father had left the office one afternoon to escort a funeral procession to Flagler Memorial Cemetery.

She'd learned later from one of his deputies that he'd insisted on driving at the front of the procession. She made inquiries around the courthouse about the deceased person. No one knew much, but she learned it was a woman. Someone had thought she'd lived in Flagler as a child, moved away, returned as a young woman, moved away again, and, a couple of years before her untimely death, had returned. Someone else thought she'd been writing a book.

"The letters — anything else in them a surprise to you?"

"Just how little I really know about a place where I've lived all my life."

CHAPTER 50

Dr. Simpson-Mayes wasn't difficult to find. She was standing beside her seated receptionist when I entered her office suite. The look in her eyes wasn't a welcoming one. "Urge to kill" gazes tend not to be. I'd not expected anything different.

I told her there were reasons I'd not called for an appointment. I wanted to be sure I'd have a chance to share some things I knew she'd want to know.

She kept her head — her whole body — as still as dead air on Sunday, but her eye contact was steady. Was she about to erupt and rage at me for entering her office without a warrant or an appointment? Or was something potent and eye-opening about to happen?

I knew it could go either way, and I thought I was handling the matter well. Then I realized my chest wasn't moving. Holding your breath will do that.

She whipped her svelte body around in a half-circle like her hips were spring-loaded and headed for her office door. She walked through the threshold, leaving the door open behind her. Was it a sign that I was meant to follow?

One way to find out.

I entered her office and shut the door behind me. Removed my hat. Took a scat on the couch. Crossed my legs to the extent that my jeans would permit and placed my hat on my lap. I figured the less she could see of my pelvis, the better. And decided that voicing a simple truth was going to be the best way to find out if a dialogue was possible.

"I have reason to believe that Professor Huntgardner is a serial killer."

The déjà vu was instantaneous. She went still as a tombstone again. Kept her eye contact steely. Offered nary a clue about how she intended to react.

There wasn't one until her chin slumped to her chest and she began to wave her head back and forth like a metronome. I gathered I was being asked what part of "no" didn't I understand.

She threw me a glance I'd describe as one part consternation and one part revulsion and began shaking her head again. "We really, really need to get to the bottom of this."

I wanted to mirror her newfound spirit of cooperation. Shifted forward to the edge of the couch. Put both feet flat on the floor. Straightened my back and leaned forward. "Then let's talk about the old warehouse."

"What old warehouse?"

"The one downtown. The one Huntgardner and his cronies have outfitted for their atrocities. I mean, torture chambers? Holding cells? Human experimentation?"

I'd read enough about Dr. Simpson-Mayes on the internet to know that she was a newer humanistic version of the old psychoanalyst. Straight talk between patient and shrink about root issues was her shtick. Her years of training and practice at handling surprising things people said in her presence were now failing her.

She wasn't thinking much at the moment. I could see that in her face. It had lost most of its color. Her eyes were spacey. She was the victim of runaway emotions. If she showed signs of fainting, I'd have to go straight across the top of her desk. Hopefully, I could catch her before she hurt herself.

Seeing that I had time, I hurried around the desk. Squatted down beside her chair. Took a gentle grasp of one arm. And told her to take deep breaths.

She gave it a try.

The better part of a minute passed. Then she said in a quiet voice, "Thank you."

I asked if she'd like a drink of water. She would. I left the room to ask the receptionist to get her one. The request alarmed her employee. I assured her that the good doctor was going to be all right.

When color returned to Dr. Simpson-Mayes's face, I told her I was willing to postpone the discussion.

For the second time, she said that we needed to get to the bottom of this. "This has all gone so wrong. So dangerously, dangerously wrong."

I returned to the couch. Sat at one end. Motioned that she would be welcome to sit at the other. She placed her water glass on her desk and moved to join me. I didn't need to remind myself to tread this path on cat's feet. "Would you like to start at the beginning?"

Her head bobbled up and down for the briefest moment, then switched to a firm no. "Wouldn't be fair."

"Fair to whom?"

"Fair to you. To the people who elected you. To everyone who lives in this innocent, naive little place. Fair to me, to my family. Fair to the professor. Fair to the people who died in his house."

I begged to disagree. "If our naive little town is full of well-heeled serial killers, it's already lost its innocence. Isn't it time we faced the truth and dealt with the facts?"

Some of the electricity returned to Dr. Simpson-Mayes's

voice. "Oh, don't be so goody-goody, Sheriff. You're absolutely clueless about what's going on."

"So that warehouse isn't a factory for abusing people?"

"That warehouse may be nothing at all. On the other hand, it could turn out to be one of the most brilliant ideas in history. Or at least, it could have been."

"And you can tell me why?"

We'd reached another crossroads in our conversation. I could tell because of what she did with her hands. She began rubbing her wrists. First on one hand, then the other. Not gestures of confidence. She was uncertain. Maybe afraid. Until she decided which way to go, I'd best say as little as possible.

In the end, Dr. Simpson-Mayes didn't take either fork in the road. She split the difference.

"I can tell you a story."

Okay, if I did it carefully, I could join the conversation. "I would welcome a story."

"A hypothetical story."

"Hypothetical would be nice."

"More like a fairy tale."

"A fairy tale would do."

"Let's say that a young troubadour came to your little village in the far-away woods. He came with a strange object and a strange tale."

I managed to keep my lips zipped. But wasn't able to keep the smart-ass who hides away in the back closet of my mind in check. *Sure, lady, and the angel Gabriel rode into town in a flaming red convertible and demanded a double meat cheeseburger.*

She'd noticed my eyebrows rise. For the first time since my arrival, she permitted herself a sliver of a smile. "Remember, you said a fairy tale would do."

"Always loved fairy tales."

"The young troubadour didn't tell his strange tale to just

anyone. Only a carefully chosen few. He made up another story to tell everybody else."

This time, I shared a smile, hoping it didn't come off as condescending. "Sounds like a cagey guy."

That didn't get much of a response because Dr. Simpson-Mayes appeared to be deciding where she was going next with her obfuscations. And, likely, how she was going to handle my response to them. "What was even weirder was what he did with the strange object."

I blinked. Stayed quiet like a good kindergarten student should at story time. Waited. And waited. She didn't seem to know where she wanted to go next.

The trained interrogator in me couldn't stay in the corner any longer. "So what did he do with the strange object?"

"Nobody knows. That's what has torn this county apart for the past seventy years. I've begun to wonder if there was ever any strange object to begin with."

"And the warehouse?"

"Oh, if the warehouse is ever used for what it's designed for, all the strangeness will disappear. And new wonders will have arrived. Flagler will be transfigured. And world-famous. Forever."

That "transfigured" word again. Was my head going to swim like this every time I heard it?

It seemed wise at the moment to sink a hand into the couch cushion and steady myself. My equilibrium felt threatened.

I saw my father being lowered into his grave. Saw him telling me about his friend, the professor. Saw him being hugged by a woman with no features. Saw his name on a weathered belt and his initials on a gaudy belt buckle. Saw him pinning his star on his young son, the family's third sheriff. Saw Dr. Carmichael's bones in the cedar box with my dad's belt around his neck.

A story had been nice. But the time for fairy tales had passed. I had questions that this woman could answer. Questions that needed sheriff-type answers, not a kindergarten make-believe-style story.

"Okay, I get some of that. The stranger in your story, he's Professor Huntgardner, right?"

She plucked something off her dark pantsuit, flicked it into space, and gave me a shoulder shrug. She wasn't saying.

From that point forward, our conversation became tit-for-tat. I served first. "He's been another of your clients."

"I have many clients."

"He's told you the real story of why he came to Flagler and what he expects to happen."

"You know I can't talk about what clients tell me."

"Then what have you been doing in this conversation?"

"I've been telling you a hypothetical story."

"Why don't you just tell me where the professor is? Is he dead or alive?"

"What makes you think I would know that?"

I almost ended the exchange there. It had reached the stage where it felt like I was arguing with a drunk.

I had two choices. I could reach for my handcuffs, frog-march Dr. Simpson-Mayes out of her office, and lock her in a jail cell until she was willing to be straight with me. But if I pushed too hard, I'd most likely lose access forever to her unique understanding of Flagler's deadly march toward — what? Transfiguration?

Gazing at her, I saw a look in her eyes that I'd seen twice before. It seemed to run in the Mayes family. *The tree doesn't grow far from the apple.*

I did answer her question. And it may not have surprised her, but it did me. When had my mind locked in on this insight?

"I think you know because the Mayes family is all that stands between the professor and a bullet."

CHAPTER 51

D r. Simpson-Mayes remained on my mind long after our talk. It wasn't the woman herself I kept thinking about. But rather the complications that her choices in life were now bringing her way. I realized that I was experiencing something similar. Complications from my choices in life.

One complication was that I'd not put a ring on Angie's finger yet because of a problem with the finger. I didn't know how long I could expect it to be around.

It was the thorny old issue that two ambitious, successful people in love so often faced. If they pledged to live their lives together, which of their careers was going to get priority?

I'd probably run again for sheriff, so I wasn't planning to go anywhere soon. And Angie could be transferred out of Flagler to Timbuktu on any given Monday. She'd never said it with emphasis, but she didn't need to. She was planning a career with the FBI unless something bigger and better came along. And that wasn't likely to happen in Flagler.

The odds were high that her next assignment would be to the bureau's national headquarters in D.C. Should she choose not to climb the ladder there, she could expect the opportunity to come in one of the outfit's premier big-city bureaus — New York, Boston, Chicago, Los Angeles, Miami. What was a countrified one-eyed sheriff from the Texas outback going to do with himself in places like that?

The problem was so knotty that we'd avoided talking about it. At all. It was just about the only serious thing between us that we hadn't treated as an open book.

But deciding our future wasn't what was staring me in the face. How much was I going to tell Angie about what had happened in the three days she'd been gone?

The more I'd thought about it, the stronger my resolve had become. There wasn't a lot I could tell her. It wasn't that I didn't trust her. It was more that I didn't know what information or which of my sources I could trust.

She'd want to get involved. It was her nature. And I didn't need another wild-card player. Besides, Flagler was a tenuous place at the moment. I didn't want her in danger. And I didn't want her proactive disposition endangering me.

I needed a little time.

Maybe putting it to her that way would be enough if the subject came up. And, knowing Angie, it would.

Dealing with the potential drama of Special Agent Steele's return had crowded everything else out of my mind. So much so that, with my missing eye, I never noticed the suitcase.

The one lying flat on the floor two steps inside the door leading from my garage into my kitchen.

The one I tripped over, creating a minor Vesuvius.

The suitcase toppled over with a loud slap and skidded a couple of yards. I stumbled into the kitchen like a spavined kangaroo.

Because I'd thrown out my arms to keep from slamming into the bar counter, I'd lost my grip on my briefcase. It sailed halfway into the den and kept sliding on the floor tiles. Each time one of the metal-reinforced corners encountered a tile joint, it made a loud clicking noise. Clickety-de-click-de-click.

Angie looked on wide-eyed from where she was arranging our eating utensils on the bar counter.

When she saw no signs of lasting damage, she did the Angie thing. Turned it into a joke. Her question, I realized, was going to be a standard laugh line for us as long as we had a relationship. "Sheriff Luther Stephens McWhorter, this another official daft day for you?"

Then she grasped how serious this could have been. "Lordy, I'm so sorry, Luke. I was carrying my own briefcase, juggling enchiladas, tugging my suitcase and I . . . Oh, sweetheart, I need a seeing eye dog."

That struck me as funnier than her crack about official daft days. "No, the one-eyed sheriff needs a seeing eye dog, hopefully with two eyes."

What the one-eyed sheriff really needed hadn't changed since he'd spotted the buzzards eating the defleshed corpses. He needed answers. And he needed to be careful about the Niagara of conflicting facts and suspicions he'd faced ever since.

More were coming. Delivered by a secret emissary from no less than the president of the United States. For now, I had to keep Angie in the dark about a lot of this. And hope I could keep it from doing lasting damage to our dreams for a future together.

CHAPTER 52

We'd each consumed one of Casa Mariachi's green-chili-sauce-soaked enchiladas when Angie dropped her bombshell. It was as telling a lesson as I could remember on the dangers of assuming you can know what to expect of a close companion.

"I alerted the bureau's Nationwide Suspicious Activity Reporting Initiative people that you might be calling. About what you and the assistant fire marshal found in the old Cromwell Company warehouse."

I didn't drop my fork.

I managed to prop it against the other enchilada on my plate.

Now that both hands were free, I could reach for the over-sized paper napkin in my lap. Pretend that it needed dividing in half. Reinforce the fold by keeping one of the triangular corners I'd created clamped in my left hand so I could run the thumb and index finger of my right hand along the nascent crease until I reached the end. This made a nice crease.

I felt that this elaborate display was sufficient cover for not glancing right away at my dinner companion.

I looked up at her, assuming that Angie would have her eyes glued to my face so she could gauge my reaction to her announcement. Instead, her attention was on the tortilla chips that had come with the enchiladas. This was the over familiarity demon at work again.

She offered me the bag. I took a few, grateful for the diversion. Not that I'd needed more than a second or two to work out the implications of her offhand comment about the warehouse. I'd not mentioned the warehouse to her. Our phone conversation had been too brief. Our texting had dealt only with her travel schedule.

The assistant fire marshal and I had agreed to keep any mention of it off social media for now, and there had been no news coverage yet. The conclusion was unavoidable. *She wasn't dependent on me for her information about Flagler's freakish outbreak of criminality and chaos. Not all of it anyway. She had her own sources.*

But then, why not? — she was a special agent of the Federal Bureau of Investigation.

Who knew what else she'd told her colleagues in Washington. Or the full extent of what she knew about what was happening in Flagler. My next thought brought an involuntary flinch to my shoulders. *Or whether she was one of the people that a presidential envoy was on his way to Flagler to warn me about?*

In those few moments, it dawned on me how naive I'd been.

This beguiling creature I was sharing enchiladas with had more ways to cover up secrets — and to uncover them — than Carter's has liver pills. More ways than I had in my little boondocks satchel of crime-fighting resources. More than I'd ever have.

Rather than keep her from knowing my secrets, I'd be advised to see how many of hers she'd be willing to share. But I didn't have to probe for the next one. She volunteered it right before she hopped off her bar stool. She was getting up to put the enchiladas and tortilla chips back in the oven.

She did that kind of thing a lot. She liked her cold foods well chilled and her hot foods well heated. And she liked the world around her to offer endless variety and intrigue.

The flight to Flagler had provided some, she noted after returning to her perch and reaching for the hot sauce bottle. "You expecting a secret super-sleuth from Dallas or somewhere?"

This time, she did shoot me a glance. Then she put the hot sauce bottle down with a solid thump without releasing her grip on it. Swiveled back and forth a couple of times on her stool while hanging onto it, never once removing her unblinking eyes from my blank face. "Oh, boy. I've stepped in it, haven't I?"

That was when she told me about the strange guy she'd sat next to on the plane.

□□□

I wasn't going to mention the call from the president. And I knew she wasn't going to resurrect the subject of strange visitors to Flagler. There was plenty else to talk about. She needed a cue, so I gave her one. "Your trip was sudden."

Angie seemed relieved at my new choice of conversation topic. "The murders of all those physicists is a bigger deal than you may have realized."

I asked her to clarify that remark. "America's short of physicists?"

As usual, she gave me a history lesson. "Not short so much — although there never seem to be enough big bang chasers around to satisfy the Department of Defense. It's more that America is paranoid about what happens to its physicists. Has been ever since the Manhattan Project."

I felt the moment could use a little coyness. "And your bosses thought ten physicists reduced to bones in the Texas badlands meant — what? The Russians had landed?"

My flippant comment irritated her. Or so I'd thought. Turned out it was something else. "The Russians would never expect to find anything of interest in Texas."

I reached for her hand. And scrambled for the right words. "Mea culpa. I'm beginning to sense that all was not peace and light for you on this trip to J. Edgar Hoover land."

"There were tensions."

"So you walked into a hornet's nest of spook-think about our dead physicists?"

She continued to scowl. "That's the thing. If ten physicists had been murdered in the northeast, say, or California, the bureau's brass would be glued to their computer screens and smartphones. And willing to kill for a chance to talk with an agent fresh from the scene. But this didn't happen. They acted like these guys went bird hunting out in the Texas sticks then celebrated overmuch with some bad hillbilly hooch or something and died from it."

"You told them we have CSI teams and medical examiners out west of the Brazos?"

The momentum she gave the hot sauce bottle carried it to the far end of the counter. "Nope. Wasn't that circumspect. Told them if they ever came to Flagler to bring toilet paper so they wouldn't have to use corn cobs."

"Bet that got a laugh."

"Well, it did after I explained what else a corn cob could be used for."

That got a laugh out of me. Then our conversation got serious again. "You went to D.C. wanting something."

Angie did a complete whirl on her swivel stool. Stopped herself by grabbing the edge of the countertop. "Look." She raised both hands, ready to count off something on her fingers.

"We have thirty-five thousand employees in the bureau. The CIA has twenty-two thousand. The Drug Enforcement Administration, eleven thousand. The Secret Service, seven thousand. The Bureau of Alcohol, Tobacco, Firearms, and Explosives, five thousand. The IRS's Criminal Investigation Division, twenty-five hundred." Then she seemed to realize she needed to lighten her tone. "I just wanted a little help for a really terrific sheriff in a nice little West Central Texas city and his ditzy FBI special agent girlfriend."

I sought to help her keep things light. "And I bet you finally wore them down. The Marines *are* coming to Flagler."

"Fat chance. I don't think I could have gotten their attention if I'd gone to D.C. with Gideon's Trumpet."

I don't think she noticed how close I came to choking. A sudden coughing spell and a fist raised to cover my mouth bought me sufficient cover. I glanced at her for what I feared had been a couple of seconds too long, but she had gotten up to pour me a glass of water.

I concluded that her comment had probably been one of total innocence. She wasn't likely to know that Gideon's Trumpet was the code name for the secret informant coming to Flagler.

Coming to Flagler?

Horse pucky. It appeared he was already here.

CHAPTER 53

I'd not managed to take a swallow of the morning's first mason jar of iced tea when my phone rang. First caller of the day.

The owner of the brisk, confident voice on the other end of the line said he was collecting donations for the Overwatch Group. "Prithee, good sire, can we meet?"

I told the president's guy I'd need thirty minutes. Gave him the name of the street and told him how to find it. Instructed him to proceed west until he came to the BewaretheJunkyardDogs Company's abandoned salvage yard. The gate would look like it was locked, but it wasn't. He should flip the rusty padlock open. Remove it from the chain. Pull the chain through the gate. Let himself in. Close the gate behind him. Replace the chain and lock. And continue to the shabby old tin shack in the far back corner.

I'd be joining him soon.

He'd ended our conversation with a comment as zany as the one that had started it. "My foot's already in the stirrup and the cows are in the corn, Herr Maestro."

●●●

It took me only twenty minutes to grab my hat, bolt out the door, effect a brisker pace to my car than usual, and speed off to BewaretheJunkyardDogs Company's vacated salvage yard. I'd not been expecting the president's man to call during the day. After all, most of the original Deep Throat's meetings with the *Washington Post* guys had been late at night. The faster we got our encounter over, the less we'd have to endure the heat in the old shack.

Meanwhile, my mind wouldn't give it a rest. It kept trying to find a picture, any person, any memory that would stand in for the individual I'd talked to on the phone.

My mind settled on an image from an old movie I'd watched on one of the streaming services a few weeks back. One made in the '50s. Danny Kaye had played a court jester. Most of the time, he'd been decked out in a motley-colored fool's hat with three droopy points, each with a bell at the end.

I'd found one snippet of dialogue in the movie so ridiculous, I was going to be repeating it to myself forever. Especially in light of what had happened at Professor Huntgardner's house. "The pellet with the poison's in the vessel with the pestle; the chalice from the palace has the brew that is true!"

He was already there. Sitting on a crate by a window. Looking nothing like Danny Kaye. Or a court jester. Or, for that matter, like an emissary from the president of the United States. He looked like someone who had defeated the best efforts of central casting to supply an actor who looked like, well, anything but a secret operative. No wonder Angie had been intrigued by him.

There was his size.

When he stood, my first thought was that he was taller than most starting point guards in the NBA. Plus three inches. That extra height was courtesy of the towering, swept-back expanse of blondish-gray hair that dared you to guess at his age. Anywhere between fifty and sixty-five, I was guessing.

Then there were his duds.

A print-splashed vintage '90s-style yellow Hawaiian shirt. Asparagus green cargo pants. And a pair of brown pseudo–work boots that zipped up the back.

He had a hand extended. "Heeeelllloooo! The code word, I believe, is Gideon's Trumpet. If that doesn't work for you, you can tikka masala and shove it up your ashram."

He laughed so loud that the rickety little shed shook.

CHAPTER 54

"**Y**ou're probably wondering about the clothes."

If he was going to be this abrupt, he might not need any warning that our conversation had to be a short one. "Well, yes. And why you're here."

"Never been to Texas before. Didn't know quite how to dress. Heard it's hot out here." He fingered the collar on the ridiculous shirt. "Something cool, eh? And, it's a rough-and-ready place." He stuck his hands in the side pockets of his cargo pants and pulled his pants legs wider. "And" — he pointed toward his cognac-colored shoe gear — "everybody wears boots."

I couldn't tell if he was pulling my leg, so I settled on politeness. "Very nice."

My reply didn't seem to matter to him. He was moving on. "What do you know about UFOs?"

I thought he was about to make me the butt of a joke. "You're about to tell me you brought one of those too, right? Because we're used to things out here that go boo in the night."

My sarcasm earned me a rebuke. "Sheriff, you need to consider all this consequential, or I've made this trip for nothing."

He looked as serious as a funeral, so I decided to humor him. I assured him that all I knew about UFOs is what I heard on the news. "Never seen one myself."

"The president wants you to understand something about the *Sturm und Drang* you've been experiencing in Abbot County all these years."

"And what would that be?"

"That it's all been a seventy-plus-years-long battle over what to believe about UFOs and extraterrestrial creatures. Aliens."

"In Flagler?"

"Well, think about it. President Fletcher says Flagler has been one of the strangest places on Earth since the Truman administration."

"What happened during the Truman administration?"

"Among other things, Roswell."

What my legs did next surprised both of us. They flung me to my feet and back-pedaled me to the far wall of the ramshackle little building. When I leaned against it, I realized that if I wasn't careful, I'd break through it. "You've come all the way from Washington, D.C., to talk about the —"

"Right. The Roswell UFO crash and the little people they found with the wreckage."

"And how is Flagler involved in all this?"

"That's what twelve presidents of the United States . . . no, make that thirteen now . . . have been trying to figure out. And they're not the only ones."

"Who else?"

"Well, the British, the Germans, the French, the Russians, the Scandinavian countries, the Belgians, the Brazilians. And, in their time, the old Soviet Union and the eastern bloc communist countries. Not that I've named everybody."

I debated whether to keep standing, but my knees didn't feel that trustworthy, so I went back to my crate. The instant I sat down, Mr. Gideon's Trumpet stood up.

Too quickly. He collided with the corrugated tin roof. The impact knocked one of its sheets loose. It stayed attached on one end. The rest of it came back down. Catawampused.

"And both your father and your grandfather — how do you say it in Texas? — almost busted a gusset trying to figure it out."

"What a fatuous gasbag you are." The retort was out of my mouth before the thought was well formed in my brain. I was being treated like a schoolboy. Not a very bright one, either.

The serious-as-a-funeral face was back. "I'm not explaining this well."

"Either that, or I'm not in the mood for fairy tales."

He glanced at the hole in the roof. "Do I take you through events step by step? Or do I start with a simple statement about why President Fletcher has sent me here?" He seemed to be speaking to himself.

I held up two fingers. The second idea sounded like it would get us out of the shed's suffocating heat sooner. *Tell me what matters to Flagler now.*

That's when he told me point-blank that the U.S. government had lied to the American people about the Roswell incident — and was still lying about it. The Roswell crash hadn't involved a weather balloon as the military claimed. It had, indeed, involved an extraterrestrial craft. A UFO. One carrying ETs. Aliens.

The people closest to the Roswell events had been right that momentous July week in 1947. One live alien and several aliens' bodies had been recovered at the main crash scene on a ranch northwest of town. They had been spirited away to an Ohio air base, never to be seen in public again. The lies had begun then and had never stopped.

But not everything found at the crash site had been recovered by the troops sent to scoop up the wreckage. A strange piece of debris had taken a roundabout route and ended up in the hands of a young Thaddeus Huntgardner. He claimed to have brought it to Flagler when he left for college and hidden it somewhere.

The current president of the United States believed the same thing his twelve predecessors had believed. At least, those who had known much about it. That this bizarre object from outer space might be the most prized artifact in our corner of the universe.

I couldn't hold my incredulity in any longer. I had questions. The first one turned out to be both hydra-headed and bitchy.

"What," I started off, "is so important about this so-called object? For that matter, what is it? Part of the UFO itself? Something it had been carrying? Or had it been inside an Extraterrestrial Parcel Service package addressed to the Honorable Thaddeus "Thad" Johans Schreck Huntgardner, Planet Earth?"

Gideon's Trumpet again looked vexed. I had an immediate regret. And a realization. He was finding this difficult, and not treating him and his explanations with rapt seriousness might be a mistake. "I'm sorry . . . this object — what does it look like?"

"Good question. If it's real, it may not have been debris. It may have been cargo — something the UFO was carrying. Or something else entirely. But the rumors in Roswell said it was like nothing you or I have ever seen before. Like nothing anyone who saw it had ever seen."

"It's metal?"

He shrugged. "Maybe. Yes, probably. But nothing like any of our metals on Earth. The rumor in Roswell was that you could crumple the stuff up into a ball, then lay it down and watch it straighten itself out without any help. Erase every crease, so that it's completely flat and smooth again. And that they'd tried to damage it. Hit it with hammers. Couldn't make a dent in it. Not a mark."

This time, I couldn't hide my skepticism. "And that's it — a weird piece of metal? This is what has turned my backwoods county into a zoo of warring factions? One that powerful people in half the world have been watching obsessively for seventy-plus years?"

This time, my conversation partner's pained look didn't last as long. "No, it's apparently more than a weird piece of metal. The bigger mystery, or so they said, is what happens to the psyche of the person looking at the fragment or whatever it is. Oh, and one other thing. Supposedly, something exotic keeps happening to its color. One moment, it's black, and the next it's something else."

"But you say all this is only a rumor?"

"Just what a few people claimed. I'm not aware of any real evidence."

"So, what's the excitement about?"

"It's Huntgardner's doing, really. What he says he was told by people in Roswell after the UFO incident."

"And what did the good people of New Mexico tell him?"

"That the alien who survived promised that some of its exoplanet buddies would come for the object on the seventy-fifth anniversary of their landing in Roswell. And when they did, they'd share new knowledge of how the universe works, shed light on a bunch of scientific mysteries, and tell us how wars and conflicts can be avoided. The kinds of things that would shake up everything from religion to politics and governments to science and cosmology."

"So, what is Huntgardner supposed to have done with the fragment?"

He fingered his shirt collar, tugging it open to let more air in. "Isn't that the question?"

CHAPTER 55

I told him I had my own questions. He needed to keep his answers brief or we were both going to die from heat stroke in the BewaretheJunkyardDogs Company's stifling old tin shack. He agreed that he would.

I asked him if the president knew why ten physicists had been slain in or around Professor Huntgardner's house.

He offered a half-shrug. "The president assumes it had something to do with the fragment, but he isn't sure. His greatest fear is that the killing isn't over. That's why he dispatched me to tell you what he knows."

I asked if the president had any recent evidence that any of the story I'd been listening to was, in fact, real. Not really, he said.

He said evidence of UFOs and alien contacts had been hidden with great success from all thirteen presidents since Roswell. But with the purported new visitation date getting closer, the leaks were growing. One tantalizing claim was about a supposed late-night meeting between President Eisenhower and ET leaders at California's Edwards Air Force Base on February 20, 1954.

I asked how the president was getting his information about what had been happening in Flagler. He wasn't at liberty to say.

I asked if he knew if Professor Huntgardner was alive and, if so, where he was. No idea, he said.

I asked if the federal government had sent any other secret agents to Flagler. Didn't know, but I should assume that it had. And that one or more of them might still be here.

I asked what they would be like. He said he could only guess. But he'd expect them to try to fit themselves into the local fabric. Set up a business, maybe. Get to know as many of the town's and county's leaders as possible. Take on appearances that made them look like they were anything but what they were.

I asked if he knew anything about a secret torture and incarceration chamber in Flagler. That earned me an incredulous look — followed by a quick shake of the head.

His next comment made it clear that he was getting to the heart of his message from the president. "You need to have a chat with a couple of people."

"People who know what this is about, I trust."

"Better than that. The people who are causing most of your problems, I think."

"Like murdering people in remote old brick houses?"

"Or setting themselves up to be murdered, not sure which. President Fletcher isn't either. But he didn't want to stand by and leave you unaware of what some folks in the highest reaches of the U.S. intelligence community have been telling him."

This was when he told me the names of the two secret religious societies long in conflict in Flagler over Thaddeus Huntgardner's mysterious fragment. And the names of the persons believed to be in charge.

I didn't bother to tell him that this information was not news to me. I let him explain how, with Professor Huntgardner suffering from dementia, the Unus Mundus Masters was commanded by Dr. Judson T. Mayes II. And Dr. Malachi Jepp Rawls was still calling the shots for the

Society of Ezekiel's Wheel, as he had for many years. Incidentally, he had founded it.

Gideon's Trumpet said both individuals kept secrets about their groups better than Madame Defarge. So he shared rule number one of the American intelligence community. If you can't get your targets to talk about themselves, get their enemies to talk about them.

I thanked him for coming. Asked him to express my appreciation to President Fletcher for his concern. Encouraged him to provide me with any new information. And asked him to leave Flagler.

"Now. 'Chop, chop,' as you'd probably put it. Book a seat on the next flight out. Don't talk to anyone you don't have to before you depart. Keep to yourself on the plane at least as far as Dallas/Fort Worth. And report only to the president when you get back to Washington. Don't be offended, but I don't need another drama-maker in Abbot County's deadly Circus Maximus."

My guest shot to his feet and headed out the door without a single glance back. But he did fling one further bit of advice over his shoulder. "Beware of Karmageddon and goat meat tacos when you're herding doggies to Dodge City."

Given what else had been happening in Flagler, that sounded like good advice.

I watched Gideon's Trumpet stride all the way to the gate, fit his large frame into his boxy lime-green rental car, and back it up in fits and starts, missing the neighboring brickyard's towering wooden fence by mere inches.

I stared at the space his car had vacated for a couple of minutes. Went back inside the shack and eased the loose roofing slat into place as best I could. Pulled the noisy, decrepit door shut as tight as it would go. And beat my own path to the fence, the street, and my parked patrol cruiser at a pace more suitable for a man walking a poky old dog.

Not at all what you'd expect from a guy who needed to be acting like Frank Hamer chasing Bonnie and Clyde.

I was buying time. And trying to decide what to do with the anger stinging my chest like heartburn from bad chili.

I had been hoping for more answers from the unexpected visitor from Washington, D.C. Hoping that he would be a frontal system helping to clear the skies of some of Flagler's more mystifying skulduggeries.

Hadn't happened.

Rather than the air-clearing insights I'd hoped for, Gideon's Trumpet had lobbed one new puzzling revelation after another at my shell-shocked sensibilities. In his wake, Abbot County's revolving door of bombshell developments was whirling faster than ever. And most of it still made less sense than kamikaze pilots wearing crash helmets.

Gideon's Trumpet had been right about one thing. There were a couple of people who owed me explanations. I'd start with the one I'd once thought I could trust with my life.

CHAPTER 56

The first question I wanted to ask Dr. Malachi Rawls was if he'd taken advantage of my grief seventeen years ago.

Because when the South Tower had gone down, my fiancée, Mary Austin, was in New York. She and her visiting cousin from San Angelo had been on either the 107th or 110th observation floor.

Mary Austin and I had been engaged for four months. We'd planned to marry the following summer. She'd have finished her master's degree in divinity at Union Theological Seminary by then and I'd have finished mine at Yale. We planned to honeymoon in France. Then she planned to work while I did further graduate study at the University of Tübingen.

Blinded by grief, I'd called the Prophet to tell him I was dropping out of Yale and coming home. He'd persuaded me to stay and finish my degree.

The following summer, my father announced that his health was forcing him to quit his job. To my disbelief, the Prophet said he was going to ask the county commissioners to appoint me to fill my father's place. They'd done that. This was why, six weeks later, I'd become the third member of the McWhorter family to pin on an Abbot County star. Those had been emotional times. It had seemed like the right thing to do.

Professor Rawls had his chair pushed back from his desk. His knees were jammed together to support the book he was holding open with one hand in his lap. The other hand was holding a cell phone up to his ear. When he saw me walk through the door, he greeted me with a quick nod. Leaned forward in his chair. Moved the book to his desk. Concluded his phone conversation with a few words. And laid the phone on his blotter pad.

I wanted to keep the benefit of surprise on my side. "You've been lying to me from the first."

I was expecting to see at least mild shock in his face at my bluntness and audacity. That never arrived. What I saw instead was calculation. A look not unlike what I'd learned to watch for in Jude Mayes's face when he was starting to dissemble.

Only, this person wasn't a still maturing man-child trying his best to deceive. If Gideon's Trumpet was to be believed, this individual was part asp. A master practitioner of the deception game. A dangerous one. One so accomplished at the game that powerful people in far-flung places would stop at nothing to discover what he was planning next. Not to mention those closer to home.

Professor Rawls's forehead wrinkled. "What 'first' would that be?"

Good.

This was where I wanted our contest to begin.

I could have taken a chair, but I wanted the benefit of the higher ground. I approached his desk, placed both hands on it, and leaned forward. "That tirade you launched on the phone, lo those many years ago. About religion ruining Abbot County's arteries. About how if fresh blood wasn't brought in, we were going to be naming our parks after the twelve apostles and the thieves on the cross. And playing golf at the Five Loaves and Two Fishes Country Club."

He squeezed his eyes shut as if remembering. "Kind of

ridiculous, I admit. But why would those hyperbolic assertions be on your mind now?"

"Because I now realize what you were doing."

"You need to tell me."

"You were plotting to get the Abbot County Sheriff's Department in your hip pocket. Worked too. I came, you saw, you conquered."

"Why would I want the sheriff's department in, as you put it, my hip pocket?"

Now was time to spring the trapdoor. "Because of the benefits you thought it would bring the Society of Ezekiel's Wheel."

I'd been expecting him to deny he'd ever heard of something called the Society of Ezekiel's Wheel. Or I'd thought he might make light of it. Call it Ezekiel's Sewing Circle or some such and profess concern about my mental health. Suggest I talk to a shrink about my paranoia. What I didn't expect was the torrent of frank admissions that began to tumble from his mouth.

"Yes, you're right. I wanted you here. Thought you were a godsend. You may still be. If there was ever a place in America that needs a sheriff who understands the hearts of people religious to the point of being farcical, it was Flagler.

"It still does. What I didn't count on was how smitten you'd be with law enforcement. Figured you'd serve out your daddy's term, maybe win one of your own, and then be off to Germany. I thought by the time you left, Flagler would have matured a little."

Would playing dumb keep this informative skein going? I decided to see. "Lots of little podunk towns in America have never gotten around to taking down the Jesus directional signs at their city limits."

His head bounced a couple of times. "But only one of them holds the destiny of humanity in its hands."

I wrinkled one side of my mouth. "You truly buy into that? I mean, you really think Thaddeus Huntgardner's purported piece of alien junk puts the world's major belief systems at risk?"

He closed his eyes again, left them closed, stayed silent. Then opened them. "Dear Thaddeus. Such a tragedy. Who'd have thought he would literally lose his mind over this?"

"So you know about his fragment?"

His smile was tight but not as strained as his voice. "If ever there was a word to be careful with, it's the word *know*. You could be asking if I've seen Thaddeus's reputed fragment. Or you could be asking if I believe there is such a thing. Or inquiring if I truly understand his fragment. There's so much in life to know about knowing."

Ah, so the academician was back in the room. "Works for me. You pick one. What can you tell me about this fragment?"

He actually turned his back on me and directed his gaze out the window. "Very little. Personally, I'm not sure it exists. The whole thing may be a figment of a very diseased imagination."

CHAPTER 57

I was about to make my first visit ever to the clinic of Dr. Judson Mayes II, primary care physician and gerontologist. And, judging by the growing testimony, someone who saw himself as a world-class ufologist and alien greeter. His offices were close to Flagler General Hospital, so I was going to make one other stop en route. This way, I could relieve a concern that had been keeping me awake at night.

Had our poisoner or poisoners struck again?

I needed to brief the hospital's staff on aldicarb poisoning. And make sure they hadn't seen any signs of it.

I could have parked close to the hospital's ED unloading bay. Gone through the swinging doors. Dodged at least two teams of paramedics whose ambulance rigs were parked near the emergency entrance. And been only steps away from the ED director's offices.

But that would have violated my rule. One that had served me well the past sixteen years. *Better to look like a little shot who can keep shooting than act like a big shot.*

So I parked in a visitor's parking spot at the front of the hospital. I was getting ready to walk into the lobby when I spotted a familiar truck pulling into a parking spot not far from me. I slowed my gait and waited to let the lumbering young Judson Thomas Mayes III approach me.

Only he didn't. When he saw me, he froze in place and stared. So I closed the gap. "Judson, somebody ill in your family?"

At first, he didn't respond. When he did speak, his voice was tremulous. Squeaky. He cleared his throat. "No."

"So you're visiting someone?"

"No."

"Don't tell me you volunteer here too."

"No."

"You're meeting someone?"

It had been awhile since I'd seen someone look this cornered. He kept half-turning to glance back down the hallway. "Professor Huntgardner."

"You're meeting Professor Huntgardner here?"

"No, we brought him here. He's had a stroke."

"Where is he?"

He glanced over his shoulder again and pointed toward the corridor he'd emerged from. "Intensive Care."

We were both walking toward that wing of the hospital when a massive figure rounded into view.

I'd always thought of myself as tall, but this was the second individual I'd met today who left me feeling malnourished. The look on Jude's face was a giveaway. At last, I was about to meet the elusive Dr. Judson Thomas Mayes II.

I knew this was one of those guys who always ended up standing in the middle in group pictures. He was a good four or five inches taller than I was and had to have weighed almost as much as his son.

But he was sculpted from a different mold. He was bald all the way to the North Pole. Had puffy dimples like Santa Claus. Close-clipped gray whiskers at the bottom of his chin. And the confident air of someone who always expected to be the authority figure in the room.

The good doctor put a huge arm around his huge son. Gave him a playful hug. Then extended a hand as wide as a ping-pong paddle toward me. Then he retrieved his other arm from around his son and laid that hand over mine too.

I felt like I was in the grasp of a giant, fleshy clam. He shook hands like a born politician. He didn't just follow up with a smile. He'd started with the smile. "Dr. Simpson-Mayes tells me you've been wanting to talk about airborne teacups."

I retrieved my hand and flexed my fingers. They still worked. I had no patience for his feeble joke about flying saucers. "No, sir. Not really. I'm focused at the moment on finding who's been killing people in our county. That is, once I understand what's been happening to Professor Huntgardner. Judson tells me you're just the person I need to talk to."

The doctor gave his son a dark look. "Judson's at his happiest when he can be helpful."

I chanced a chuckle, hoping it would defuse matters a bit. "It's a relief to know where the professor is. Can I assume that he's okay?"

This brought a nod from Dr. Mayes. "Just old."

"And where exactly is he?"

"Room one eighteen."

"And you're directing his care?"

"I am."

"So may I kindly ask you to fill me in on what this is all about?"

His right hand moved to his well-manicured chin and began to stroke it. I recognized the movement as a tic. He was nervous. I'd noticed the same repetitive tendency in his son. "You've heard of Jerusalem's Wailing Wall, Sheriff?"

I didn't answer. Didn't move. Couldn't imagine where Dr. Mayes was going with that.

He continued anyway. "It was a unique moment in history when the temples fell. A sad moment for the Jewish people. Unimaginably strange as it is, Flagler is facing a similar crisis."

Mayes's smile had not diminished. Not in the slightest. I was finding that as distracting as his improbable tale.

"Question is, is Flagler going to be a place where people come for the rest of history to wail? Or a place where they celebrate because this is where the new future of the universe began? Your ten victims at the Huntgardner place are martyrs to the latter possibility, Sheriff. Your job and mine is to see that they didn't die in vain. And do our damnedest to see that no one else does."

When puzzled or stressed, I tended to purse my lips. If necessary, chomp down a bit on the lower one. I had to say something. *When in doubt, swing the conversation about.* I repeated Mayes's words. "Martyrs to the future of the universe, eh?"

"I'm not sure you're understanding me, Sheriff."

"That's entirely possible, Dr. Mayes. I've been having a lot of trouble understanding people lately."

"I think we need some place more private, so we can talk."

"Couldn't agree more."

I'd been resisting the urge to load both big Mayes men into my patrol car and continue on to my office for in-depth conversations, but I was feeling a distinct sense of urgency. The Mayeses knew things I needed to know, and the quicker I knew them, the better.

Dr. Mayes hugged his son again and asked him to tell his mother that he'd be back as soon as he could. Then he grasped my arm and pulled me down the corridor like a dentist trying to extract a reluctant molar. "I know just the place."

To our benefit, the hospital chapel was empty.

Instead of pews, folding chairs provided its seating. Mayes moved two chairs out into the open space in front of the modest altar. Turned to face each other. Widened the space between them once, perhaps appreciating for the first time that he needed to show a bit more respect for the law.

"I've been talking a lot. Your turn now," he said.

I had to take a moment to gather my thoughts. I was forced to review my options, particularly what I'd do if I needed to slap handcuffs on this huge fellow and he resisted.

CHAPTER 58

I'd been in this chapel several times before. On each of those occasions, it was to deliver bad news to families of a deceased person. My tendency was to do it with dispatch. It felt right to do that with Mayes. This encounter needed to get to the point.

"Do you think Professor Huntgardner is a serial killer?"

I was going to have to start renting myself out as a refrigerator. My questions kept causing people to freeze. He struggled for words. "Professor Huntgardner . . . you think . . . Oh, my goodness! No, no, no, no. Dear God, where did that idea come from?"

"The old warehouse."

At those three words, the doctor's face instantly changed. As the men in the Mayes family tended to do, he was considering whether to equivocate. He started to. "Old warehouse?"

"The old Cromwell Company building, down by the railroad tracks. It's owned by one of Huntgardner's physicist pals. Somebody's been remodeling it. Somebody with the most depraved mind since the Borgias, from the looks of what's inside." The sharp edge to my voice told him I was in no mood to play games.

"And you think it's going to be used for what?"

"Like I say, housing and torturing people earmarked for murder. What I want to know is this: are Huntgardner and his pals behind all of this? And if so, how did they get away with their depraved activities for so long? Without somebody knowing? Without *me* knowing?"

"Sheriff, you've got this all wrong — so very, very wrong."

"Then, Doctor, you need to help me get it right."

"Yes, I most surely do."

The doctor clenched, unclenched, then re-clenched his fists. Then parked them on his legs, still clenched. "Dear God ... Dear God ... Dear God."

The theatrics were getting a little old. "Look, Doctor. Some information might be helpful. You seem to be wanting to tell me the warehouse isn't what I think it is."

"Oh, it's not. Most definitely not." He seemed to decide he had no choice but to tell it like it was. "It's about housing and protecting extraterrestrials. Beings that aren't from our neck of the universe, you know. ETs. Aliens. The warehouse is all about keeping alien visitors safe and secure in Flagler. If and when they come."

Expletives were becoming a staple in our conversation. The next one was mine. "Jesus H. Christ! Please don't tell me you're serious."

He said he needed to explain.

I agreed.

CHAPTER 59

Mayes started with a single word. "Thaddeus."

Not a bad choice of beginnings. Because it sounded like I was about to get the professor's life story, *Reader's Digest* version.

"Bright lad. Born and raised on a ranch northwest of Roswell, New Mexico. You've probably heard how he liked to get up early and watch the sun rise. Because of this, he witnessed the light from the world's first atomic explosion — the Trinity test. You've probably heard that story too."

I gave him a nod.

"Affected him profoundly. He was about to be a junior in high school. Talked about the experience incessantly to his classmates for the next two years. That was what led to what happened the summer before he left for college. That was the summer the UFO crashed northwest of Roswell. Late July 1947. The flying saucer crash was confirmed by the government, then denied. First told reporters it was a flying disk, then passed it off as a weather balloon."

Mayes explained how the military tried to gather all the debris from the crash. One of Huntgardner's classmates, a teenage girl, lived on a neighboring ranch. One of her daddy's ranch hands found a strange metal fragment with mysterious

266

writing on it. He believed it was from the crash and showed it to her. Somehow, she'd managed to hide it. By and by, she'd heard Thaddeus describe seeing the Trinity test in one of her classes. Knew he was interested in science. Sought him out. And gave the fragment to him.

"And Thaddeus did what with it?"

Mayes gave an outsized shrug. "Wish I knew. But I can tell you he brought it with him when he came to Flagler to go to college. And then spent most of his time over the next sixty years consumed by the object. Obsessing, actually, over what he thought he was meant to do because it had ended up in his possession."

I knew my eyes must have gotten wider. "And that was what?"

"Get Flagler ready for the aliens' next visit."

"Who told him they were coming back? More than that, coming to Flagler?"

"Nobody that I know of. But eventually in his physics studies, Thaddeus learned about dark matter and dark energy. They intrigued him. He got it in his head that the fragment held an explanation for that."

"Surely, he had some reason to think so."

"Well, he could spin quite a yarn. Said the fragment was a weird piece of — he called it liquid metal. Metal-like, at least. A sheet of it. Not large. Maybe eighteen or twenty inches square, but nothing like any metal we know about."

Mayes pressed his steepled fingers against his chin. Stared at me as if he was still deciding if I could be trusted with what he was about to say.

I passed the test, whatever it was. Because he started describing what Huntgardner had said the sheet was like. He told me nothing I hadn't already heard from others. Except for one thing — he said it was the writing on one side of the sheet that had intrigued the professor most.

"Strange markings, like hieroglyphics, scientific notation, that kind of thing. Somehow, he had the notion that these characters held one of the great secrets of the universe. And that it was all going to be revealed to us Earthlings when intelligences superior to ours returned to explain what the characters meant. And it was going to happen in Flagler."

"Doctor, you're no dummy. You believed all this?"

He leaned forward slightly, seeming more determined than ever to be understood. "Well, for years and years, my wife and I viewed Thaddeus and his schemes as a kind of experiment in human nature."

I'd taken my notebook and ballpoint from my shirt pocket earlier, but I realized I wasn't ready to include this kind of information in my report, so I put them back. "That explains why you got so drawn into all this."

"Some of it. All of us, including the professor, were astounded that the rumors about the fragment spread in certain circles so quickly and were greeted with such hostility. And that so many of the people disturbed by it seemed to be playing for keeps. If we were going to survive, we realized, that was the way we needed to play."

He said his snoops — the actual word he used — ferreted out information that Huntgardner's claims were the reason Dr. Rawls had mobilized his Ezekiel's Wheel secret society. Other forces he'd never understood put Flagler in their crosshairs too. Townspeople were being hurt, threatened, burglarized, burned out. On at least one occasion, one of them disappeared.

"So that's why you formed the Unus Mundus Masters?"

"In part, it was. But the closer we got to the seventy-fifth anniversary of the Roswell event, the more my wife and I sensed that we might be caught up in something authentic and historic. That Flagler might be about to become the stage for something enormously important. And that somebody was increasingly unhappy about it. Maybe a bunch of somebodies."

I wasn't bothering to hide my skepticism. But Mayes wasn't noticing. He was still caught up in his story. "I guess I didn't totally get aboard until Thaddeus's friends started contacting my wife."

"What was that about?"

"They wanted her help therapeutically with their dreams."

"Dreams?"

"Yes."

"Dreams about what?"

"About flashing blue lights. About being abducted by aliens. Being transported up into UFOs and told to get ready. About Flagler becoming the site of a kind of a . . . Second Coming."

Should I tell him about the flashing blue light that had been left in my house by an intruder? I thought about it, then decided it would disrupt the flow of our conversation. Instead, I decided to get to the point. "So was that why so many physicists were at Huntgardner's house the other Friday?"

He kept his head still, but his answer equivocated. "Yes and no. It explains why they were all in Flagler that weekend. My wife felt they'd benefit from hearing one another share their experiences with the dreams. But I don't know whose idea it was to go to the old Huntgardner house."

"Do you know what they were doing?"

This time, he dipped his head, paused, then answered. "I do know that. They thought Thaddeus might have hidden the fragment somewhere on the property."

At that moment, my eye fell on a painting someone had hung on the chapel wall. It showed the baby Jesus in his manger. The observation sent my thoughts scrambling. Here we were once again, dealing with something that could lead to a deadly conclusion. Again, the cause was something alien, or so religious people had argued for eons. Only, this time, it wasn't a baby. It was a piece of space junk. I could feel my forehead wanting to switch to its "oh, really" face, but I repressed it. "Do you think that was why they were killed — because they found it?"

"I wish to God I knew."

I still wasn't clear about the remodeled building. "Tell me if I've got this right. That elaborate warehouse and all the electronics and the steel bars on the doors and the armored bus — you created that to keep alien visitors in?"

He shook his head with enough vigor to make his large earlobes flap. "My heavens, no! The bars aren't there to keep the aliens in. They're there to keep people who would harm our visitors out. We don't want what happened in Roswell repeating itself. Not in Flagler."

That was when my "Thaddeus awakening" began. The light exploded on the horizon. I had the beginnings of an epiphany. And the immediate craving for context.

"So, the conflict, the chaos, the mayhem, the endless lawlessness of the past seventy years in Flagler has been a jurisdictional conflict."

Mayes bobbed his head five times, moving his chin farther along an imaginary line each time. I knew what he was doing. He was advancing through my word "jurisdictional" syllable by syllable. Five syllables, five head bobs. By the time he got to the final one, he'd decided. "Jurisdictional? Yes, that's one way to put it."

I felt the need to explain. "I mean, the brouhaha has mostly been over who's going to take charge of our so-called alien visitors if and when they show up. Right?"

The doctor was still. When he spoke, his rhythm was slow, his tones resigned, almost mournful. "No, not that. It's been a bit more diabolical. It's been over whether our alien visitors will be protected or whether they'll be destroyed."

So this was what an epiphany felt like. I didn't like the feeling. I'd much prefer to be back in a classroom or around a seminar table dealing with history that was already cut and dried. Arguing about insights that had been parceled out to me chapter by neat chapter. Having time in between the arrival of unexpected insights to cogitate and evaluate.

I looked at my watch. Eighteen minutes. That's how long it had taken to go from Thaddeus Huntgardner's birth to the death of my naiveté about what solving Flagler's crimes and mysteries was going to require.

I might have been able to ask more questions if my dispatcher's voice hadn't interrupted. He was calling on my walkie-talkie. Wanted me to get to the hospital ASAP.

I told him I was already here.

He said an ambulance was incoming. Helen was riding in it. She'd explain everything.

CHAPTER 60

Helen wasn't on a stretcher. She was seated on one of the ambulance's benches, close to the person being transported. A woman. I recognized her the moment I looked up into the ambulance. It was Cassandrea Caraballo. "Cassie" to her friends. Caraballo was Abbot County's supervisor of voter registration and elections.

Most mornings, the sassy dark-haired import from Brooklyn breezed into our offices from hers across the hall. She and Helen had a name for themselves. The courthouse beverage sommeliers. She'd announce that it was time for the sommeliers to meet and would ask if the "cawfee" was hot. She called Helen her "fren," which she was. A good one. And she would sometimes slip back into pure Brooklynese and announce she was going to the "terlet."

I helped my office manager step down from the ambulance. I didn't get a good look at Caraballo as she was wheeled passed me on the stretcher. The paramedics were already waiting with her at the nurse's station when I caught up. They needed to know to which treatment room they were being assigned.

Their patient was unconscious. And a mess despite their efforts to clean up after her. She'd been vomiting. And had the runs. All our noses were indicating that her bowels were dealing with something they couldn't tolerate. Her face was bathed in perspiration. The paramedics were calling out her other symptoms as she was surrounded by ED personnel. Some of it I understood. Most of it I didn't.

"Pulse rate forty-six." I knew that wasn't critical. Not by itself. A normal resting heart rate is between sixty and one hundred beats a minute. Most times, forty-six beats a minute would be considered a healthy pulse.

"Blood pressure one eighty over one ten." That signaled hypertension — high blood pressure. Very high blood pressure. I'd discussed the condition enough with my own GP to know a reading that high was not a good sign. Not unless it was a normal reaction to stress or something severe, like a stroke.

Then one of the paramedics rattled off a string of conditions. A few, like excessive tearing and tremors in the extremities and increased salivation, I understood. The others were Greek to me. But having one eye is an amazing goad to your auditory memory. I could often tell you what I'd just heard, whether or not I'd understood it.

Miosis. Bradycardia. Fasciculation. Then came some more plain English. The paramedic said before the patient had become unresponsive, she had been confused and agitated.

But it was what I heard him say next that told me I needed to get in the picture. "We've been doing almost constant airway aspiration. It's like this patient wants to drown herself in her own fluids."

Yes, that's one of the reasons why they call it Tres Pasitos — "three little steps." That's all the steps the unlucky rat can take before it drowns in its own fluids.

There was no one around the stretcher I knew. No one I could see in the entire emergency department whom I recognized. My top-gun impersonation was going to have to be one of the best of my career.

"Listen, people, I don't have time to explain why I know

this. But I do. You don't have much time. If you don't do the right thing, she's going to die on us."

The response came from a smooth-cheeked kid in light blue scrubs. He had the stethoscope draped around his neck like a dog collar. Any other time, I'd have admired his spunk.

But this time, he pointed toward the swinging doors I'd barged through only moments before. "You mind stepping outside, mister? We're pretty busy here."

His name tag said Dr. Wittig. Young Dr. Wittig was only seconds away from a humbling experience. For the first and perhaps only time in his still budding medical career, he was about to be levitated on the job. I intended to grab the fresh white T-shirt showing from beneath his scrubs right below his chin. Gather it tight in my fist. And jerk him upright until his feet cleared the floor. He wasn't a sizable person. I'd probably be able to dangle him for a moment in thin air.

But I wanted to try the nonviolent route one more time. Maybe I could impress him with the basic verbal currency of his profession.

Jargon.

"Aldicarb. Do you know what aldicarb is, son?"

His reply encouraged me no end. "It works like an organo-phosphate."

I had no idea if that was true or not. But already, he was showing less and less interest in calling security and having me ejected. "It's a deadly poison. Illegal in the U.S. It will kill a rat before it can take three steps."

His eyes moved from me to his patient. "She's taken rat poison?"

"I don't know that for sure. If she has, I'm almost certain she didn't know she was doing it. But if we let her die lying here in your ED, you and I are both going to have a lot of explaining to do. Not to mention, one of the greatest regrets of our careers."

He pointed to a computer and gave the nearest nurse an order. "Look up aldicarb. I haven't heard the word since my toxicology training." His next comment seemed to be an aside. "We don't get a lot of that in medical school, you know." Then he looked back at me. "Tox training — we don't get a lot of it." His eyes fell to the badge penned to my shirt. "You're not a medical person, are you?"

"No, I'm just a country sheriff. But at the moment, I probably know as much about dealing with aldicarb as anybody between Fort Worth and Phoenix."

"Then you know what we normally do first for cholinergic toxins."

"All I know, Doctor, is how different it would have been if you had been available to pump nine of our Abbot County citizens full of something called pralidoxime the other day. You could have prevented the largest aldicarb murder in American history."

"The physicists' deaths?"

"Yes, the physicists."

His attention shifted away from me, and I was thrilled to see it go. I'd done what I wanted to do. Reengaged the doctor in him.

He might have directed one further comment in my direction, though probably not. More likely, it was directed to the small army of trauma center staffers who had gathered to attend to Cassandrea Caraballo. "We may not need pralidoxime. Let's try atropine first. That'll help the secretion problem — help dry her out. Her muscles are getting weaker and weaker."

I was already moving toward Helen who had been observing the tense encounter between the ED doctor and me like a bewildered parent. Neither of us needed to encourage the other to find a place where we could speak in private. It wasn't going to happen in the emergency department. I pointed to the ambulance loading area outside the automatic double doors. Told her to wait there. I'd pick her up in just a minute.

I needed to know in minute detail what had happened to Abbot County's supervisor of voter registration and elections. From all appearances, this morning's regular meeting of the courthouse beverage sommeliers had almost killed her.

CHAPTER 61

Out in the ambulance bay, Helen didn't wait for me to come to a full stop. She chased after my cruiser. Reached for the passenger side door. Jerked it open. Leaned down into my still-moving car. And began to talk. Or tried to. She was short of breath.

I eased to a full stop. Put my vehicle in park. Waited until she was seated. Then encouraged her to take a moment and collect herself.

She was verging on tears. I didn't mind that. But it would delay my learning something that might well keep someone else in my courthouse or elsewhere in my county from going through what Cassandrea Caraballo was going through.

I reached over and squeezed her shoulder. "You did well. Looks like Cassie's going to be okay."

She shuddered as she exhaled. "I thought she was going to die."

"Tell me what happened."

She didn't do that. Not right away. Instead, she raised both her arms and began to tap the crown of her head with all four fingers on both hands. Not hard taps. But solid enough that I could hear them land.

I knew about tapping because I'd seen her doing it while seated at her desk the previous day. I asked what she was doing, and she told me about this relaxation method she'd read about in one of her health magazines.

She said the user starts at the top of the head and tap-tap-taps their way down the body's energy meridians. Said the Chinese had been doing it for 5,000 years.

I wasn't going to wait for her to proceed through the whole routine, but she knew that. Several taps to her head and several along the inner edges of her eyebrows, and she was done. "She drank a glass of the tea I made for you."

I'd had time stand still before. Once. While I was gazing into the Grand Canyon. It was the awe of it all.

I wasn't awe-stricken this time. Now, the clock stopped because I realized it was going to be impossible to do all the things that needed to be done.

I reached for the handset on my car radio. Depressed the talk button. And stopped without saying anything. I realized I needed more information from Helen. "Did Cassie drink the tea I left sitting in my office? Or did you fix her a glass for herself?"

She didn't answer at first with audible words. But it was easy enough to read her lips. "Oh, bloody hell." I'd not witnessed a stronger curse from my office manager in sixteen years. "She fixed her own glass. From the same pitcher."

"Is the glass you fixed for me still sitting on my credenza?"

This was where Helen's head began a reinforced kind of bobbing after each of my questions. It was more a scooping motion than a head bob. Chin-down, then chin right back up. The meaning was clear each time. "Oh, hell, yes."

"Is the tea still in the pitcher?"

Scoop bob.

"Is the ball infuser still in the pitcher?"

Scoop bob.

"Is the canister you keep the tea leaves in sitting in its usual place?"

Scoop bob.

"Did you take the tea leaves from that canister when you made my tea this morning?"

Scoop bob.

"Did you leave the kitchen unlocked?"

Scoop bob.

"So anybody who wants to can still drop in and help themselves to a glass of tea?"

Scoop bob.

This time, I held the switch open and gave precise instructions to Jeff Brailsford, my daytime dispatcher.

Get someone to put my office suite on lockdown, starting with the door opening from the hallway. No admittance to anyone for any reason until I got there. Crime scene tape up across the kitchen entrance and my personal office. CSI unit standing by for my arrival in the first-floor hallway. And no one should drink any tea. No explanations to anyone about what was going on. I'd be there shortly, code 1.

○○○

As I walked toward the courthouse, I couldn't help but be aware of the pandemonium that my instructions to Jeff had triggered. In my rush to ensure that no one else got near the kitchen, I'd set off a near-panic in the courthouse. It wasn't only the kitchen that had been put off-limits. Two deputies were stringing crime scene tape at the foot of the courthouse stairs. Already, a small crowd had gathered, blocked from entering the building.

It took a moment for all this to sink in. I was too busy processing my awe. I'd just had a near-brush with death. If Gideon's Trumpet hadn't called at the exact moment he had,

I'd have done the same thing I did to start every day at the office. Had my morning iced tea.

It had become obvious in the ED that no one had briefed them yet about Tres Pasitos. By the time they would have figured out they needed to inject me with pralidoxime, or maybe the doctor's atropine, it was not stretching the facts to fear that it would have been too late.

It almost had been. Cassandrea Caraballo had been a hapless bystander to the intended outcome of these events.

My sense of awe dissipated almost as fast as it had arrived. The Grand Canyon it left behind was of a different kind. An abyss opened up by my own ignorance. Few of my assumptions about the murders at Professor Huntgardner's house held water any longer.

As I entered the courthouse, one look at the visitor waiting for me at the door to my department told me more of them might be about to spring a leak.

CHAPTER 62

Garrick Drasher had traded his natty *GQ*-worthy outfit for duds more suitable for a country courthouse. Faded jeans. Checkered long-sleeved shirt. Ordinary T-shirt. Wide black belt. Scuffed western boots. And a plain straw cowboy hat.

The fact that he was holding the wide-brimmed hat in his hand as he watched me approach made me clue into something I'd not seen in him before.

Humility, maybe?

The thought was reinforced by his jeans. It was as if the pants had seen honest labor. They showed wear. His change in appearance lowered my defenses. A little. He still had an expensive laptop case sitting on the step beside him. He put his hat on and picked up the case. He held it sideways in front of him with both hands, making it look like he was wearing a fraternal lodge's ceremonial apron.

His first words were spoken like he was taking great care not to be overheard. It didn't matter. Our cavernous half-granite courthouse hallways amplified all voices, in particular male voices. Drasher might as well have used a megaphone. "I need to tell you who I really am."

That made me curious. But it was not enough to convince me he needed to be a priority. Not on a day when I needed to be ten places at once.

He noticed that and upped the ante. "I need to tell you about something. Or rather, someone. I'm not sure, but I might be able to shed some new light on your murder investigation."

It seems he still didn't see reassuring signs that he had my attention, so he appealed to my sense of duty. "Do you really want this kind of nonsense to keep happening, Sheriff?"

He didn't seem to be aware of the events in our department kitchen this morning. If he'd known of the attempt on my life and the near-fatal consequences for one of our county administrators, he'd not have reduced our Abbot County turmoil to "this kind of nonsense."

I pointed down the hall to the other entrance to our offices. "Ten minutes."

"We'll need privacy."

I steered him to my interrogation room.

He took his seat. Leaned his laptop case against a table leg. Placed his hands on the tabletop with the fingers on both spread wide. Went silent. And stayed silent. Then said, "Thought I had most of this figured out."

In normal times, I might have been more patient. Forbearance during interrogations can pay off. But this wasn't an interrogation. This was an indulgence. And letting a person who had elbowed his way into my schedule decide when to tell me what "this" meant wasn't going to cut it. Not on a day teeming with this-es.

I made no effort to mask my growing irritation. "Eight minutes."

This time, the part of Drasher's anatomy he thrust at me over the table wasn't his hands. It was his elbows.

He used them to anchor his arms as he folded them in front of his trim torso and leaned toward me. Once again, I found myself interpreting the gesture. This one seemed to signal a decision on his part to persevere against my irritability.

He started with a question. A weird one. "Are you aware that Wide Sky Country is pockmarked with old Atlas missile silos?"

I answered by holding up one finger on my right hand and two fingers on the other. Yes, I knew about the twelve massive holes in the ground, any one of which could have fired a nuclear warhead at the Soviet Union at the height of the Cold War.

He wasn't through.

"And do you know what some of Flagler's finest have made elaborate plans to do with one of those empty silos?"

He took the blank look on my face for what it was. Total ignorance.

"I didn't think so."

That was when he told me about the Ezekiel's Wheel group's plan to build an elaborate holding area for extraterrestrial visitors in one of the silos.

If Flagler ever hosted the alien visitors that Professor Huntgardner had so often predicted, they were going to be transported to the silo. Taken into its 180-foot-plus depths. Entrapped behind the heavy interior doors at the bottom of the stairs. And left entombed forever.

Once again, a look of disbelief flashed across the table. This time, it originated from my face.

My visitor got to his feet and leaned against the wall. "Like I said, it's time to put an end to his nonsense."

For the first time since we'd entered the room, I was no longer thinking about how much time was left on the clock. "So you need to tell me who you are."

"I'll do that, but first, there's someone I'd like to ask to join us."

He teased his smartphone out of his pants. Waited a few seconds and spoke a few words. "The party will be with us shortly."

CHAPTER 63

I made no effort to hide my surprise.

Not when she walked through the door without knocking. Not when she pulled a chair around to my side of the table and sat down. Not when she placed her faux leather tote bag on the floor beside her chair. Not when she looked in the direction of the room's other occupant and addressed him. "About time, Garrick."

Drasher shot me a glance before looking back at her. "I know, Special Agent Steele."

Angie was in no mood to be polite. "You may have put him in unnecessary danger by waiting."

He knew better than to push the issue. "So I just learned. No more secrets, at least between the three of us."

She snorted. This was something she often did when she smelled a rat, an incompetent, or a schemer. In this case, judging from what she said next, she considered Drasher the third. "You wouldn't know how to go about not having secrets. You've been underground too long."

Drasher had placed his phone on the table. He was flipping it back and forth. "Can't argue. Like I told Sheriff Luke, it's one reason I'm here. Feels like it's time to come in from the cold, at least where he's concerned."

I cleared my throat. "Obviously, you two have met."

Got dual nods.

Now it was my time to play the politeness card, less I lose my cool. "Obviously, you, Garrick, have other employment besides your day job."

That brought a hands-thrown-skyward "what can I say?" gesture from Mr. Pretty Face.

The other person in this conversation looked like she was about ready to sit on her hands. "And, obviously, the two of you have had conversations before about our problems in Abbot County."

Drasher waved a palm at Angie, and she met it with a wave of her own. Neither spoke, but then I could surmise that speaking was something they both liked to avoid. Drasher because there were apparently a lot of things he still wanted to keep secret. Angie because she'd realized there were things she should have told me much sooner. And she had to be wondering what else Drasher had bothered to tell me about himself and his presence in Flagler.

I pressed him. With a guess. "You're actually FBI?"

"Sometimes I wish."

"CIA?"

His head shake said no.

"Defense Intelligence Agency?"

This time, his head did the metronome thing. Moved in a brief arc. Meaning what? I guessed yes and no. He confirmed it. "Closer. But the fact that you and I are even talking about this should tell you I'm not with any of our national intelligence agencies. Because *you* don't have a security clearance."

I acknowledged that.

"Angie and I have been working to get you one. Really all that's left is for you to fill out the paperwork. But I don't even work for the government. If I did, I'd probably never be able to tell you what I'm about to tell you."

"So you don't do secret work at all?"

"Oh, but I do. Let me explain what an IRAD is."

"IRAD?"

"Stands for Independent Research and Development."

"Sounds a private company."

"Exactly. It's a kind of private CIA, though nowhere near that elaborate. Or that big. Or that visible, believe it or not. The Defense Department uses them all the time — just not for this purpose."

"So who runs yours?"

Drasher glanced at Angie. She raised her eyebrows and gave her head a tiny tilt. His call. "One of our major U.S. aerospace companies runs it."

"And its purpose is what?"

"First and foremost, to cover any government official's ass that needs covering."

"Sounds like a big job. Any particular ass-covering specialty?"

He unleashed a huge sigh. Laid his hands in his lap. And entwined his fingers. More silence. Maybe he was deciding on his answer. Or deciding whether he was going to answer. Or deciding whether to abort his whole mission.

Then he seemed to realize he'd already crossed this Rubicon and needed to get to the point. "We operate at the bottom of the rabbit hole."

"No idea where to go with that."

Drasher said his private intelligence agency's responsibility was to investigate UFO sightings, legitimate or otherwise. In the U.S. or anywhere else in the world when something interested them. Sightings by civilians, military personnel, local law enforcement, pilots, or, as had once happened, the governor of Arizona. Sightings by anyone. But especially, sightings by anyone who might be intimidated by the noxious attitudes in the federal government.

That was the rabbit hole.

The need for it could be traced all the way back to Roswell. Within hours of that momentous summer day in 1947, the generals who ran the Army Air Forces were running for cover. Petrified by the fear that anyone might think they thought they were dealing with a real UFO crash.

Lying about what had happened in the remote New Mexico countryside. Confiscating every piece of evidence of the crashed UFO they could lay hands on. Warning witnesses of the most drastic penalties if they ever breathed a word about what they had seen. Insisting that people should forget that their lying eyes had seen anything.

Seventy-plus years later, he said, little had changed. To this day, nothing spooked officials at all levels of the American government more than being accused of treating UFOs and extraterrestrial visitors as real possibilities. Thus, the rabbit hole.

He couldn't — or wouldn't — tell me which POTUS had created the IRAD solution. Said Truman would have if he'd thought of it. Or Eisenhower. Even Nixon.

"But one of them finally realized we needed a rabbit hole. Literally. A hole in our intelligence capabilities where serious UFO and alien visitation researchers could disappear and deal with their data in total privacy. That's what IRAD does. It's been the only way to get around the official timidity and look seriously at the evidence."

"Your IRAD squad. It's been active in Flagler for a while?"

"We've come and gone and come and gone and, now, we've been back for three years. Chalk it up mostly to the erratic Professor Huntgardner and his claims about his fragment. They're like Tootle the Little Engine — they just keep going. And coming. And now they're getting people killed. One of our people too to our profound regret."

The shock in my voice was genuine. "One of your agents was killed in Flagler?"

"Your tenth victim at Professor Huntgardner's house. Wyatt

Donovan was his name. One of our best undercover people. Had a degree in physics, incidentally. Infiltrated the Unus Mundus Masters group about two years ago. Unless you've figured it out, we still don't know what happened to him. And we weren't able to tell you anything for fear of blowing our cover."

Drasher's bombshell revelation about his slain agent put our meeting on a different heading. But it would have gotten there anyway. Because of what he said next.

"You've had one other direct exposure to one of my guys. Pretty sure you didn't know it, though." He said his spook had installed a clock with a hidden surveillance camera on one of the walls in our locker room.

I knew about the clock. The so-called manufacturer's rep had said the company was donating one to every department in the courthouse. I'd suggested they hang ours in the locker room because it had available wall space.

Until now, I didn't know that the donation story was a fabrication. And that the manufacturer's rep had been bogus. Or that a spy camera had been part of the package. Or that it had been installed because Drasher was beginning to suspect that the sheriff's department's hands might not be clean in Abbot County's ongoing bloodthirsty shenanigans.

Drasher said the camera was hidden in the zero in the number ten. The tiny camera lens captured anything that moved within its 120-degree viewing range. The images were then stored on a SD memory card.

The removable cards were one of the reasons that he and the special agent had planned this meeting. He had some of the cards in his briefcase, but the current card was still in the clock.

Before we looked at anything stored on them, he wanted to raise one more issue. He wanted to know if, in my investigations into "all of Abbot County's troubles," as he put it, I'd ever come across a particular person.

The mysterious author's pen name was the Prairie Canary.

CHAPTER 64

While I'd not been told about the spy camera in the clock-face, Angie must have been. And she should have been in the loop on other issues of importance in Drasher's investigation. But I wasn't seeing confidence of that on her face.

On the other hand, Angie had kept secrets from him. She'd known about the Prairie Canary because we'd both read the Canary's letters to my father — the ones stuffed in No Cock Crowed Box No. 6.

I didn't know what Drasher had conjectured about Angie's willingness to confide in him, but I'd detected more than professional collegiality between the two since Angie had entered the room. Now, courtesy of the long-departed Prairie Canary, he was about to get another inkling of how he might have misinterpreted their relationship.

Where I was concerned, it couldn't be clearer. Neither of them had chosen to make me a full partner in probing Abbot County's criminal matters, whatever their reasons.

Drasher's motives for this were obviously professional. Already, he'd made it clear that he had one of the strangest jobs in American governmental spook-dom. Or was it non-governmental spook-dom?

But the extent that the woman I loved had gone to avoid leveling with me was an eye-opener.

We'd have to talk about it. At length. In private. When our buddy on the other side of the table had crawled back into his rabbit hole.

My other trust problem was more immediate. How much, if any, of the information in my father's No Cock Crowed boxes should Angie and I share with Drasher?

Neither Angie nor I had responded to his question about the Prairie Canary.

He took that to mean we didn't know anything about her. He moved on.

"Luckiest thing, in a way. But then again, who's going to know more about the history of a place than the local librarian?"

I watched while Angie took a breath. She knew as well as I did what Drasher was about to tell us. He'd found the Prairie Canary's manuscript. In the county library.

It was all I could do to keep my balance in my chair.

I wanted to know everything Drasher knew about the Prairie Canary. Had already framed my response in my mind. "I'm pretty sure you didn't just sashay into the library and ask if they had any secret files."

I wasn't expecting his reply. "Kind of did, actually. Asked if they had any materials about the county's history that didn't circulate."

Interesting.

I'd never have thought about doing this. And I'd known Miss Ruthie Kollberg, the county librarian, since I was in the third grade.

"You did this because the idea fairy in the rabbit hole suggested it."

Drasher reacted with a contrived chuckle. And decided a smart-ass question deserved a smart-ass answer. "No, I did it because I love sniffing other people's unwashed underwear."

Angie blushed. I found myself tongue-tied with embarrassment. Not with him. With myself. *That was dumb, Sheriff. You need to get this back on track, pronto, Tonto.* I tried a compliment. But it landed like a pig's grunt. "Brilliant idea — who'd have thunk it?"

He was still smart-assing. "Nobody but a student in junior high school English, most likely."

Angie rode to the rescue. The way she sent a blocking shoulder in my direction signaled she wanted Drasher to think she was diverting all her attention his way. "The Prairie Canary, she was an author?"

Her intervention put his agitation on the sidelines. "A really talented one. I've not read anything quite so spellbinding since I read . . . well, Mary Karr's *The Liars' Club*. Or maybe Ruth Wariner's *The Sound of Gravel*."

I was a reader. I'd read both those works. Both were engrossing. Emotional, deeply personal books. But how odd that he'd cite works by talented authors who'd grown up in wildly unconventional circumstances. One in a dysfunctional east Texas oil patch family. The other in a polygamist cult.

Angie hadn't taken her eyes off him. "Is the author's name on the title page?"

"All it says is 'By the Prairie Canary.' The library doesn't know the author's name, either. They said the manuscript was mailed to them anonymously years ago."

I had a question for him. "You compared it to the two memoirs by women authors. So this is a non-fiction work by a woman too?"

He confirmed that it was. "The book is called *The Expiator's Curse: A Memoir about the Pain of Caring Too Much*. But you're the one who keeps referring to the author as a woman. Why are you thinking that?"

At this point, I'd have understood if Angie had considered

her cover blown. Said, "Whoops!" and started telling Drasher what we knew about the Prairie Canary.

Instead, she turned into an instant literary critic. "Her choice of a nom de plume, Garrick. Usually, men wouldn't call themselves canaries. If you or Luke had written this using a pseudonym styled after an animal, it would have been something like the Vigilant Eagle or the Wolf That Never Blinks. Something manly, you know."

She was out of the trap. But she wasn't finished.

"The title also hints at that. It positively radiates a woman's perspective. We females are sensitive to being left with the guilt of a relationship that falls apart, no matter whose fault it was."

"Human Relations 101." The words popped out of my mouth.

Another smart-ass wisecrack wasn't the way I'd planned to return to the dialogue. But now that I was back, I wanted to get clarity on one issue. Drasher's answer was going to determine whether our discussion about the Prairie Canary and *The Expiator's Curse* continued in my interrogation room. "I asked if the book was non-fiction, and you didn't answer."

He flicked his eyes to the corner of the room before sweeping them across each of our faces.

"My guess is that it's mostly the truth, at least as the author saw it. But true or not, it's still stranger than fiction."

Drasher said he would never forget the book's opening sentence. Six short words.

They are going to kill me.

After reading that, he said he'd turned to the last page and read the book's closing paragraphs.

The Prairie Canary had written she wanted to get the manuscript to the post office while she could, so she could be sure it would reach the library.

She was going to ask the library to respect her privacy until Professor Huntgardner's death or for twenty years, whichever came first. Even then, she would ask that any mention of the book's existence be kept low-key. They could list it in their card catalog but without any publicity.

I'd thought he was finished telling us about the manuscript, but he wasn't. "There's one more paragraph. One that seems to be trying to shoehorn the previous three hundred pages into a few sentences."

As best he could remember, the closing paragraph said something like this:

"The professor no longer knows what is a lie and what is the truth. Or maybe it's all lies. The one thing I know for certain is that he made me love him. For that, I gave him a son. Then he threw us both away. His fabulous fragment may have suffered the same fate. You can decide for yourself, now that you've read my book. Or not. But this is all I know."

CHAPTER 65

To say I was irritated with Garrick Drasher would have been one of the millennium's ranking understatements.

I was betting he'd spent several hours immersed in the manuscript. Maybe several days. All the while, leaving life-and-death-influencing events and the people who controlled them to make their own way. Meander in the meadow of real life like pixie fairies chasing butterflies. At their own risk. Flying blind.

What an idiot!

I wasn't sure my face was prepared to shield my anger. I extracted my flip-over-the-top notebook from my shirt pocket. Flipped over a page. Then another one. And pretended to study the next one until I felt like I could wing it.

Decided to risk saying something. "Does the manuscript tell us anything about who else might be a target?"

Didn't work. My voice broke. Drasher noticed. "You're pissed about something, aren't you?"

It was a relief to realize I was going to be able to answer like an adult. "Feeling the stress, Garrick. Feeling the stress."

He seemed relieved. "Targets? Could be. The author herself said she had become a target. She thought she knew too much about a lot of things going on in Flagler. But especially about Huntgardner. And his fragment. If she's still around, she could be a target, but for all we know, she's long since dead. Let's talk about that guy you dug up west of town the other day. What was his name?"

"Carmichael."

"She says Carmichael was a part of Professor Huntgardner's secret group. Or clique, or cult — whatever you want to call it."

I helped his narrative along. "The Unus Mundus Masters. Or just the Masters."

He continued with his story. "She says by the time she got involved, they'd become a bunch of obsessed, self-righteous killers. Says Carmichael wasn't really a part of it. Just a hanger-on — one who got too nosy. And careless. Left one evening for the Dairy Queen to get burgers for everybody and was never seen again."

"Why did the Prairie Canary come to Flagler?"

"Like I say, she was a writer. She wanted to do a book about a community where the UFO alien buzz was creating a stir. Starting about 1990, people began to write book after book about the so-called Roswell incident. She wanted to write about a place with UFO excitement not named Roswell."

"She knew about Flagler how?"

"All Professor Huntgardner's tongue-wagging about his precious fragment. Newspapers loved the story. Especially the British tabloids."

"So the Prairie Canary was British?"

He gave a quick head shake. "Came from the Midwest, I think. Ohio maybe."

"So she spent a lot of time in Professor Huntgardner's company?"

"Not only his company but his bed as well."

"Let me guess — a lot of her narrative involves pillow talk."

"Well, remember, they did other things too."

"Oh, that's right. Does she indicate what happened to the child?"

"Said he wouldn't let her keep it. Said if their relationship was to continue, she'd have to make it disappear. Seems to have been profoundly relieved that he didn't kill it."

"So what'd she do with the child?"

"Local adoption agency took it. One of the real tearjerker moments in her book is where she describes holding her newborn for the only time. The child had a large strawberry-shaped birthmark, right in the middle of its back. Huge mark. She tells how she massaged it for long minutes before surrendering him to a nurse. And then for years, dreamed about running her fingers over the mark on the new infant's back."

I glanced at Angie. "So what happened to her relationship with the professor?"

Her look at Drasher told him she expected him to answer.

He thought about it for a moment. "The woman came to see what a monster he was. More than that, she learned too many of his darkest secrets."

"Such as?"

He thought for a moment. "What he'd done to people because of his obsession with the fragment and his belief that aliens were coming to Flagler to retrieve it. She said he was paranoid about what Malachi Rawls and his Society of Ezekiel's Wheel might do to extraterrestrials if they actually descended on the town. Said Huntgardner and Rawls often acted like opposing Mafia chiefs in a turf war with each other."

Now that he'd mentioned it, I wanted one more piece of information. "What about the fragment? Did she think it was real? Or have any idea where it might be?"

"You really need to read the manuscript for yourself."

I intended to do that at the earliest opportunity. Drasher wasn't giving me the kind of revelatory insights I'd been hoping for. And because I still had too many questions. For one thing, I wanted to know if the Prairie Canary's book ever mentioned my father. And whether it offered the slightest clue as to why and how Sheriff John's beloved belt had ended up around Professor Carmichael's neck.

I wondered if, during all their pillow talk, Huntgardner had mentioned dreaming about being visited by aliens himself. Or had had such a dream while lying asleep next to her.

I was eager to know if the manuscript pointed to other places in the county I should invite Reverend to come perform his sniffing magic.

And I had one other expectation, or I would have never have allowed this discussion to stretch this long on a day like today. I was desperate for clues to who was killing or trying to kill my county's residents.

Once again, it was Angie who moved us ahead. She suggested we'd all be derelict if we didn't soon look at the images captured by the spy camera in my department locker room clock. Drasher reached into his satchel and removed a small coin envelope. Shook the SD cards it contained into his palm. Looked at the ultra-fine felt-tip markings on them. Selected one. And handed it to Angie.

CHAPTER 66

There was only one reason I was willing to spend a few minutes watching the video. I needed to find out who had poisoned Cassandrea Caraballo. I *would* be a fool if I ignored the possibility that Flagler's mass murderer had been operating under my nose all along.

I watched as Angie took the SD card and inserted it in the adapter on her laptop. The picture show began. No popcorn. Or small talk. No talk in the room at all for a while. But there wasn't much to see. Our department's locker room was a far duller place than I'd realized.

In most instances, our people used it for storage. Uniforms or street clothes. Their duty belts. Their duty guns if they had a smaller off-duty gun to take home. And anything else they desired to lock away. It was not meant to be a dressing or changing room, so we weren't viewing my employees in dishabille. We had changing rooms.

We were treated to a scenario where two of my deputies stayed in front of their locker door mirrors so long it looked like they were homesteading.

Both kept drawing their lips back, engrossed with their teeth. One actually took time to floss. Drasher took note.

"And this year's Emmy for Best Preening Before Appearing in the Ready Room goes to . . ."

My chief deputy, Sawyers Tanner, was the next person to come into view. As he deposited his backpack on a nearby bench, I felt discomfort at what we were doing for the first time. Observing my employees and their personal storage spaces without them knowing it does not generally leave me feeling like a voyeur. I had a right to this kind of surveillance. It said so, in so many words, in their employment contracts. And how was this any different from walking through my department's work spaces with an observant eye, on the lookout for anything I should be concerned about? But watching Sawyers Tanner open his locker door without his knowledge wasn't the same.

It felt like what it was. Spying.

It felt disloyal.

Other than Angie, there was no one in Flagler I trusted more. Even though we'd only worked together for five years. Numerous times, I'd asked him to ride shotgun with me for one reason only: respect. My respect for his judgment, his policing skills, and his character. It was a way of saying that I trusted him with my life. Watching him shelve and unshelve items in his open locker, I still felt that. I was still feeling it when Drasher spoke up again. "I know him."

"What about him?"

"He delivers stuff for Pecan Mountain's caterers when our vans are tied up."

I recalled Tanner telling me about his part-time gig as a delivery guy. We watched as Sawyers removed his dress shirt. Like me, he preferred dressing in mufti — wearing civvies seemed less threatening to people. And we both felt that it kept the laundry bill a little lower.

As our spy camera trained its prying eye on him, hygiene seemed to be what was on Sawyers's mind.

He'd reached for a deodorant stick on one of his locker shelves. Unscrewed the cap. Lifted the bottom of his T-shirt enough that he could roll the deodorant under his armpit. Raised his arm to sniff the results. Appeared to get a whiff from his T-shirt that he didn't like. Reached inside his backpack. Found a replacement. And tugged the T-shirt he was wearing over his head with his back to the camera.

We all saw it at the same time.

Gasped.

And stared.

No, gaped. At the huge birthmark in the center of his back.

Still shaped like a rose-port-wine strawberry, just as the Prairie Canary had described.

I issued an order. "Freeze that." It occurred to me, regardless of any deceptions that had been between us, suddenly we were all on the same team. "Can we enlarge it?"

She didn't need me to identify the "it." She maneuvered the birthmark into the center of the screen. Then magnified it until the mass of abnormal blood vessels filled most of the picture.

I think we all felt the urge to touch it, but Angie was closest to the screen. She reached out and began to trace the edges of the birthmark with her fingers. I knew we were all thinking about the grief of a new mother. The one who had again and again traced the birthmark on the back of the infant she'd just given birth to. A newborn baby who was about to be lost to her forever.

I looked at Drasher. "Does your company ever deliver food to the Huntgardner house?"

He met my eyes and nodded slowly.

The spy camera in my department locker room had found him. My chief deputy had to be Professor Huntgardner's illegitimate son. And my instincts, and the growing ball of nerves in the pit of my stomach, told me he was probably something else. Abbot County's mass murderer.

CHAPTER 67

I should be able to call Tanner on his walkie. Talk to him directly. Ask him to return to the courthouse. And reassure me that my growing concerns about where he'd been and what he'd been doing were baseless.

I tried.

No answer.

For the first time, I realized I didn't know when the spy camera video we'd been watching had been recorded. I asked Garrick. He said it was a replay from a few weeks ago. He reminded us that today's memory card was still in the clock. I'd overlooked that. Had assumed that we'd been watching Sawyers getting ready for work this morning.

I asked Angie to restart the video and return the view to normal size. It showed my chief deputy leaving the screen, toting his fresh T-shirt, his long-sleeved work shirt, and his backpack. He headed for the men's change room.

I asked Angie to rewind and focus on Sawyers's locker again — in particular, the two shelves near the top. I was interested in a closer look at what else was there.

Stuff.

Not everything was visible. But I could see his deodorant stick. A couple of cologne bottles. A box of bullets — or at least the kind of box bullets came in. A heavy-duty flashlight. A small bound-at-the-side coil notebook. Two balled-up pairs of socks. And some small doodads I couldn't identify.

I turned to suggest that we all head for the locker room, but Angie was already on her way. I became number two in the entourage. Drasher followed in our footsteps.

My accomplices yielded to protocol when we reached the door to the department's locker room. Actually, they didn't have any choice. I was the only one in the group who had a key. When Tanner's locker door didn't yield to a tug on its handle, my mind engaged in a bit of wordplay: *The locker, dear diary, dear diary, was locked.* As it should have been. Fortunately, I had a key to our janitor's supply room. Somewhere.

It took four tries before I found the right key, fit it in the storage room door, and gave it a turn. Next, I needed a tool. A large screwdriver would suffice. I located one and rejoined Angie and Drasher, who were waiting expectantly in front of Tanner's locker. This wasn't Fort Knox, and the door yielded easily. I swung it open. Both my colleagues waited politely for me to take charge, but they were crowding close to see over my shoulder.

The gaping open space beneath the locker shelving contained a couple of items. One was a shipping box with the U.S. postal service's red-over-white international markings. It wasn't a small box. You could have lowered a six-pack into the carton with room left over. The sealing tape was broken, and the lid was partially open, but this didn't afford a view of what was inside. We'd have to bend the lid back to see what the box contained.

Another container was leaning against one of the locker's back corners. An odd-sized mailing tube? Maybe. The object was white, about two feet long and three inches in diameter. A plastic cap was inserted in the one end that was visible. The tube had no markings that I could see. Once again, we were going to have to remove the lid to examine the contents.

But none of this interested me as much as what I found folded up on the top shelf of Sawyers's locker.

It was a map. But not a printed map like those we receive from tourist bureaus. Or from the state's transportation people showing construction projects. Or a highway map — not as such. And not an official one.

It appeared to be a map that Chief Deputy Tanner had made himself: a hand-drawn map of the location of the region's twelve abandoned missile silos. The ones controlled during the Cold War from the air base north of Flagler.

My colleagues made the mental leap at the same time I did.

Dasher cursed. Stood straighter. Parked his hands on his hips. And bent forward to take another look. "You wanted to know about targets. I'd bet somebody's told him about how the Rawls group plans to deal with any alien visitors. I'd move Professor Rawls to target number one."

Angie continued to stare at the map. Her gaze settled on the silo site closest to Flagler.

It was a few miles south and a little east of the U.S. highway that ran through town. On Sawyers's map, the filled-in circle that marked its location had an asterisk beside it. A large one. Angie pointed to it. "I agree. We need to find Professor Rawls."

I'd already reached for my portable radio. "First, I want to see if my dispatcher knows where the chief deputy is."

Jeff Brailsford was his usual all-business self. "The chief dep's taken a vacation day. But —"

But this was one of those occasions when brevity wasn't enough. "Where's SpyTrackers showing his car?"

"Eden Junction 'Y.' I'd guess his car is parked in the bar and grill lot."

I instructed my dispatcher to try to raise Sawyers on the radio. And check to see if any of our other personnel knew his whereabouts.

Next, I deputized Drasher. A simple thing to do. He didn't have to raise his right hand or swear to anything. All that the law required was for him to acknowledge that I'd asked for his help and that he'd agreed to do so.

I asked him if he had a gun. He raised his arms as if he was about to be frisked. "Not on me, obviously. But I've got one in the car."

He said it was a Walther P22 pistol he used for target shooting and kept in his glove compartment. Said he had one of the new Texas Licenses to Carry, but he'd never carried a handgun on his person. I told him to try not to need his pistol for self-defense because it was a peashooter. But to stick the weapon in his belt and head for Flagler General Hospital. My dispatcher would tell hospital security he was coming. And have deputies join him as soon as possible. If Professor Rawls was target number one, Professor Huntgardner and any — or all — of the Mayes family may be next in the line of fire.

Angie was on her cell phone. My guess was that she was updating her bosses in D.C. I laid a hand on her arm. She moved the phone away from her head. I told her I was requesting the assistance of the Federal Bureau of Investigation.

She indicated her phone. "They heard that. It's official."

"See if you can find Professor Rawls. As soon as you get a location, join him. And give me a call so I know where the two of you are."

She asked where I was going.

I told her to the Eden Junction Bar and Grill. Since my chief deputy's car was in the parking lot, I was hoping that I knew where he'd spent half the afternoon. At the restaurant's bar emptying bottles of Strothers Brothers Dry Stout, his favorite brew.

I'd not gotten more than a block from the courthouse before my dispatcher reported in. He'd phoned the restaurant. Sawyers was nowhere to be found. The bartender could find no one who had seen him at the establishment since shortly after lunch.

I still wanted to check out the location myself.

So I continued to the Eden Junction turnoff. Parked next to Sawyers's patrol car. Glanced inside it. Saw nothing out of place. Went inside to talk to the bartender.

He said my chief deputy had sat alone at a booth eating a burger around noon. He'd been in his street clothes. No sign of his badge, duty belt, gun, or anything else official. Before leaving the establishment, he'd asked to have his thermos filled with hot coffee. Then walked out the front door.

Now, a couple of hours later, I was walking out the same door. Each step toward my car seemed to remind me of how little I'd known about the man who had been serving all these years as my second in command.

As the minutes passed, Sawyers Tanner was becoming more and more a stranger. The sheriff part of me served notice, not that it was needed, that it was going to be essential to penetrate those mysteries as quickly as possible. But the theologian-trained part of me couldn't resist pointing out how dependably the human soul can be counted on to reveal its true nature. Hard as we might try to avoid it, sooner or later, our inner self seems to be destined to show its cards.

CHAPTER 68

My dispatcher and I were interrupted from time to time, but for the most part, I had Jeff Brailsford to myself. He'd responded to my staccato barrage of instructions with his usual equipoise and quick grasp. A request made, a request delivered. A question asked, an answer forthcoming. An opportunity provided, an opportunity fulfilled. He had a rhythm to his thought processes that reached out to the person on the other side of the broadcast tower and engaged you. A kind of entrancement. Or maybe it was an entrapment. But no matter the chaos in the field, a few exchanges with Jeff seemed to help you sort out what needed to happen next.

I asked him to issue a BOLO. That was law enforcement speak for a "be on the outlook" announcement.

I also asked that he send a deputy to each of the county's abandoned missile silos. There were four of them — the other eight that had been located in West Central Texas were in other counties. He was to tell our deputies not to enter. Not the silos themselves and not even the outside fence gates. They didn't need to get out of their cars at all. All I wanted to know was if there were any vehicles parked close by. If they spotted any, they were to run the license plate numbers past the motor vehicle people in Austin. If one of them belonged to Chief Deputy Tanner, they were to notify me right away. If they saw a vehicle but it wasn't registered to the chief deputy, they were to run the license plate number in case we needed it later. I sensed that I was overexplaining my expectations, but Jeff didn't complain. He wouldn't. Wasn't his style. But he did need to know where all the county's abandoned silos were. I gave him a crash course in local missile silo geography, and left him alone for several minutes to carry out my order.

I wanted to talk to TxDMV myself.

I knew Sawyers's main personal conveyance was a spiffy new chocolate-colored Chevrolet Tahoe SUV. He kept it immaculate. Spent more time at the car wash than he spent in the shower himself. Always parked it in the farthest available corner of any parking lot. Any observant person would realize that leaving a mark on it would be a fearful act if my chief deputy found out who'd committed the crime.

I could issue a BOLO for the Tahoe. But I wanted to be sure of something else first. I wanted to see if my chief deputy was listed as the owner of any other kind of vehicle.

I called the motor vehicle office and identified myself. The clerk said Sawyers Frank Tanner was listed as the owner of a white 1999 Ford F-150 pickup. Said I could run the pickup's VIN through the National Motor Vehicle Title Information System. Tell if the vehicle had been salvaged, rebuilt, or damaged in a flood.

On most occasions, I had people who took care of these kinds of matters for me. But I was in a hurry.

I took down the website link she recommended. Decided it would be safer if I steered my car to the side of the road before I started punching in the data. Pulled over on the shoulder. Entered the link on my car's computer console. Punched in the information it requested. Waited for it to be processed. And tried to steel myself for another punch in the solar plexus.

It arrived on schedule.

Sawyers had filed an insurance claim for collision damage to the front end of his pickup a week ago Monday. He'd claimed to have crashed into a tree while trying to avoid a deer.

Maybe that was true. But my stomach had wrapped itself in an instant around the suspicion that he'd hit something else first. Our tenth Huntgardner house victim.

I had one more crucial stop to make before I put my dispatcher into action again.

Sawyers's house.

He had good taste. Lived in the same neighborhood I did. I'd passed the entrance to our subdivision on the way to the Eden Junction "Y" and was approaching it again now that I was returning to town. Ninety seconds more and I'd know for sure.

"For sure" meant that I'd either find my chief deputy's new Chevrolet Tahoe SUV parked in his circular driveway, or I wouldn't.

I did.

Ringing his doorbell twice brought no response. A peek through the windows across the top of his garage door told me that the garage contained no vehicles. In particular, I wasn't seeing a Ford F-150 pickup getting more ancient with every passing day.

I returned to my car. Reached for my radio. Noted that my dispatcher's response was as crisp and proper as a starched shirt collar.

I could have clued him in on what I'd learned since we'd last talked. But going straight to the bottom line accomplished the same end. "Jeff, we need to get a BOLO out for Chief Deputy Tanner."

That brought a pause in our exchange that surprised me. It shouldn't have. I was asking that an all-points bulletin that shined a dead-serious law enforcement spotlight be issued on one of our own. Jeff wanted to be sure he understood. "BOLO? Or just a request that they keep an eye out for him?"

I'd already considered this. We didn't need a friendly tip that Sawyers had been sighted or his pickup spotted somewhere. We needed to apprehend him. So an all-points bulletin was what I wanted. "BOLO, Jeff."

"Should it say he's armed and dangerous?"

"Yes, say he's armed and dangerous."

"Should we say what he's been charged with?"

My dispatcher had me stumped on that one. I was charging full speed ahead in pursuit of a person I'd have been willing to turn control of my department over to. And I was doing so without having, to this point, charged him with a crime. "Let's say we consider him a person of extreme interest in multiple deaths in Abbot County, Texas, Jeff."

That was true.

The language in our BOLO stayed that way for about forty-five minutes. The next time I heard it, Jeff had taken it on his own to interject a new sense of urgency.

It warned anyone listening to be on the lookout for an extremely dangerous individual. A veteran West Central Texas law officer believed to be driving a 1999 white F-150 pickup with a damaged front fender and turn signal light. Also believed to be heavily armed.

But it wasn't Jeff's upgraded BOLO that froze my blood. It was what I heard next. The snippet of an over-the-air exchange between him and one of my deputies. The reception wasn't that good, so I'd caught only the tail end of the deputy's comments — something about a campus shooting. But Jeff's reply thundered out of my car radio speaker and vibrated in my brain like a hard-plucked guitar string.

"We need to find out what happened to our FBI agent."

CHAPTER 69

I wasn't that far from the entrance to the University of the Hills. By the time I sped by the Whosoever Rock, I had a bare-bones idea of what I was going to see next.

Two campus security officers were blocking the entrance to the Bible Building parking lot. One of them came to my window. There was no mistaking the urgent look on his face. "Thank God you're here, Sheriff Luke. There's been a couple of fatalities."

He said the gunman had fled the scene.

As I drove into the grounds, it was clear the campus was in turmoil. And there were far more uncertainties than sureties about what had gone down.

I braked to a stop near a half dozen other cop cars. They lined the curb bordering the building entrance's concrete fore-court. In the intense afternoon sunlight, the circling red and blue beams of their emergency lights were bouncing off the building's dazzling plate glass exterior. Each time they did so, they doubled themselves in the windows.

I met the paramedics already leaving the building, carrying their emergency trauma bags looking like they'd not been unzipped. Their tomato-red spine board was empty.

Detective Salazar was stringing crime scene tape at the foot of the stairs to the second floor. Detective Coltrane and several other officers were clustered at the top of the stairs.

He and three others were holding up blue plastic sheeting. They were shielding whatever was lying on the wide hallway's second-floor landing. Onlookers — young people and shaken-looking faculty — jammed office doors, craning for a better look. Two more officers were in deep conversation that involved frequent pointing at places that were not visible to me.

My CSI team was not there yet. But Jeff would have summoned them. Given them directions. Shared the bare facts of what he knew.

I needed to stay a professional. People were expecting that. I could tell — or I thought I could — that I was being monitored by a hundred eyes.

One of the deputies consulting with the others at the head of the stairs was Detective Moody. I took the stairs two steps at a time. Grasped her forearm. Tugged her to follow me with more vigor than was needed.

But she understood the reason behind my brusqueness. My near-panic. I released her arm, and she followed me down the hall and around the nearest corner.

This time, she was the one who laid her hand on my forearm. She left it there for a moment. The brisk shaking of her head sideways had started when we rounded the corner, and it hadn't stopped. "It's not her."

"So where is she?"

"She's gone."

"Where's Professor Rawls?"

"Dead."

"Who's the other one?"

"Not sure, but they're saying it's one of his faculty colleagues."

"But what happened to Angie?"

"He took her."

"Sawyers, you mean?"

"Yes, Sawyers."

Now I was the one holding her arm, hard, as if I could squeeze the information out of her. "Took her how?"

"Witnesses said he dragged her to his pickup with her hands cuffed behind her."

CHAPTER 70

A number of deputies began rushing to their cars, and on my walkie, I could hear Jeff reassigning them. It was clear what he was trying to do. Establish a perimeter at Flagler's city limits.

That made sense. At least until someone could confirm that Chief Deputy Tanner and his hostage had moved past it.

But he knew what I knew. What all the people in our department knew. Like most towns and cities in Texas, Flagler mostly reached out, not up. Our out-in-the-boonies community covered more than a hundred square miles in its relentless reaching out.

We had only two main highways that ran in and out of all this real estate. We could put roadblocks on those and were doing so, but there were a dozen other ways to sneak out of town, and I was sure Sawyers Tanner knew all of them.

If my chief deputy . . .

Whoa.

Should I still be thinking of him like that? As chief deputy?

Probably so, until someone in authority managed to get their hands on his badge and gun. Or incapacitated him. Or killed him.

But *my* chief deputy?

In that instant, I realized I had another reason to keep thinking about him that way. It kept me from closing any useful doors to all those years of close observation of the man, his habits, his manner, his obsessions, his needs.

Closing the door to that would have been easy to do. A lot of those memories felt under siege. But there would be a time for second-guessing, for being judgmental.

This wasn't it.

I needed everything I knew about Sawyers Tanner to help fathom what was happening in his mind. What his endgame was now that he had claimed two more victims. Dragged an FBI special agent to his pickup with her hands cuffed behind her. And had a whole cityful of folks locking their doors and sitting glued to their radios, TVs, or computer screens. Those who weren't out hunting for him.

If I didn't figure that endgame out, then I might not ever get a chance to decide whether to offer Angie a ring.

So did I need to hurry?

I did.

Did I need to make a decision in haste?

I mustn't.

I needed to do what I'd had a reputation for doing at Yale in a seminar room filled with bright young theological minds. Provide a twist that nobody else, including my professors, saw coming.

And where did these twists come from?

My hunches. From deep in my brain. Maybe all the way from my cerebellum. Sometimes, it seemed, all the way from China.

I had a hunch that Sawyers's murderous behavior was a kind of tidying up. One that made perfect sense to him, no matter how unnecessary it seemed to others. Or how much it cost them. My first thought was of Professor Huntgardner. Now that Sawyers had put a fatal bullet in Professor Rawls, even with Angie in tow, I thought he might go after Huntgardner, even though the professor was already at death's door.

In normal circumstances, I'd have aimed my patrol cruiser toward the hospital in east Flagler at high speed. And asked for backup.

But that wasn't what my hunch was telling me to do.

It had me in the firm grip of another idea, wild as it was. I had a hunch that my chief deputy's next act of tidying up was going to happen on the opposite side of town. At a location made for tidying things up.

Flagler Memorial Cemetery.

CHAPTER 71

I'd have spotted the pickup quicker if not for a prim little decorative tree. You could see under it only for a short distance. The groundskeepers at Flagler Memorial Cemetary had shaped its branches like the bangs that Moe of the Three Stooges wore. Once I'd eased past the tree, the pickup was in clear view on one of the cemetery's winding dirt roads. The passenger side door was open. The vehicle appeared to be empty.

Driving right up behind it would have taken only seconds. Or I could have walked the distance in less than a minute. Instead, I killed my engine. Radioed Jeff. Told him to have backup deputies approach the cemetery without lights and sirens and remain out of sight. One of them needed to be a sniper. He should take up a discreet position with a clear line of sight to where I was at all times but do nothing unless I called for help or he saw circumstances turning dire.

I made small pivoting movements with my head to give my one eye the widest view possible. Otherwise, I sat still as a yogi. I wanted to see my chief deputy and his captive before they saw me.

That might take awhile because I was gazing into an ocean of granite slabs. There had to be hundreds, maybe more. I wasn't certain I'd be able to pick Sawyers and his captive out unless they started moving.

Then I saw him.

My chief deputy stood up.

Angie was still not in view, but I could see Sawyers looking down. Once, he pointed at something. That had to mean he was pointing it out *to* someone.

The last thing I wanted either individual to feel was the kind of surprise that would panic them. That ruled out triggering my siren. Or calling out on my car's loudspeaker. Or sneaking up on them unawares and announcing myself.

I decided the least threatening way to reveal my presence was to slam my car door. Not in dramatic fashion. Like a normal exit. Then stand by my vehicle, unmoving. And see how my chief deputy reacted.

The sound caused Sawyers to crane his head in my direction. When he saw who it was, his next move was decisive and threatening.

He reached down behind the sizable red-granite tombstone he'd popped up from behind and half-jerked, half-hoisted Angie into view. She was still handcuffed, and he was using the chain on the cuffs like a handle. No doubt, as they'd walked, he'd steered her first one way, then another. It had to have been exhausting for her. I was too far away to tell how she was taking it.

I knew what a TV detective would do in a moment like this. Avoid being a hero. The strategy seemed apt.

I stepped away from my car and made an exaggerated show of unbuckling my duty belt. I opened my rear door and laid the belt, my gun still in its holster, on the seat. The only thing I clipped on the back of my pants belt was my walkie-talkie.

I was ready as I was ever going to be to make the longest walk of my life.

317

CHAPTER 72

I was guessing my chief deputy hadn't deliberately taken Angie as a hostage. He'd probably needed a shield to get himself through a gauntlet of law officers, and she was the first person he could grab.

In that case, he shouldn't be vested in keeping her. That was going to be my most immediate goal. Get him to release her. Start her walking to my car. Then stay behind and see if we could go to work on finding solutions to his immediate problems. That was standard negotiating procedure.

I couldn't have been more wrong.

I was still twenty feet away from the pair when Sawyers made it clear that kidnapping Angie herself had been part of a plan. "Now you know how it feels."

"How what feels, Sawyers?"

"Having someone you love fall into evil hands."

I had no idea what he was talking about. "Sounds like you do."

His voice was soaked with menace. "Don't try that with me. I've had as much training in talking crazies back from the edge as you have."

"Probably more."

"That's right." Then he laughed. Not in a pleasant way. A rueful way. "That's what they train us to do, isn't it? Get the bad guy to thinking he's being understood."

I'd arrived at this dangerous juncture wearing too many hats. When you are dealing with a hostage-taker, the scene commander and the negotiator need to be two different people. Here, I was both. More than that, I was a victim. Three roles.

Not good at all.

And we'd had no standoff phase. No time when the kidnapper made his demands. Sawyers had made none so far. Unless there was an oblique demand wrapped in the cryptic comment he'd greeted me with.

I wanted to ask for more information from him. But he was right. I'd never known how it felt to have a person you love handcuffed to a mass murderer. But I'd lost someone I loved dearly to 9/11. And on this very day, I'd experienced moments when I didn't know whether Angie was dead or alive or whether she would make it through the events that were unfolding.

Until now. And the fear from the thought of this was paralyzing my tongue. So I said nothing.

The pause kept dragging out. Maybe that was what made it powerful.

Other than the three people involved in this standoff, the one participant that couldn't be ignored was the fair-sized red-granite marker at Sawyers's and Angie's feet.

The closer I'd gotten to it, the more I'd suspected this was what my hunch had been about. To confirm that, I needed to be able to view it from the other side. See what was engraved on it. Then I should know. "There's a reason why we're here, isn't there?"

Sawyers squinted. "Don't play the dumb game with me."

I chewed on that for a couple of heartbeats. "No games being played."

"Always games. In this town, they never quit."

I was about to ask for an example when Angie caught my eye. Gave her head a flick so slight I almost missed it. I had no idea what it could mean other than go in another direction.

I decided to try a neutral comment. "I'm in the dark here."

He waved a hand toward the grave marker. "You really didn't know about this?"

"Don't know what this is about — I've never been in this part of the cemetery before."

The tug Sawyers gave the handcuffs forced Angie to look up at him. "He's lying, isn't he?"

Angie's voice squeaked, causing her to clear her throat. "Don't think so." Then added something I'm certain neither Sawyers nor I expected. "But I'm too far away to tell."

"You're what?"

"I can't see his nostrils that well. When he lies, they flare, you know."

My chief deputy gave up a sharp, unexpected laugh that came all the way from his belly. "They do, don't they."

Looking back later, I'd come to see this abrupt departure from the script as the turning point. But at the time it happened, it was only one more unexpected moment. Another one in a day already overflowing with them.

The next one followed right on its heels.

Sawyers steered Angie backwards for several feet. Then motioned that I could advance around the marker to the point where I could read what was engraved on it.

I'm sure everyone present — Angie, Sawyers, and the police I'd called for stationed secretly around the perimeter — sensed my hesitancy in moving forward. My feet felt like they were chained to an anchor. The marker had been a dike, holding back all those secrets, games, and lies that Sawyers had been inveighing against. Now, the dike was about to be breached.

Sawyers and Angie were standing stock-still, their eyes scrutinizing my face. And that was the last thing I remembered before realizing that I was squatting before the polished tombstone. Running my fingers over the rough channels cut by the graver's chisel. And feeling my heart race at the implications of all that was written there.

Star Renae Stark McWhorter
"The Prairie Canary"
1948–1998
she sang of truth & hope

The tone in Sawyers's voice was that of a man who realized too much water had flowed under the bridge.

"Don't know if it'd have made any difference if we'd known a long time ago. But after your mom died, your dad married mine."

CHAPTER 73

After resting a hand on the gravestone for a few moments, I felt compelled to stand. Put my head in motion. Sweep it back and forth. Give my eye every assistance in taking stock of where this grave was located.

Enlarging my field of vision didn't help. I saw nothing that helped me understand. I'd never had reason to visit this part of the cemetery. My parents were buried closer to the entrance. And I'd attended no other burials in this part of the graveyard.

But you don't serve four terms as sheriff without crossing paths with a sizable army of willing scouts. The name McWhorter wasn't a common one. Someone would have seen this. Someone would have told me about it. But no one had.

I confessed as much to the two people watching me. "Can't believe I never knew about this headstone."

Angie half-turned to her captor, forcing him to look at her. "Don't do this, Sawyers. Tell him."

My chief deputy shifted his weight. The adrenaline of the chase was waning. He was getting tired. "Hasn't been here that long."

This wasn't enough information to satisfy the FBI special agent. I noted the new assertiveness in her voice. "The upright marker was only delivered yesterday, Luke. Before that, there was just a flat grass marker here."

That helped a little, but it didn't begin to explain how the information being claimed on this upright slab had eluded me. "People read flat markers too. Any marker with the name McWhorter in this cemetery is eventually going to be noticed by somebody."

Angie glanced at Tanner, then turned away to the extent that she could move her shoulders. It was his story. She was inviting him to tell it.

"Your family's precious name wasn't on the grass marker."

I ran with that — to where I knew not. There were a half dozen major mysteries extant in that gravestone inscription, maybe more. "So the grave has been marked all these years as belonging to Star Renae Stark."

"My mother."

"And the Prairie Canary?"

"That's the byline she put on her book."

This confirmed another of my growing suspicions. He'd read the manuscript. But how long ago? "When did you order the new marker?"

"About three months ago."

"So you've been planning all these killings that long?"

"Ever since I read the book."

"Why'd you wait?"

"Wanted to be sure the grave was properly marked. And I don't know, maybe I wanted to have this little reunion. My adoptive parents didn't provide much in the way of a family. In a way, the McWhorters have always been the only family I've ever had. Even if I didn't know it."

This ruthless killer now seemed to be suffering, if not remorse, at least late-arriving feelings of humanity. I noticed it. Angie noticed it. And there was one more question that begged to be answered.

Why had he turned against the only family he said he'd ever known? Attempted to poison its only surviving member? And might still put a bullet in both Angie and me?

I stepped forward slightly. "What else did you learn from the Prairie Canary's book?"

"So you haven't read it?"

"Haven't. Two hours ago, I didn't even know it existed."

He pointed toward the headstone. "Did you know about her before?"

I saw Angie's chest rise, pause, then fall. The movement in her chin wasn't quite so pronounced but the pattern was the same. She realized my dilemma. And wasn't sure what I was going to say. Wasn't sure, I sensed, what I *should* say.

That made two of us.

The man with the gun was unstable. Volatile. He'd killed on several occasions already. Twice on this day alone. He might be on the brink of killing again.

I could lie to him here. But that might be more dangerous than telling the truth. "I did know, though not very much."

"Because your dad told you?"

"No. He saved her letters to him. But it was twenty years after her death before I found them. Just the other day, in fact."

"Did she mention me?"

"She did. But only in passing." That sounded harsh. Knowing he was hungry for context, I tried to provide him with some. "Her reference to you was brief. But she loved you. It wasn't her choice to give you up."

"The book told me that." That comment was for me. The next one seemed to be for his own personal consumption. "Told me a lot of things."

I let him have his private moment, not that there was anything strategic in my silence. Once again, in this encounter, I was at a loss about what to say, where to try to steer this conversation. Sawyers knew all the ropes of hostage negotiating. My training felt useless.

I was about to see if the family angle would provide any leverage when he brought it up again himself. "You know, one thing the book doesn't explain."

"Ask me."

"What did she see in your father?"

"In her words?"

"That would be nice."

"She said he was a man of principle in a town full of liars, cheats, and criminals."

The look on Sawyers's face was still quizzical. "I wonder what she'd have thought if she'd known Professor Carmichael was strangled with your dad's belt."

There was no hesitation in my reply. "I think she did know."

"She mentioned it in her letters?"

"Not in so many words. But she warned him to watch his back — told him he'd crossed a line that had put him in peril."

I saw a sneer start to develop on Sawyers's face. But it was quickly replaced with confusion. "So, you don't think Sheriff John was a murderer?"

"No, never. I think his belt was placed around the professor's neck to control him. Blackmail him. Somebody else killed Carmichael."

Knowing my father's penchant for steering directly into a headwind, I had one other suspicion. When I read the Prairie Canary's book, I might find out otherwise. Or I might never know. But I didn't sense that now would be a good time to tell Sawyers about that particular suspicion. That my father had married his mother because it was the most effective way he could think of to tell both sides in Flagler's religious wars where they could stuff it. And that they'd better be careful when and how they did it.

The Prairie Canary's journalistic skills were going to blow the lid off secrets that none of Flagler's deranged religious combatants wanted revealed. But Sheriff John had wagered they'd not harm the lady if she was married to the man who wore the star.

Not wanting to add to Sawyers's gremlins, I went another route. "And I think I know why he married your mother."

"Why was that?"

"Because he loved her."

▫ ▫ ▫

That short exchange broke the log jam. The quickness of his replies suggested he was eager to share his story. And the lack of tension in his voice hinted that he was holding nothing back. I decided to push the envelope. See how much I could learn. This might be my one and only chance.

"How did you know about the manuscript?"

"Miss Ruthie."

"Our county librarian thought you needed to know about it?"

"I was the one who brought it up."

"You went to her asking about a work called *The Expiator's Curse*?"

"Didn't know about anything like that. I went to her asking if she had anything in her files about Professor Huntgardner's beloved fragment."

"Why the sudden interest in the fragment?"

He worked his jaw before answering. "I started out as a detective, remember? And it wasn't sudden."

"So you've been investigating the fragment all along?"

"Investigating? Don't think you could call it that. Well, maybe you could. But mainly, I was curious."

"About what?"

"What a myth can do to a town."

Why hadn't I realized how perceptive my easygoing chief deputy was beneath that aw-shucks demeanor of his?

Our town *had* been in the clutches of myths, half-truths, and malicious rumors. More than a few, in fact. For more than seventy years. Ever since the arrival of that one man. The one associated with the fragment.

And Sawyers had hit the other bull's-eye too.

These myths and half-truths and rumors had deadened our imagination and left us a sterile shadow of what we could have been. He'd voiced the reality in eight meaning-packed words. And I was supposed to be the one with the graduate degree in the value of ideas and ideas about values.

I couldn't stop now. "When did you decide Professor Huntgardner had fabricated a myth?"

"That's what makes my mother's book so powerful. So beautiful."

"She shows the fragment was a myth?"

"Doesn't do that. Don't know that she thought the fragment was a myth. Something else, really. She explains why if you can't help someone you love realize what their myths and lies have done to them, you have to move on."

"So she did? Move on?"

"Yes. And in ways I'll never know the truth about, it cost her her life."

"You've been settling scores?"

"Some of that. But I view it differently. I've been removing the causes of the cancer that infects this town."

As this conversation unfolded, my awareness never left Angie. I was watching her for a clue to how I needed to respond to her presence. So far, she was trying to be as invisible as possible. She obviously realized that offering Sawyers's deranged mind a reminder who it was he had in his grasp would be a development fraught with danger.

That caused my mind to make one of those instantaneous transports it's capable of making. A feeling of déjà vu washed over me.

I was back at the cattle guard near the original crime scene at Professor Huntgardner's house. In Angie's SUV. Listening to Sawyers's suggestion that the nine corpses might be victims of somebody's vindictiveness. I recalled what my thought had been then: *Lordy, is this whole thing about somebody's sour grapes?*

Now, I realized he had been talking about himself. Thanks to his mother's book, his past had been dumped on him without warning like a collapsing mountainside. The power of the Prairie Canary's prose had swept away his ability to think rationally. And in its place, a Niagara of rage had been loosened. He'd been taking his revenge against people who had mistreated him. Some of them were the crucial players mentioned in the Prairie Canary's book.

I wasn't one of those, but he'd doctored my tea with a near-fatal dose of rat poison. Nearly killed someone who frequented my office. And he still might put a bullet in me. Or Angie. "You think I'm one of the causes?"

What he did next washed through my awareness like battery acid. He glanced down at Angie with a look that was almost loving. "I did until I talked to this lady."

It was the same kind of look I'd seen less than three hours before — when Garrick Drasher had watched Angie enter my interrogation room. On that occasion, my mesmerizing FBI special agent girlfriend had taken matters into her own hands.

She did it again.

"Sawyers, these cuffs are getting unbearable. You need to let me go."

When he answered, he seemed to be addressing the tombstone more than Angie. "It's time, isn't it?"

He freed her and let the handcuffs fall to the ground. Angie walked over to me, took my hand, and whispered something only I could hear. "Tell him you're going to let him have a moment with his mom."

I did that. And we continued toward my car.

We were halfway to my patrol cruiser when my sniper fired. Later, he said Sawyers had raised his revolver and was pointing it straight at us.

CHAPTER 74

I was still sitting in my patrol cruiser when I got word from my dispatcher that Professor Huntgardner had died at Flagler General. It had happened at almost the same time Chief Deputy Tanner's life had been snuffed out by our sniper's bullet.

My thoughts flitted instantly to Leviticus 24. To those four verses where the Old Testament lawgiver spells out the consequences for doing injury to your neighbor. Under the Tribe of Levi's rules, you got equal payback. Fracture for fracture. Eye for eye. Tooth for tooth. And now, perhaps, death for death. But who did I consider the primary instigator — the most serious offender — in this instance? The professor? Or Sawyers? And was it my right, or my role, to conclude that it was more one than the other?

I'd always choose to think my chief deputy had killed himself — suicide by cop. Believing he'd have shot me or Angie, or the both of us, in the back was beyond my comprehension.

Officially, he was a murderer. A mass killer. That was in my public world.

In my private world, which I'd need not explain to anyone, he'd always be my friend and a loyal employee. I wouldn't be explaining to very many people how painful it was to be forced to own both realities.

As for Huntgardner, to the extent that I knew, I had no further role to play. No doubt, as he'd become more and more self-obsessed, the physicist had committed more than one serious crime, murder included. But the statute of limitations on most of these offenses had run out. There wasn't a statute of limitations for murder. But I had no evidence of that to forward to a prosecutor.

Besides, the man was dead.

I planned to attend the professor's memorial service. Might even send a deputy with a smartphone to make a record of who showed up. But Dr. Mayes, the physician, had been the professor's legal guardian. I'd leave it to him to sort out the demented old man's affairs.

And that's where matters stood, until they didn't.

CHAPTER 75

The phone call from Dr. Mayes came about midmorning. There was urgency in his voice. "The local paper was just here."

That didn't surprise me, and I told my caller so. "Dr. Huntgardner was a bit larger than life in these parts. Has been for a long time."

"Most of the questions weren't for his obituary."

"Let me guess. They're doing an article on the fragment."

"More than that. They're doing an entire section on it in tomorrow's paper."

I did a double take he couldn't see. "An entire section?"

His rush to tell me the whole story was obvious. "Listen to the headline. 'Ten Places to Search for Abbot County's Most Famous Space Junk.'"

Mayes couldn't see me shaking my head. But he heard my expletive.

He had more to tell me. "They're offering a five hundred dollar cash prize to anyone who finds it."

I couldn't hold back my invective. "Motherless oafs!"

"And that's not the crux of the trouble, Sheriff."

"What might that be?"

"They've hit the nail on the head with one of those ten sites."

"You're saying you know where the fragment is?"

"I think I do."

"And you know this how?"

"I've just opened up the professor's safety deposit box. Read his will. It gives precise directions to where he buried the fragment."

□ □ □

I thought this was one of those situations where less would be more. What that boiled down to was one of each.

One person in charge. That was me. One legal representative of the family — Dr. Mayes, who was riding with me. One surveyor, because we were going to need precise measurements. One dual wheeled pickup driver, a friend of Mayes. He'd also operate the ditch digger on the trailer he was pulling. And one of our CSI team, coming in his own vehicle, bringing a video camera.

It wasn't until we'd left the Sweetwater Highway turnoff two miles behind and were making our first curve to the west that I noticed a fifth vehicle keeping pace with our little caravan. Not crowding it. But not falling off the pace any, either.

The vehicle puzzled me. From what I could see in the mirror, it looked official. One of those black Chevy Suburbans that federal government law enforcement favors.

Angie drove one.

The thought that it might be hers was why I didn't react to it. Didn't bring our entourage to a halt and check the SUV and its occupants out.

Instead, we kept raising dust. Reached the point where Judson's yellow-flagged stakes had begun. Turned west and motored to the circle of aristocrat pear trees.

The black Suburban didn't follow us all the way to the clearing. It hung back about 150 yards and came to a stop on the prairie. Two people emerged from it. They leaned against the vehicle, watching us through binoculars.

According to Dr. Mayes, the fragment was buried twenty-seven meters and 140 degrees west of a tree located at due east in the circle of trees. We'd know the exact one because it had been flagged. A survey marker had been embedded fourteen inches due west of where the tree emerged from the ground.

The surveyor in our party found the marker. Set up his equipment. And was soon driving a stake into the white stones that were part of the top oval "eye."

He was off by only a few inches.

The operator on Dr. Mayes's ditch digger needed less than five minutes to expose a large, heavy-duty army-green military surplus case. Two feet long. Almost that wide. A foot-and-a-half high. Its recessed handles made it easy to attach cables at each end. The boom on the ditch digger made it easy to lift the case free and place it on the ground.

The doctor brushed the remaining dirt off the case's thick lid. Undid its five latches. Thrust the weighty lid back on its three hinges. And began removing the packing material jammed inside.

The rest of us crowded around, keen to observe. The equipment operator stayed on his knees. I bent over Dr. Mayes's shoulder. My CSI staffer had his eye pressed to his camera viewfinder.

We were all so focused on what was happening with the case we'd uncovered that none of us maintained any kind of a lookout.

I had an excuse for not noticing unavailable to the others. The activity we missed was taking place on my blind side. I'd had to have turned my head at least a third of a circle to have realized that the black Suburban had edged forward to the trees. And its occupants had dismounted.

What our little entourage was riveted on was what was in

the case. Beneath the packing straw, Dr. Mayes had found an elongated white shroud. Something was wrapped tight within it. The doctor slipped his hands underneath the bundle, palms up. Lifted it free of the case. And laid it on the ground with care.

Two white cords held the shroud in place, one at each end. Each was tied with a bow. The doctor tugged both bows loose. Let the ends of the cords drop. And began opening the shroud. That was another reason why all of us lost touch with what was going on around us. The whole engagement felt funereal — like we were recovering the body of a long-dead infant.

We got only a quick look. I'd check with my companions later to see if they agreed with my reaction. Gazing down at the object in the shroud felt like peering into a bottomless portal. And getting a glimpse of something that didn't belong to our world.

The object had a color to it, but its hues vacillated.

Oscillated.

One moment they might be the darkened grays of anodized aluminum and the next, the coal-blacks of the cast-iron skillet in my kitchen. Yet, there seemed to be an unmistakable luminosity being generated. Funny, but as I stared at it, I kept thinking of Professor Huntgardner's comment to Professor Rawls. The one about how much the dark can tell you if you don't get blinded by the light.

What we saw was an entity — if that's the right word — that seemed to be drinking up its surroundings instead of taking its rightful place among them.

Another way to say it?

The substance that the entity was made of caused it to stand apart from everything around it, including the shroud that had been its protection. The entity was directing no yea and no nay — to anything. But I wasn't seeing any of those markings about which the professor had made such a big deal. At least, there were none in view on the part of the entity visible to us.

Our impressions might have been more substantial if we'd had more time. And if we'd not been interrupted with such jarring rudeness.

Four figures approached us. All of them wore tactical fatigues. Splotches of dark gray on a sea of white. And sunglasses. And dark green berets. But no insignias of any kind.

Not even on Garrick Drasher's clothing.

Because of the sunglasses, I couldn't tell if he ever looked me in the eye. But he was the one who reached down and scooped up the shroud and its contents. The other three were heavily armed with machine pistols. As Drasher headed for the eastern edge of the trees, clutching the object he'd just purloined to his chest, the others fell in protectively around him.

I took a couple of seconds to process surprise. I considered pulling my revolver. But knew I'd not pull the trigger.

For three reasons.

One, we were badly outgunned.

Two, I was concerned about hitting the object in the shroud, not to mention shooting someone in the back.

The third reason was the noisy beast that swooped in over the circle of trees from the west. It made a low pass over the clearing and lowered itself onto the prairie a few dozen feet to the east of the trees.

The bulb-nosed UH-60 Black Hawk helicopter had dived down on us like — well, like a hawk. I knew what it was because I'd seen the intimidating crafts darting around the Army's firing range west of Burford DeBlanc Air Force Base.

The chopper disturbed the air. Disturbed the grasses. Disturbed the closest trees. Disturbed our peace of mind.

One of the crew extended his hands through a wide-open door halfway down the chopper's side. Our absconder passed along his plundered cargo. Other hands were extended to him and his companions. One at a time, they scooted into the craft on their stomachs.

In less than a minute, the helicopter was disappearing over the ridge in the direction of Mexico.

My first words were to Dr. Mayes. "I'm pretty sure that was the professor's fragment."

EPILOGUE

The appearance, then the disappearance, of the Black Hawk might have signaled the end to the reign of mysteries in Abbot County.

Not meaning we'd found convincing explanations for any of the others. We hadn't. Nada. Nary a one. And it wasn't for lack of trying.

By my department. By Angie's FBI. By Pentagon investigators and other hifalutin government gumshoes I'd been told about and some I hadn't been. At least, if the other agencies had come across any culprits or motives, they hadn't shared them with me.

But there was one important breakthrough.

One Thursday night after Angie's and my regular "date night" meal, I suggested that we motor up Make-Out Mountain. The peak was a favorite spooning location with Flagler's teenagers. It was only about fifteen minutes' drive east of my house.

Angie and I had been there enjoying the twinkling lights of the city below and the starry hosts of the heavens above for about twenty minutes when I suggested we get out. Walk around to the front of the car. Commune with the moment and the elements without being surrounded by a cage of automotive steel.

I slipped an arm around the extraordinary woman I was with and drew her close. Kept the flashlight I'd exited the car with out of her sight. Removed my arm. Reached inside a pant pocket and extracted the ring box I'd kept jammed down in my car seat. Stepped in front of her in the darkness. Dropped to one knee. Flicked on the flashlight. Opened the box. And asked her to marry me.

She said yes and burst — spectacularly, I thought — into tears.

No sooner had I slipped the ring on her finger than Angie looked up and pointed. "Luke, are you seeing this?"

I stood up and spun around.

Five blue lights in a ragged *V* formation were approaching Flagler from over the prairie. One occupied the nose position. The others filled out a Delta-wing-like shape, two on each side. Their speed slowed to a crawl, and the entire *V* started a slow, wide spin. Like it was trapped at the edge of a huge whirlpool.

To our further astonishment, one of the lights broke off from the formation. Dipped low over our little city. Made three passes in all. Then returned to its place in the *V*. That was when the formation broke apart — like a slow-motion firework — and each of the five blue lights departed in a different direction.

When she spoke, Angie's voice sounded small and wondrous. "What was that?"

I smiled. "The weather people must have sent their balloons again. They sure have a weird sense of humor." I paused. "You buying that explanation?"

Angie smiled back.

I drew her close, kissed her, then joined her gazing at the now empty sky. No more blue lights. No more weather balloons. No more flying saucers. Just a million, billion twinkling stars.

ACKNOWLEDGMENTS

My lifelong companion and business partner, Sherry, has spent an untold number of hours vetting every twist and turn in this work. Her sense of how the world works is uncanny and her imagination is boundless. So is my love for her and my appreciation for what her selfless spirit and zest for living bring to my work.

I'm indebted to these other individuals for their assistance with the Sheriff Luke McWhorter Mystery Series:

Brandon Allen, MD, Assistant Medical Director, Adult Emergency Department, University of Florida Shands Hospital, Gainesville, Florida. ED procedures and terminology.

Amy L. Beam, EdD, owner of Mount Ararat Trek travel agency of Dogubayazit, Turkey, and Barbados. The realities of climbing Mt. Ararat.

Jennifer Blanton and Penny Goering, Texas Search and Rescue, Austin, Texas. Care and handling of cadaver dogs.

Jack David, Co-Publisher; Rachel Ironstone, Managing Editor; Amy Smith, Marketing Manager; Jen Knoch, Senior Editor; Jessica Albert, Art Director; Jen Albert, Production Editor; Crissy Calhoun, Proofreader; Susannah Ames, Publicity Manager; Emily Ferko, Sales Director, ECW Press, Toronto, Canada. Publishing, marketing, and general hand-holding.

Leo Halepli, Istanbul and Green Bank, West Virginia, the first Turkish citizen of Armenian descent ("a Bolsohay") to be offered a position in Turkey's Secretariat General for EU Affairs. Turkish geography and culture.

Heather A. Reed, Site Manager, Buffalo Gap Historic Village, McWhiney History Education Group, Buffalo Gap, Texas. History and geography of the Callahan Divide area of West Texas.

Marco Samadelli, PhD, Researcher at the Institute for Mummies and the Iceman, South Tyrol Museum of Archaeology, Bolzano, Italy. Mummy preservation and all things Italian.

Emily Schultz, Brooklyn, New York. Superb editing instincts, insights, and mastery of the English language.

Steven Schwartz, Sarah Jane Freymann Literary Agency, New York, New York. Finding a publisher and negotiating financial aspects.

My grateful thanks to Charles Boulos and Michèle Carrier of Montreal, Quebec, Canada; Gary John, EdD, of Dallas, Texas; and my brother, Stanley Wayne Lynch of Phoenix, Arizona, for providing quality control for this work in spades.

Other friends, family, and/or fellow authors who generously answered questions and/or critiqued early drafts include Jay Brandon, Dan Coleman, Skipper Duncan, Stephanie Jaye Evans, Perry Flippin, Larry Hahn, Joe Holley, Victor L. Hunter, Howard R. Johnson, Scott Kinnaird, Larry Lourcey, Major General Don Lynch (U.S. Marine Corps, Retired), Robert M. Randolph, and Harold Straughn.

My thanks to staffers at the *Roswell Daily Record* and the International UFO Museum and Research Center in Roswell for responding to questions about the 1947 incident.

Several individuals have my lasting gratitude for their outsized contributions to developing my writing skills. In the order they appeared in my life:

Mildred Downs, Journalism Teacher, Pharr-San Juan-Alamo High School, Pharr, Texas.

Heber Taylor, PhD, and Charles Marler, PhD, Journalism Professors, Abilene Christian College (now University), Abilene, Texas.

John Ludka, Journalism Professor, Eastern New Mexico University, Portales, New Mexico.

DeWitt Carter Reddick, PhD, Journalism Professor, the University of Texas at Austin, Austin, Texas.

Ernest A. Sharpe, PhD, Journalism Professor, the University of Texas at Austin, Austin, Texas.

Joe B. Frantz, PhD, History Professor, the University of Texas at Austin, Austin, Texas.

Gordon K. Greaves, Editor, *Portales News-Tribune*, Portales, New Mexico.

T. Jay Harris, Editor, *Lubbock Avalanche-Journal*, Lubbock, Texas.

Howard (Bud) DeWald, Editor, *Arizona Republic Sunday Magazine*, Phoenix, Arizona.

Etta Jones Lynch, Biographer and Writing Skills Developer, Lubbock and Houston, Texas.

The contents of this work are the sole responsibility of the author. Any inaccuracies or other shortcomings are his alone.

© LARRY LOURCEY

DUDLEY LYNCH was born in Tennessee but raised in an oft-moving preacher's family, mostly on the southern Great Plains. He has written sixteen non-fiction books, including a biography of Lyndon Johnson and a study of Texas tornadoes. This is Dudley's first book of fiction; he is currently at work on the second book in the Sheriff Luke McWhorter Mystery series, *A Good and Deadly Deed*. He lives in Gainesville, Florida.